East on Sunset

Also by Ken Mercer

Slow Fire

East on Sunset

Ken Mercer

Minotaur Books ❧ New York

This is a work of fiction. All of the characters, organizations, and events portrayed in this novel are either products of the author's imagination or are used fictitiously.

EAST ON SUNSET. Copyright © 2011 by Greenland Creative, LLC. All rights reserved. Printed in the United States of America. For information, address St. Martin's Press, 175 Fifth Avenue, New York, N.Y. 10010.

www.minotaurbooks.com

Library of Congress Cataloging-in-Publication Data

Mercer, Ken, 1962–
    East on Sunset : a Will Magowan novel / Ken Mercer. — 1st ed.
        p.   cm.
    ISBN 978-0-312-55837-6 (alk. paper)
    1. Ex-police officers—Fiction.   I. Title.
PS3613.E7E37   2011
813'.6—dc22

2011005104

First Edition: June 2011

10   9   8   7   6   5   4   3   2   1

East on Sunset

ONE

It's amazing how quickly your whole day can turn to shit.

Will Magowan let out his breath as he fought to steer his now hobbled Volvo station wagon into the parking lot of the mini mall.

Things had all been going according to plan: He'd put on his best shirt and a pressed pair of khaki pants and left the house right on schedule. He was driving east on Victory through Van Nuys, the traffic moving for a change, when it happened.

The white Daewoo cut into his lane without warning, and he was forced to jerk the steering wheel to the right to avoid ramming into it. He felt his front wheel hit the curb, then the front end of his car dropped as the tire blew. The steering wheel began to shudder in his hands.

As a general rule, he hated mini malls, considered them to be a blight on the land, part of the plot to pave over every last inch of Greater Los Angeles. But he had to admit he was pleased to spot this particular one, a way for him to get off the busy street.

He turned into the parking lot and switched off the ignition. He got out of the car and went around the front of it. The passenger side front tire was now a shapeless mass of deflated rubber.

A car horn blared behind him. Will turned and saw the white Daewoo idling by the entrance to the parking lot. He went over to it. The passenger side window cranked down, revealing a dark-skinned man behind the wheel.

"I am so sorry." The man spoke with an accent, Indian or maybe Pakistani.

Will leaned into the passenger window. The backseat of the car was covered with translucent plastic shopping bags filled with takeout containers. The smell of curry wafted out through the open window.

Will tried to tamp down his anger before he spoke. "You need to watch where you're going."

The man nodded. "I am so sorry. Please no police? I will lose my job."

"Maybe you should have thought about that before you cut me off."

"Please, forgive me."

Will glanced back at his disabled car. The tire was toast, but the rim looked like it would live to fight another day.

He turned back to the man. "It was an accident, right?"

The man nodded again. "It was quite unintentional."

Will straightened up. "Then don't worry about it."

The man thanked him and shook Will's hand through the window before driving away, disappearing into the traffic and exhaust fumes on Victory.

Will walked back toward his car. Of course, he'd just let the AAA membership lapse in a cost-cutting move, figuring he hadn't used it in years. Which meant that he'd be the one getting down on the oil- and Slushee-coated pavement himself. In his dress clothes.

He reached inside the car for his cell phone and date book. He opened the book and turned the pages until he came to today's date. He punched in the number he'd written down, then hit CALL.

A young woman's voice answered. "Los Angeles Dodgers."

"Joe Gibbs, please."

Will was put on hold. Instead of music, he was treated to a recording of Vin Scully doing play-by-play. The sun beat down on the blacktop, and he began to sweat in the afternoon heat.

The other man came on the line.

"Joe, it's Will Magowan, I've got a meeting with you at four—"

"You mean an *interview*."

"Right. Listen, I'm having some car trouble and I'm still out in the Valley." He flipped open the date book. "Can we reschedule?"

"No."

Will thought that maybe he hadn't heard right, the crappy cell phone reception and all. "Sorry?"

"Sorry won't cut it. I need people that are dependable."

"I *am* dependable. I just got a flat tire."

"You can't even make it to the job interview, what's that supposed to tell me?"

Will started to wonder if he really wanted to work for this dick. He stared out at the soot-covered stucco buildings of the mini mall: a Vietnamese nail joint, check cashing store, a Del Taco.

"I'm sorry." Will thought that he was starting to sound a lot like the Indian delivery dude. "I'm really interested in the job."

"Well, you sure got a funny way of showing it."

Will inhaled the smell of frying oil from the Del Taco. Up ahead at the corner, a Mexican man wearing an Angels cap stood in the hot sun selling oranges in green mesh sacks. "Please, just meet me in person. You won't be sorry."

"Look, I was only seeing you as a favor."

"What do you want me to tell Charlie?"

"It was Charlie Miesmer referred you?"

"That's right."

Even over the static of the cell phone connection, Will could hear the other man let out a breath.

"You used to be a cop?"

Will nodded. "I was a detective with LAPD."

A rusting VW camper van with a longboard strapped to the roof pulled into the spot next to him. A faded decal on the driver's window had a pastel-colored map of California above the words SUMMERTIME ALL THE TIME.

"Tell you what. Chuckles sent you, you can't be all bad. You think you can manage to get your ass in here at ten on Monday?"

Will didn't bother to check his book. "No problem."

"I certainly hope not," the other man said before hanging up.

TWO

Erik Crandall sat on the bench inside the old wooden bus shelter and watched the Receiving and Releasing van drive away.

The guards were supposed to stay and make sure you actually got on the bus, but it was close to lunchtime, and after dropping him here they had just left. Crandall took this to be a positive development, because now he wouldn't have to lay out the cash for a bus ticket.

He only had $160 of his gate money left, since they'd already deducted the $40 for the gray sweats he was wearing. Most guys had their family send them release clothes, but Erik didn't have anyone to do that for him. At least the sweats were halfway decent. The labels said they were Russell. One problem, the pants had no pockets, so he had to carry his possessions around inside a small cardboard box.

He turned his head and looked at the tan stucco buildings of San Quentin. He could see the red roof of D-Block and a guard tower standing empty by the West Gate. It didn't look so bad from out here, not compared to what it was like inside.

The bus shelter was built from redwood, like a small cabin. The damp air inside reeked of mildew and fermenting piss. The Plexiglas windows were fogged from years of salt spray coming off the bay.

He stuck his head out through the open doorway, scanning the road. He knew he needed to wait, make sure the van wasn't going to come back. He took the top off the cardboard box. Not much inside: his gate money, a toothbrush, the heel of a bar of Irish Spring. He pulled out a worn blue plastic stress ball and began to work it in his left hand.

When it felt like enough time had passed, he got up and walked out onto the shoulder of the road. He tucked the box under his left arm and stuck out his right thumb.

A cold wind blew the thick fog around. Almost May and it felt like the middle of fucking winter. If he never saw the Bay Area again, that would be fine by him. Of course, he really hadn't seen much of it, just what was in view from the yard. The windswept gray waters of the bay, the ferry terminal, an oil refinery on the eastern shore.

He'd been waiting for this day for almost five years. In his mind, he'd pictured it differently; always with bright blue skies, birds chirping from the trees as he tooled down the road in a convertible.

Cars sped by, accelerating as they went up the small hill. He tried to make eye contact, the drivers alone inside their cars, pretending that they didn't see him. Like it was easy to miss a 245-pound baldheaded man standing there on the side of the road.

He made sure to face forward so the oncoming drivers couldn't see the back of his shaved head. He'd had a biker inside tattoo a pair of eyes onto the back side of his head, and he didn't want to freak out any potential rides.

The tattooed eyes were in full color, not like most of the jailhouse tats, just blue ink from a ballpoint pen. They perched on the rear of his skull, the same height as his real eyes.

A blonde driving some kind of fancy BMW truck looked out at him through her windshield. She wore tight-fitting workout clothes, the seat belt separating her big set of jugs. Erik gave his best smile and held his thumb up higher, working the stress ball in his other hand. This babe picked him up, she'd be the one going for the ride.

She turned her head away as she accelerated, leaving him staring at the back end of her car. A bumper sticker on the rear window had a picture of one of those smiley faces, except it wasn't smiling. Next to it were printed the words MEAN PEOPLE SUCK.

He felt like a dork standing out here in the sweats, wondered if he should try walking to a store, find some more suitable threads.

It was Friday morning. He had until Monday afternoon to make it down to L.A., check in with his parole officer. He had a job lined up down there, driving a limo. He needed to get his driver's license renewed, not a big deal since his correctional counselor had been helping him study for the test as part of his pre-release classes.

He'd get that going, then turn his attention to more important things.

He flinched at the loud squeal of air brakes, looked up to see the semi pulling onto the shoulder up ahead of him. He jogged toward it, hopping up onto the step of the cab as the door swung open.

Crandall climbed into the passenger seat, placing the cardboard box on his lap. The truck driver was fat and had a bushy mustache that reminded Crandall of Tom Selleck in *Magnum, P.I.* The inside of the cab reeked of sweat and onions.

Crandall shut the door. At least he was on his way.

THREE

Will sat in the dining room of his house in Van Nuys. On the table in front of him was a paperback copy of *What Color Is Your Parachute?*

The book told him that the reason most job hunters fail to get their dream job is that they don't know enough about themselves. Following the instructions in the book, he took a blank sheet of paper and wrote at the top:

Who Am I?

He stared down at the words, tapping the eraser of his pencil against the table.

The breeze picked up, rustling the fronds of the sago palm that grew outside the window. He could hear the cars on Burbank Boulevard, commuters fighting their way through the Valley traffic, trying to get home for the weekend. He got up and shut the window.

He sat back down and took another look at the question. He picked up his pencil and wrote, "I am . . ." Then he stopped, trying to think of what words should come next.

He was interrupted when the front door opened and Laurie walked in. Buddy, their golden retriever, got up from his bed and trotted over to greet her.

"What're you working on?" she asked.

He shut the book with the front cover facing down. "Nothing."

Laurie walked over to the table and put her hand on Will's shoulder. He looked up at her face. Her skin seemed to glow. He'd noticed that this would happen sometimes when she came home from the yoga studio. She was still wearing her yoga clothes, the stretch fabric clinging to her torso.

"What?" she said.

"Nothing."

She shook her head. "Is that all you can say? How'd the interview go?"

"It didn't."

"What do you mean?"

He told her about the delivery driver, the flat tire, the telephone call. When he got to the part about how he succeeded in talking Gibbs into giving him another chance, she cut him off.

"Why do you care so much? It's just a job as a security guard."

"We could use the money."

"Don't you think you're a little overqualified?"

He put down the pencil and let out his breath. "Do we really have to go through this again?"

"I don't know, it's just that I worry about you. You've been back over a year now, you haven't done anything."

"I've *done* things." He ticked off items on his fingers as he ran through them. "I rebuilt the deck. I painted the bedroom. I started my book."

"Come on, Will. Some days I come home at one in the afternoon, you're still in your pajamas. After Sean died, you had a good excuse for not doing anything, but what about now?"

He stood up and went to the refrigerator. He reached inside and took out a bottle of nonalcoholic beer. He twisted off the cap and grimaced as he took a sip. He could never get used to the taste of the fake stuff, but he wasn't supposed to drink alcohol.

"I thought you didn't want me to go back to being a cop," he said. "Not that anyone would hire me now, anyway."

"There are plenty of other things you could do."

"Like what?"

"You have a lot of talents, Will. All these things to offer."

"Such as?"

"You understand people, what makes them tick. You can think on your feet. You can talk your way out of anything."

He took another hit of the fake beer. "Maybe I should become a Realtor."

She picked up her yoga bag and started to walk away, toward the bedroom. "If you can't be serious, then forget it."

"I'm sorry," he said. "I just don't know what the hell to do."

She turned around and looked at him.

He played with the label on the bottle. "It's just that I've spent my whole life killing myself, trying to accomplish something. And I haven't gotten anywhere."

"You were a good cop."

"Maybe being a cop isn't what I thought it would be."

"What did you think it would be?"

"I don't know." He played with the label some more. "Maybe about justice."

"Strip away all the bullshit, isn't that what it is about?"

"That's the point. You *can't* strip away the bullshit."

She sat down at the table. "Maybe you should go to work for a non-profit. Do drug counseling, something like that. Help people stay off drugs."

"I'm not sure I've got that one completely figured out for myself."

The dog came over and laid his head in her lap. "Then why don't you go back to law school?"

"My version of hell—spending all day surrounded by lawyers."

"You're forty-two years old, Will. You've got almost your whole life ahead of you. You can accomplish whatever you want."

He looked at her. "What if I don't want to accomplish anything? What if I just want to live a normal life, like other people? You know, settle down and lead a life of quiet desperation."

She shook her head. "I'm getting tired of your sarcasm."

"Sorry, I was trying for irony."

He reached out and took hold of her hand. "Look, this is something I really want to do. I've always loved baseball, I'm happy when I'm at the ballpark. I like being around all the families."

"Fine."

He looked at her. "What do you mean?"

"Don't you get it? I don't care how much money you make. I don't care what kind of career you have. I just want you to be content with your life."

"Content," he said. "Why not happy?"

She pulled a stainless steel water bottle from her yoga bag and took a sip. "I think the Western idea of happiness is misleading. It's just this notion that's been fed to us by TV commercials. Smiling, happy people jumping into the air in front of their shiny new cars. Chasing after it is what makes us suffer."

Will smiled at her, wondering how he had ever been so stupid, to let her slip out of his life. The sun had set now. Buddy had fallen asleep, his head still in her lap, drool spreading out on her yoga pants.

Will lifted his bottle and held it out to her in a toast.

She looked confused but picked up her water bottle.

He clinked his bottle against hers. "To contentment."

FOUR

The truck dropped Crandall off on the outskirts of a shit-kicker dump of a town near Bakersfield.

He stood in the parking lot of a convenience store holding his cardboard box. The sun had just set, but it was still warm out here in the dusty heart of the Central Valley. The air smelled of cow shit.

He went inside the store, a set of bells jangling as the door swung open, the blast of air-conditioning like stepping inside an igloo.

The refrigerator cases had glass doors that let him look inside at the shelves of cans and bottles. He was searching for a six-pack of beer, maybe even two. All those years inside, he'd been dreaming of this moment every day: walking into a store, buying some beers, getting hammered.

There were all different kinds of bottled water—he wondered who the fuck could taste the difference—cans of soda, tall bottles of iced tea. He came to the final cooler, but it was only filled with containers of milk and no beer.

The man behind the counter was old and wrinkled, some kind of Chinese.

"Where's your beer at?" Crandall asked.

The man shook his head. "No beer."

"Then give me a pint of Jägermeister."

The man shook his head again.

"Why not?" Crandall asked.

"No license."

Crandall worked the stress ball in his left hand. What kind of convenience store doesn't have a liquor license? How the fuck did this guy manage to stay in business?

The guy pointed out through the door. "You go in town."

"Where's that?"

"Four mile."

"I don't have a car," Crandall said.

"You go," the man said.

Crandall worked the stress ball faster. "Moo goo gai pan." It was the first thing that popped into his head.

The Chinese guy stepped back from the counter, like he was nervous.

"You wait," he said. Then he turned and disappeared through a door on the far side of the counter.

Crandall stood there in the empty store, wondering if the guy had gone to call the cops. A framed photo hung on the wall, the Chinese dude standing with a woman and two young girls, the background blue and mottled like what they used at Sears.

The guy came back out carrying a tall but flat cardboard box. Through the cellophane front panel, Crandall could see tiny bottles of different kinds of booze. Like you'd get on an airplane, but even smaller.

When the man set the box on the counter, Crandall saw that the bottles were made out of brightly colored tinfoil.

"What's this?" Crandall asked.

"Chocolate," the man said. "But inside real."

"Say what?"

The man pointed out the tiny bottles. "Brandy . . . vodka . . . crème de menthe . . . very good."

Crandall looked at the package again. The label said the bottles were filled with an assortment of fine liqueurs from around the globe.

"It's actual booze?"

The man nodded. "Yes. Very good."

"How much?"

"Fifteen dollar."

Crandall hesitated, unsure. Then he took the lid off his cardboard box and counted out the money.

The night air had started to cool. Crandall wished he had something else to wear other than the goddamned sweat suit.

He went around the corner of the store and sat down on the walkway, his back against the rough cinder-block wall. His skin looked yellow under the security lights.

He tore the cellophane from the box and examined the tiny bottles. He selected something called Asbach Uralt and pulled it from its slot in the green plastic backing. He tore off the tinfoil wrapper to uncover a piece of chocolate shaped like a bottle.

He held it up to his ear and shook it, heard the sound of liquid sloshing around inside. He bit the nipple from the bottle and spit it out on the walkway. Then he tipped his head back and drained the contents. The liquid was rich and warm and made his eyes water.

He threw the empty chocolate bottle away under a dried-out bush and pulled a bottle of orange-flavored Stolichnaya from the box. It burned his throat a little going down, but nothing like the pruno they made inside. That shit was worse than Liquid-Plumr.

The swinging dicks at Quentin all liked to brag about how it didn't matter how long your sentence was. That you only did two days: the day you went in, and the day you came out. He knew that was complete and utter bullshit.

The day he went in he got gassed. The guard was walking him

along the tier when some Mexican locked inside his cell tossed a plastic cup filled with piss at him. Things only went downhill from there.

Twenty-four years old, white and skinny, he never even had a chance. When he'd landed in Medical with a torn rectum, he figured it would finally stop, that the guards would put an end to it. But the doctor just stitched him up and gave him a box of suppositories. The next day he was back in mainline.

A truck rumbled by on I-5, drowning out the sound of the crickets. He reached another one of the tiny bottles from the container, not bothering to look at the label.

In the prison yard, he'd started lifting weights, trying to make himself stronger. When a biker offered to sell him some 'roids, he said yes.

He gained forty pounds of muscle in the first two months. He used whatever he could get his hands on: Dianabol, Anadrol, testosterone, a veterinary steroid called Equipoise. He stacked it all in ever-shifting combinations.

On the bench press, he was able to do rep after rep, no fatigue. His arms swelled, his weight went from 160 to 200 and kept climbing. There were the other changes, too. He went bald, but hair started sprouting in odd places on his body. His head got bigger. His back and chest became covered with a weeping acne that was like a rash.

And there was the other thing. *The Rage.*

One morning in the yard, some gangbanger had started something with him. Without even willing it to happen, Crandall threw a punch, his entire vision going red, pressure building inside his skull. Then his fists were a blur, pounding into flesh, bone and cartilage snapping, knuckles gone red and slippery.

When the guards managed to pull him off, he couldn't remember how he'd gotten down there on the ground, on top of the guy who seemed to have no face now. Just one glassy eye staring up from out of a pile of bloody hamburger.

The judge had stacked a manslaughter rap on top of the original drug charge. Crandall had done most of it in Ad-Seg, locked all by himself inside a tiny cell with a solid door. Left alone with nothing but his push-ups and sit-ups and anger.

A trustee kept the supply of steroids coming. Trapped inside his cell, Crandall kept growing bigger and stronger, imagining the coming day of reckoning when he'd rip the steel door from its frame and stalk down the corridor, tearing the guards' arms from their torsos, blood spouting up into the air like geysers.

He took another chocolate bottle out of the package. They were almost all gone now. He felt warm, the lights of the parking lot starting to vibrate.

He bit the top off the bottle, but then didn't feel like drinking any more. He felt sick to his stomach, probably from all the different kinds of booze mixing together. He dumped the liquid out on the concrete.

His eyelids grew heavy and started to close. He figured he'd crash here for a while, then walk over to the 5, thumb a ride south.

He just needed to get back down to L.A., get himself set up. After that, he didn't think it would be all that hard to track down the *lying-thieving-conniving-asshole* cop.

FIVE

On Monday morning, Will left the house before eight thirty to play it safe.

He drove away down his street, lawn sprinklers casting out arcs of water. Postwar stucco homes were packed together on small lots, aluminum awnings perched over windows for relief from the relentless Southern California sun. Orange trees grew in front yards.

He headed east through the Valley, then took the 5 toward downtown. The car windows were down. The air smelled fresh, and there were still patches of green from the winter rains up in the hills. The peaks of red tile roofs rose up from the other side of the freeway's concrete sound wall.

He took the Stadium Way exit. He was early for his meeting with Gibbs, so he decided to drive around Elysian Park. He drove beneath a corridor of date palms until he reached the old Barlow Sanitarium. He turned around in the parking lot and drove past the buildings of the LAPD Academy.

The ticket booths at Dodger Stadium were closed, but he told the guard why he was there and was waved through.

The stadium sat atop a knoll that featured a panoramic view of the city. The parking lot had light fixtures that were made to look like baseballs. He found the one with the number nine painted on it and parked beneath it.

Joe Gibbs's office smelled of his cologne, the walls covered with framed photographs of Gibbs posing beside famous ball players. Gibbs was a short African American man with a pencil mustache riding on top of his upper lip. He wore a suit and tie, a silk pocket square tucked into the front of his jacket.

"So how do you know Charlie?" Gibbs asked.

"We were both detectives working out of Rampart. He was Vice, I was Narcotics."

"You look pretty young to have your thirty."

"I don't," Will said. "I left."

"Why's that?"

Will looked at him. "Charlie didn't tell you?"

Gibbs took a sip from a mug of coffee but didn't offer Will anything. "Tell me what?"

"That I was terminated."

"How come?"

Will tried to think of the best way to frame his answer. "I had a substance abuse problem."

Gibbs frowned. "What about now?"

Will nodded. "I'm clean."

"For how long?"

"Four years." Will knew he was stretching things a bit, but if you ignored the pills, it was true.

"When did you leave the department?" Gibbs asked.

"In 2003."

Gibbs picked up a gold-plated pen and made a note. "So what have you been doing? I mean since then?"

"Different stuff," Will said. "I was chief of police for a small town up north."

Gibbs set down the pen and pushed back his chair. "Well, thanks for coming in. Tell Chuckles I said hey."

Will struggled to keep his voice even. "What do you mean? I thought you said you'd see me."

Gibbs opened his palms. "And I have."

Will tried to think of something to say. After talking things through with Laurie, he'd felt like this job was the right thing for him. If it didn't happen, he didn't know what he was going to do. If he couldn't even get a job as a security guard, what was in store for him?

"I drove all the way down here from the Valley," Will said.

"I don't know what you want me to say. You're just not right for the position."

"Why not?"

Gibbs looked at his watch. "You're overqualified."

"You know, I've never really understood that. I mean, isn't it better than hiring someone who's *underqualified*?"

Gibbs straightened his tie. "Listen, there's no crimes to be solved around here. Mostly, it's just keeping yahoos who knocked back one too many High Lifes from running out onto the field."

Will took a breath. "I understand that. But please just tell me why you think I wouldn't do a good job."

"I need people who will take this seriously. That aren't doing it as some kind of a lark."

"I'm not." Will shook his head. "I really want this job."

"*Why?*"

"I like baseball."

"Everybody likes baseball." Gibbs picked up his pen and clipped it to his shirt pocket. "Give me one good reason I should hire you."

Will didn't know what the hell he should say. He tried to think, Gibbs staring at him. "I understand people, you know, what makes them tick. I can think on my feet. I can talk my way out of any-thing."

Gibbs rubbed his chin. "I can see that."

"Look," Will said. "I really think I could do a great job for you. Talk to Charlie again, he'll vouch for me. Why not just give me a chance?"

"You're not very big. Can you handle yourself?"

"The way I see it, if I let a situation get to the point where it turns physical, I've already blown it."

"Very profound," Gibbs said. "But be that as it may, what do you have in the way of self-defense training?"

"The standard LAPD stuff. And some Krav Maga."

Gibbs smiled. "That's good. Anything can turn Jews into fighters must be good stuff."

Will laughed. Not because he thought what Gibbs had said was particularly humorous, but because he thought it might help them to bond. It made him feel cheap, but he was determined not to walk out of here empty-handed.

Gibbs looked out the window, staring out at his view of the deserted parking lot like it was the eighth wonder of the world.

Will waited, sensing that it was best to give the other man room to think.

After what seemed a very long time, Gibbs turned to face him. "Tell you what, I just had to let someone go, so how 'bout if I had you come on, as a provisional hire, just until the end of the season?"

"Great," Will said.

Gibbs held up his hand. "But if it's not working out, you'll be gone well before that."

Will stood up and shook Gibbs's hand. "You won't be sorry."

"Well," Gibbs said. "Let's hope not."

SIX

Crandall steered the Lincoln Town Car with his right hand, working the stress ball with his left.

He'd just finished dropping some stiff off at LAX, was working his way back north on La Tijera because he wanted to avoid the 405. It was late afternoon, everyone on the roads, the sun beating down on the sea of cars. He'd pushed to get assigned a stretch, figuring that was the ticket to getting with the high rollers, but his boss said he'd have to work his way up.

As if he'd be sticking around that long.

He only took the job to keep his parole officer out of his ass. Once he'd taken care of business, he planned on blowing the country, heading down to Honduras.

He'd found a book about it in the library at Quentin. The book was oversized, like something meant to be left lying out on top of a coffee table. Crandall would sit there for hours at a time, staring at the pictures of deserted beaches the way the other guys would stare at shots of beaver.

He scratched at his thigh, the dark wool suit he was wearing itchy as shit. What did he expect from the five-dollar rack at Goodwill? The suit was two sizes too large, but his arms were sausages squeezed inside the jacket sleeves.

He worked the stress ball, hating the way he could feel his muscles going soft, turning to Jell-O. The last time he'd put the tape on them, his biceps measured 21 inches, his chest 57. He wasn't about to go backward. He'd been keeping up with his workouts, more or less, but he needed to score some 'roids. It'd been over a week now since his last shot. He'd been forced to leave his stash behind, bequeathed it to his cellie. It was ironic, you could get any kind of dope in the world into that prison but couldn't risk taking it out.

Most guys wouldn't be feeling the absence of the 'roids so soon, because they juiced in cycles. But Crandall didn't cycle—he'd been shotgunning nonstop for four years now.

The white Range Rover in front of him switched lanes, as if it would make any difference. Then, without even using its blinker, it cut back in front of him, wedging into the tight opening so that he was forced to jam on his brakes.

Crandall leaned on the horn. The driver's window of the Range Rover slid down, and a man's hand snaked out. Then the hand flipped him the bird.

Motherfucker. Crandall stomped on the gas and brought the front end of the Town Car right up on the guy's ass. He dropped the stress ball and used his left hand to honk the horn, his heart hammering inside his chest

The Range Rover's turn signal came on, and it moved back into the left lane.

Sure, now *you use your fucking signal.* Crandall held the wheel in a death grip, wrenching it counterclockwise, changing lanes to stay tight on the guy's bumper.

The Range Rover turned left on La Cienega. Crandall followed, moving his foot back and forth between the gas pedal and brake. He steered with one hand, pounding the horn button with the other, the pressure building inside his head, painful as a migraine.

His nostrils flared as he breathed, his vision starting to turn the color of the blood pounding inside his skull.

The light at Slauson was green, the traffic lighter here. The Range Rover accelerated, like he was trying to get away from him. Crandall stepped on the gas, staying glued to the truck's bumper, honking his horn in a metronomic rhythm.

The Range Rover hung a quick right, cutting across traffic. Crandall spun the wheel to follow. They were on a side street now. Crandall floored it, passing the Range Rover on its left. Then he cut back in front of the truck and slammed on the brakes.

The Range Rover skidded to a stop behind him. Crandall threw open his door and jumped out, striding up to the driver's window.

The guy in the driver's seat was young, maybe a couple of years older than Crandall. He wore a bright blue dress shirt and an expensive-looking pair of wraparound shades.

"What the hell are you doing?" he asked.

Crandall didn't say anything. Just stood there, staring down at the guy.

The other man brought up his hands. "Look, man. I'm sorry."

Crandall saw the man's lips moving but couldn't hear the words, the blood rushing around inside his head too loud. He reached through the open window and grabbed the sunglasses off the driver's face.

"What—"

Crandall dropped the sunglasses onto the road, then stomped them with his dress shoe, grinding his foot from side to side. The guy went to take his cell phone off the dash. Crandall reached through the window with both hands and grabbed the man around his neck.

The guy struggled and got himself tangled up in the seat belt, but Crandall just pulled harder, and the guy came free. Crandall lifted, pulling the man out through the open window, his legs kicking at the air.

Crandall set the man down on his feet, holding on to the front of his shirt with his left hand. Then he threw his right fist into his face.

The man dropped to the ground like he'd been poleaxed. This surprised Crandall, because he didn't think he'd hit him all that hard. He bent over to hit the man again.

As he did, the man moved backward on the pavement, scrambling away like a crab. Crandall tried to grab him, but the guy was too quick. He disappeared underneath the Range Rover.

Crandall's knees popped as he crouched down onto the pavement. He stuck his head under the truck just in time to see the guy crawling away on the far side.

Crandall took off after the guy, chasing him down the empty road. He could barely see now, his field of vision shrinking down, the whole world going red.

The guy was faster than Crandall. He was maybe fifty yards ahead of him now, the gap widening. But then the guy made the mistake of cutting across an empty dirt lot. The place was deserted, the dusty ground strewn with scrubby plants, food wrappers, and broken bottles. When the man tripped over a small bush, Crandall pounced on him.

The guy brought his hands up in front of his face, his eyes wide and white.

"Please," he said. "I've got a kid."

Well, good for you. Crandall slapped him hard with the back of his left hand.

The man screamed.

Crandall punched him and felt the man's nose snap. The man screamed again, the sound hurting Crandall's head.

Crandall punched harder, trying to shut the guy up. The rhythm of his blows increased and began to take on a wet sound, his knuckles becoming slick with warm blood and snot from the man's broken nose.

He threw punch after punch, alternating between his right and left fist, the man's screams turning to weak sobs. Crandall could barely hear him now, lost in the task at hand, continuing to rain down blows until the guy stopped moving.

Crandall tried to catch his breath, staring down at the man's destroyed face.

Blood flowed from his flattened nose, lips puffing up like they'd been stung by a swarm of bees, eyes already beginning to swell shut.

Christ, he couldn't even remember how he'd gotten here, like waking up from a deep sleep. He remembered the guy cutting him off, pulling the guy out of his car, but everything after that was pretty much a blank.

He scanned the area. At least no one was around. He reached one hand down and put it on the other man's chest, relieved to feel that he was still breathing.

Crandall stood up and reached a paper napkin out of his jacket pocket. He wiped the blood from his knuckles as best he could, then threw the napkin on the dusty ground.

He checked his watch. Four thirty-five. *Great,* now he was going to be late for his next pickup. He tucked in the tail of his white dress shirt and straightened his suit jacket.

Then he started to walk toward the street, trying to figure out where he'd left the car.

SEVEN

Will and Laurie walked along the beach, following the edge of the wet sand.

They'd driven out to Malibu to have an early dinner at Duke's to celebrate his new job. The night was warm, the sun still a good hour away from sinking into the Pacific. It was the first of May.

Laurie wore a summer dress, her feet bare. Her blond hair was curling from the moist air.

"Something wrong?" he asked.

She answered without looking at him. "No, why?"

"That was good champagne. You hardly touched it."

She stopped walking and turned to face him. "I'm pregnant," she said.

It took him a moment to process what she'd just said.

Then he grabbed her and pulled her close. "That's fantastic."

He was grinning like an idiot, his face buried in her hair. He'd had a glass of the champagne and was feeling pretty good to begin with, but he was blown away, the granting of a wish he'd never even allowed himself to have.

"How far along are you?"

"Three months."

He pulled back to look at her face, his arms still wrapped around her. "Three months?" he said. "How come you didn't notice anything sooner?"

"How come *you* didn't?"

He smiled. "I thought your breasts were getting bigger, but I didn't want to jinx it."

She shoved him in the shoulder with her open hand.

"So when did you find out?" he asked.

"Around Easter."

He looked at her. That was over a month ago. "Why didn't you tell me?"

"Please don't be mad."

"I'm not mad." He tried to keep the pain from his face, not wanting her to see how much she'd hurt him. "I just can't believe you'd keep this from me."

She took hold of his hand. "I'm sorry, Will. I had things I needed to work through, on my own."

"Don't you think maybe I should have been consulted here?"

"I needed to be sure."

"Sure of what?"

She talked without looking at him. "I didn't want to bring another child into this world unless I knew that they'd have a father they could count on."

She tried to start walking again, but he held on to her hand. "So what would you have done? I mean, if you decided I wasn't worthy?"

She looked away, staring down at the ground, her bare foot kicking particles of sand.

"Jesus, Laurie."

"I'm sorry, Will. But it was bad enough I had to watch my son die. But then you disappeared right in front of my eyes."

"You think I wanted that to happen?"

She shook her head. "All I know is that it did."

He closed his eyes. "I thought we were past this."

He saw the tears well up in her eyes before she turned away. "So did I. But then I got pregnant, and it all kind of came flooding back."

He remembered the house after Sean died. The way it always seemed too quiet, so that he found himself tiptoeing around in the darkness. Eventually he stopped coming home. He'd sleep inside his car, telling her he was working heavy overtime. He couldn't handle the thought of going back inside the house, the funereal silence of it.

By that time, he'd already been chipping heroin for a couple of years, just for professional reasons. Working undercover, he needed to show the bad guys that he wasn't a cop. So he'd use in front of them. It wasn't in the manual, but it had become something of a regular occurrence for him.

But after Sean's death, it became something else. He'd slip the needle into the green line of a vein and drop the plunger, and it would be like turning down a dimmer on his suffering, the only thing that could stop the thoughts that tore through his brain like razor blades.

As a narcotics detective, he had plenty of access to the stuff, which was a good thing, because before long he needed more and more of it just to keep the plates spinning. He started wearing long-sleeved shirts all the time to cover the track marks, even in the dry heat of autumn.

"Look," she said. "I'm sorry I kept this from you. But I didn't want to just go ahead with it blindly, so that I'd end up regretting it later. Now, I know how I feel."

"How you feel . . ."

"*Yes.* I'm sure now. I know it's going to work, between us. I can see how you've changed. Getting away from the stress, from the pressure of the job, I can see you're like a different person."

"I guess I'm supposed to take that as a compliment?"

She nodded. "That's how I meant it."

He put his arm around her shoulder, and they began to walk again. The waves were small, raised welts against the grayness of the Pacific.

She leaned in to him. "What would you have said?"

"About what?"

"Before, you said I should have consulted you. Do you want to have another kid?"

He didn't have to think about it. "More than anything."

"And what about us? Do you want that?"

"You know I do."

She looked at his face, her eyes searching. "You're sure?"

He thought of all the things he'd lost, remembering the days he didn't give a shit if he lived or died.

"It's like we're getting another chance here, Laurie. To be a family again. To have a life."

She kissed him on the lips. "So you'll forgive me?"

"Under one condition."

She looked at him.

"I get to name the baby."

She shook her head. "No way. You remember all those names you came up with for Sean? Elvis . . . Leroy . . . *Sailor* . . ."

He smiled. "What're you talking about? Those are great names."

She rolled her eyes.

"I'm sorry," he said. "But you made your bed . . ."

Laurie held out her hand to shake. "All right, deal."

He ignored her hand, wrapping her up in his arms and pulling her close.

EIGHT

Two weeks later, Will pulled on the blue uniform shirt and polyester pants the Dodgers had issued him. Today was his first day of work.

He clipped his bronze badge to the front of his shirt and buckled his garrison belt. He wasn't allowed to carry any weapons, the only thing on the belt a two-way radio.

He left the house a little after 4:00 P.M. and headed for the freeway. He went past blocks of low-slung apartment buildings with flat roofs that were like stucco shoe boxes. Gilded signs bolted to the stucco facades announced the building's names in cursive letters: The Tahitian Palms, Valle View, Ocean Aire Terrace.

He realized that his new job wasn't much of a career move, but he was looking forward to going behind the scenes at the ballpark. Having access to the things the public never got to see, being allowed to walk out onto the manicured grass of the infield.

He turned onto Van Nuys Boulevard, the wide street lined with tall royal palms. Storefront signs advertised taquerias, pawnshops, and an Indian grocery. Metallic streamers strung on wires flapped in the breeze above a used car lot.

He tuned the Volvo's radio to KCRW. Then he went back to work on *The List*.

He'd already begun compiling two mental lists of baby names: one for boys and the other for girls, since he and Laurie didn't know which one they were going to have.

He'd been trying not to let himself get too excited about the baby, conflicted by a sense of guilt. On some level, he had the irrational idea that having another child was somehow a disservice to Sean's memory. There were sometimes entire days now where he wouldn't think of Sean, but the memories and pain were always there, like scars.

He waited for the metering light to turn green and then merged onto the 101.

He was so caught up with his list of baby names that he failed to notice the black Lincoln Town Car that had been trailing along behind him ever since he'd left the house.

NINE

The *lying-thieving-conniving-asshole* cop was also flat-out stupid. What kind of cop actually has his address and phone number listed right there in the phone book?

Crandall followed the taillights of the Volvo station wagon. The thing had to be ten years old, but it was clean, the blue paint glossy with a coat of wax. Crandall wondered why a man would actually choose to drive a Volvo. The thing looked like a refrigerator on wheels. He knew they were supposed to be safe, but if that was the only thing that mattered to you, then stay the fuck home.

Crandall's shift had ended at noon, and he'd driven straight out to the address in Van Nuys. His Town Car was a take-home, probably the only good thing he could find about the job.

He'd changed into the new clothes he'd bought, a red Under Armour top that clung to his ripped torso like a second skin and a pair of camouflage-patterned cargo shorts that were cut loose enough for his tree trunk legs. A pair of mirrored wraparounds he'd stolen off the spinner at Safeway completed the look.

The cop's house was on a nice quiet street east of Sepulveda. It wasn't all that big, but it was still a nice crib. The shingles sported a fresh coat of yellow paint, the front lawn looking like it had just been mown. Tropical plants sprouted up from the flower beds.

He'd sat across the street for hours, was about to give up for the day when the front door of the house swung open and the cop finally stepped outside. A bronze badge was clipped to the front of his uniform. Crandall wondered why he wasn't working plainclothes anymore, figured he'd probably screwed up, been busted back down to patrolman.

As Crandall drove, he tried to keep some distance between the Town Car and the cop's Volvo, easy to do with all the traffic clogging the freeway. He wondered where the hell they were going. He had to piss like a racehorse, being cooped up in the car so long.

He worked the stress ball in his left hand while he steered the Lincoln, his anger coming to a slow simmer. All these years of waiting and planning now moments away from becoming something real.

The cop exited at Stadium Way, Crandall pulling up right behind him, so close now that he could see the back of the cop's head.

Crandall hit the switch to lower his window. He'd polished off two containers of mu shu pork while he'd been camped in front of the cop's house. The empty containers sat on the floor of the Town Car, the interior reeking like a restaurant Dumpster despite the cardboard pine tree dangling from the rearview.

He picked up his fortune cookie from the leather surface of the passenger seat, cracked it open in his palm. He extracted the strip of paper, reading it as he popped the cookie into his mouth.

YOUR PAST SUCCESS WILL BE OVERSHADOWED BY
YOUR FUTURE SUCCESS.

About goddamned time, he thought. He tucked the fortune into the pocket of his shorts, then stepped on the gas when the light turned.

The cop hung a right, heading up the hill. There were booths up

ahead, blocking the road, a sign hanging above them that read WEL-
COME TO DODGER STADIUM.

The Volvo stopped at the tollbooth for a second, then got waved
through. Crandall cursed, pounding his fist against the steering wheel,
figuring he was screwed for sure because he didn't have a ticket.

But when he pulled up to the booth, all he had to do was fork over
fifteen bucks for parking and he was on his way again.

He floored it up the hill and caught up with the Volvo near the crest.
He tried to hang back, not too many other cars around up here, the road
wrapping around the stadium.

Crandall watched the cop park the Volvo, then maneuvered the big
Town Car into an empty space in the next row.

TEN

Will slung the strap of the backpack over his shoulder and walked toward the stadium.

He whistled to himself, the tune something caught in his head, picked up from the radio. It was going to be a beautiful night for a ball game, a warm breeze rustling the fronds of the palm trees that grew beside the stadium.

A man stood at the end of the row of cars, staring at him. Will did a double take when he realized that the man was turned away, the eyes staring out from the back of his bald head. As Will came closer, he saw that the eyes were tattoos. The colors were lifelike, the details so convincing that the effect was eerie.

The man turned around and took a step, blocking Will's path. Will changed course to move around him, but the man moved at the same time, so that Will was forced to stop walking to avoid colliding with him.

"Excuse me," Will said.

The man didn't move. "*Excuse* you? That's all you've got to say?"

He was some kind of bodybuilding freak, his bulging muscles as delineated as an anatomical drawing in a medical book come to life. Greenish veins as thick as pencils protruded from his arms.

"You know who I am?" the man asked.

"Mr. Universe?" Will couldn't help it. He'd always found the whole bodybuilding thing ridiculous, guys who were trying to compensate.

The man gritted his teeth, rhythmically squeezing something concealed in his left hand. "You don't remember me?" he asked. "'Cause I sure as shit remember you."

Will took a closer look at the man's face, saw a protruding forehead above eyes that were set too far apart, like a hammerhead shark's. A spray of acne stretched across his cheekbones. Will had a slight twinge of recognition but couldn't place the guy.

"I'm sorry," Will said. "Do I know you?"

"You should," the man said. "You sent me away."

So that's what this was all about. Will had heard the stories, ex-cons nursing grudges showing up to hassle the cop who'd busted them. Nothing usually coming of it, just the need to blow off some steam.

Still, Will wanted to defuse the situation before it could turn into something more.

"I'm sorry, it's been a while. I can't remember your name."

The guy nodded his massive head. "Erik Crandall."

Will looked at the guy again. He thought he could recall the bust, but he remembered a skinny young kid. Could this really be the same guy?

"How long've you been out?" Will asked.

"Couple of weeks."

Only a couple of weeks? Will wondered why the guy would just be getting released now if he'd been sent away on the drug charge.

Will took half a step back and turned his body to the side. He didn't want to engage with this hulk but wanted to be prepared if things turned physical.

He looked into the man's eyes, trying to make a connection. "I need you to understand something, Erik. What happened? It wasn't personal. I was only doing my job. You got caught. That's how the game works."

"You think this is some kind of *game*?"

There was a twitch now, under the guy's eye, his left hand clenching and unclenching at a furious pace. Will wondered if he was some kind of tweaker, but that didn't make sense, all the meat on the guy's bones.

"Calm down, Erik." Will regretted speaking the words as soon as they'd left his mouth, knew he'd made a mistake.

Crandall spoke through clenched teeth. "I am fucking *calm*."

"What are you looking for here?" Will asked. "You want me to apologize for busting you?"

The big man blinked. "No. What good would that do?"

"Then why are you here?"

People were starting to stream into the stadium now, fathers and sons dressed in Dodgers caps and jerseys.

"I want what you stole from me," Crandall said.

"You mean *time*? That's gone, there's nothing we can do about it. But what you can do is not waste any more time on bullshit like this."

"I'm not talking about *time*. I'm talking about what you stole."

"I don't know what you mean."

"You remember when you and your partner busted me?"

Will nodded his head. He had only a hazy recollection of it, not long after Sean died, days when he'd been fucked up most of the time.

"I ended up getting charged with selling eighty grams of fentanyl."

Will nodded. "Okay."

The man spoke with his jaw clenched, his face starting to go red. "When you busted me, there was a *pound* in that duffel bag."

If Will remembered it correctly, fentanyl was a hundred times more powerful than morphine, so this guy was talking about a lot of dope.

"Let me add it up for you," Crandall said. "You busted me with a pound of fentanyl. When I appeared for my arraignment, I'm charged with distribution of eighty grams. You don't have to be a genius to figure out where the rest went."

"So why didn't you say anything back then?"

Crandall smiled. The effect was unsettling, making his huge head turn into a jack-o'-lantern. "What, tell the DA that I was actually holding *more* weight? Volunteer for a longer sentence?"

"Look, Erik, I don't know what you're talking about. But I can swear to you that—"

"Shut the fuck up and listen." A vein throbbed along Crandall's temple. "I'm going to be reasonable with you here. That was a pound of fentanyl you stole. It would have went for half a mil, easy. That's *wholesale*. But I'm not asking you for what it would go for on the street. I'm not asking for interest. You can keep all that. All I want is the five hundred K back, and we can get on with our lives."

Will was sure now that the guy was either crazy or full of shit. Either way, he could tell it wouldn't do any good to stand here and attempt to reason with him. He just needed to get rid of him, didn't want any part of this guy's mental drama.

"I don't have your five hundred K, Erik," he said. "I don't have five hundred K, period."

ELEVEN

The *lying-thieving-conniving-asshole* cop must think he was some kind of moron.

Nothing was going the way Crandall had pictured it in his mind. He'd expected the cop to shit when he got in his face, but the guy was playing it all Steve McQueen, trying to jack him around. Speaking to him in that exaggerated fake-calm voice that his correctional counselor used.

He was fighting to keep a lid on his anger, a crimson curtain drawing closed at the edges of his vision. The cop calling him *Erik*, over and over, like they were old friends. He wanted to grab the cop, pick him up like a sack of garbage, and toss him onto the roof of a parked car.

"Don't try and bullshit me," Crandall said. "I'm gonna give you some time, to think on it."

"I don't need to think, Erik. Because I didn't steal your dope. And I don't have your money."

Crandall looked at the other man. He seemed smaller than the image he'd been carrying around inside his mind all these years, as if he'd somehow been shrunken by the passage of time.

For some reason, the cop wasn't carrying a gun on his belt. Nothing there but a radio. He took a closer look at his badge. Reading it for the first time.

LOS ANGELES DODGERS

And below that:

SECURITY

Jesus, the cop wasn't even a real cop. Crandall pointed at the badge. "You really think this can protect you?"

The cop's voice was still calm. "You've made some kind of mistake."

"No, you're the one making the mistake, *jackass*. Because, believe me, you don't want me in your life."

The cop looked him in the eyes, cocking his head just a little. "Is that supposed to be some kind of threat?"

Crandall spread out his opened palms. "It is what it is."

The cop looked off, watching the people streaming into the ballpark, like he was trying to make some kind of difficult decision. Looking older now, tired.

"I need you to listen to me carefully, Erik. I don't know what you think you're doing here. But you need to understand something. If I ever see you again, I'm going to make sure you get sent back to prison. Is that what you want?"

Crandall couldn't believe the set of stones on this guy. Fucker steals his dope, then turns around and threatens *him*? It was too much to take.

The crimson curtains had drawn fully closed now, Crandall seeing the cop, the ballpark, everything through a film of red. So much pressure building up inside his head that it made him afraid his skull might crack.

He reached out to grab the front of the cop's shirt.

The cop must have been waiting for it, because without warning he kicked Crandall hard in the shin with the heel of his black dress shoe. Just below his right knee, then raking it downward.

The pain made his eyes water, freezing his thoughts.

Before he could react, the cop's open hand shot forward and shoved Crandall in the throat, more force behind it than he was expecting.

The blue sky suddenly zoomed into view as Crandall began to pitch backward. He landed on his back, the ground knocking the wind out of his lungs. His head snapped backward, and the rear of his skull bounced off the pavement.

The world spun for a moment, the tops of the palm trees rotating like they were on a carousel. Then the cop's face came into view, blocking them out.

The cop looked into his eyes, a look of concern on his face. But when he saw that Crandall was still conscious, he spoke with an edge to his voice.

"Remember what I said, Erik. Don't let me see you again."

Crandall opened his mouth, but before he could say anything the cop turned and walked away.

Crandall tried to get up, but nothing seemed to be working right, his brain unable to communicate with his limbs, *The Rage* coursing through his veins.

He managed to get himself up on his hands and knees just in time to see the cop entering the stadium, disappearing through a door that was flanked by security guards and marked EMPLOYEES ONLY.

TWELVE

The next morning, Will waited until Laurie left for her job at the yoga studio, then poured himself a mug of coffee and took it into the home office.

He turned on the computer and Googled the California Department of Corrections and Rehabilitation. When he pulled up the site, he went to the page that listed the field offices and found the telephone number for the South Central parole office.

Will punched the number into the handset of the cordless phone. When he got the receptionist, he asked to be connected with the case officer who was handling Erik Crandall.

She put him on hold. Will waited, mentally composing the voice mail message he figured he would have to leave. Buddy came into the office, took a long look around, then went underneath the desk and lay down on Will's bare feet.

"This is Tony Nguyen. How can I help you?" The voice sounded young. He pronounced the name like "Win."

"My name is Will Magowan. I'm an ex-LAPD narcotics detective." Will mumbled the word "ex," hoping the other man wouldn't pick up on it. He wasn't about to lie outright and identify himself as a police officer, since that was a crime.

"What can I do for you, Detective?" Nguyen sounded rushed. Will was thankful for this, figuring it was the reason he hadn't bothered to verify his badge number.

"I need to talk to you about one of your cases. Name's Erik Crandall. With a *K*."

"Let me pull him up," Nguyen said. Over the phone, Will heard the clattering of a computer keyboard. "That's K-R-A-N—"

"Will interrupted him. "No, it's *C-R*—"

"I thought you said *K*."

"I did, but it's at the end of his first name. Erik with a *K*."

"That's kind of unusual."

"That's why I spelled it."

Will waited, listening to the man hunt and peck.

"Found him," Nguyen said. "Just out of Quentin. Checked in with us on the twenty-eighth, right on schedule."

"In person?"

"That's the way it works."

"I'm just kind of surprised. Because I'm pretty sure you would've remembered this guy," Will said. "Big like a bodybuilder, a set of eyes tattooed on the back of his head."

"I didn't see him."

"What do you mean?"

"I took a personal day. He was seen by the officer of the day."

"So when are you going to see him?"

"We're supposed to do a home visit within ten days, but who knows."

"I don't understand."

"Guy's not High Control. Not a second-striker, or a gangbanger. We're totally swamped over here."

"But not too swamped to take a personal day." Will couldn't help it, the words slipping out on a wave of frustration.

"I'm not sure I like your tenor, Detective."

Tenor? Underneath the desk, Buddy got up, turned in a small circle, then laid back down.

"I'm sorry," Will said. "I was out of line."

"You should understand, with the state budget crunch, we've got a hiring freeze. Guy just retired, we're not even allowed to replace him, had to split up his cases. So forgive me if I don't have the time to go chasing down some little drug offender."

Will fought to keep the anger out of his voice. "I was the arresting officer on the case that sent him away. Yesterday, he showed up and threatened me."

There was a pause. "I better get your name again," Nguyen said. "And your badge number."

Shit. "My name is Will Magowan." Will shut his eyes, wishing he could hang up the phone and start fresh with this guy, play it differently. "I don't have a badge number."

"Why not? I thought you said you were LAPD."

"I was," Will said. "I'm not anymore."

There was another pause, longer this time.

"Then I shouldn't even be talking to you," Nguyen said. "I've already told you more than I should have."

"Did you hear what I just said? This guy threatened me."

"With what?"

Will thought about it. "He got in my face, told me I didn't want him in my life."

"I don't know if that really qualifies as a threat. Did he say anything specific?"

"It wasn't what he said. It was the way he said it."

"Did you file a report with the police?"

"No, I wanted to come to you first. Figured you'd want to take care of it."

"I don't know what you expect me to do. This guy checked in on schedule. He's already set up his PACT meeting. He's employed, he's got suitable living arrangements. Compared to the rest of my caseload, he's a model citizen."

"Except for the part about harassing me."

"Unfortunately, this stuff happens from time to time. Chances are, you'll never see the guy again."

"What happens if I do?"

"If he's breaking the law, go to the police."

"How about taking some preventative action, keep him from breaking the law?"

"It's a nice idea, but that's not my job."

"Maybe it should be."

"Look, I've got to go," Nguyen said. "Thanks for calling."

Will heard a click, but kept the phone to his ear for a moment, not wanting to acknowledge that the other man had just hung up on him.

THIRTEEN

Crandall steered the Town Car into the parking lot of the medical building. He'd spotted the place yesterday, out in Sherman Oaks, when he'd stopped in at the vitamin shop next door to pick up some protein powder.

The orange skull and crossbones was what had caught his eye, the bold letters spelling out the word BIOHAZARD. After that, the idea had just popped into his head.

He didn't want to escalate things with the cop, just wanted to get back his money and ride off into the sunset. But after what happened on Tuesday, what choice did he have? The dude trying to blow him off, then pulling that sneaky Jackie Chan shit on him. He couldn't let that stand.

The windows of the Town Car were up, the air-conditioning blasting out a chilled breeze against the heat of the Valley. He was playing one of the classical music CDs that they'd issued to him along with the car. It was Vivaldi. He'd come to like it, the music smoothing the rough edges off his day.

He took a slow cruise through the parking lot, moving along the rear of the building. It was two stories, covered in mustard-colored stucco that was rough with swirled trowel marks. The endocrinologist's office was on the ground floor, sandwiched between an orthodontist and a chiropractor. It looked like the office was closed, the lights turned off on the far side of the windows, but he kept the car rolling, wanting to be sure.

The metal box was right where he'd first spotted it, hanging by a metal bracket from the top of the door. The sign on the front of the box had the name of a medical lab right below the biohazard symbol.

He pulled into a space in front of the endocrinologist's office but left the engine running. The parking lot was deserted. He picked up his protein shake from the dashboard cup holder and took a gulp. It tasted like ass, like drinking sweetened sand. He'd had the woman in the health food store add a double boost of creatine powder. Not exactly 'roids, but it would have to do for the time being.

He waited a couple more minutes, still no sign of anyone. He shut off the engine and got out. He walked up to the endocrinologist's office and tried the door.

Locked.

He banged on the door, putting on an act like he was supposed to be there. "Hello?" he called. "I thought I had an appointment."

No response.

He went back to the Lincoln, popped the trunk, and took out the tire iron.

The lid of the lab box had a lip on it, so that he couldn't get the flat end of the tire iron in far enough. He reached up, using the tip of the tire iron to work at the lip, moving back and forth until he succeeded in prying up a two-inch-long section. He jammed the tire iron into the gap beneath the lid and yanked down hard. He heard the sound of the lock mechanism snap as the lid popped up.

The top of the box was above his eye level, so he couldn't see what was inside. He reached up and stuck his hand down inside the box. He rooted around, felt a plastic container. He pulled it out.

The clear jar was filled with brown urine, a sticker on the side filled out with a patient's name. Crandall set the container down on the concrete walkway, then reached back up inside the box.

This time he came out with three plastic vials that were bundled together with a rubber band and filled with dark blood. He was careful as he set them down on the walkway.

He repeated the process until he couldn't feel anything but the empty metal bottom of the box. He looked down, doing a quick count. He estimated there were close to sixty vials of blood, a dozen containers of piss.

He bent over, ignoring the urine, gathering up the blood.

Then he got back inside the Town Car and headed for the cop's house.

F O U R T E E N

The mechanical arm pivoted and rose upward. Will drove the Volvo out of the parking garage.

The Cinerama Dome was having a Douglas Sirk retrospective, and he and Laurie had gone to see *All That Heaven Allows*. Then they'd spent the last twenty minutes stuck in the mob of traffic trying to exit the parking structure.

He hit the switch to lower his window. The night air was humid and carried a vague hint of the sea. He turned left on Hollywood Boulevard, lots of people out on the sidewalks, a mixture of wide-eyed tourists and homeless men pushing shopping carts stolen from Safeway.

Laurie wore a white linen shirt that set off her tanned skin. "How's The Names Project coming?"

He knew what she meant but played dumb. "I'm not sure what you're referring to."

"The name. For our baby."

"Oh, *those* names. I'm making good progress."

"Care to give me a preview?"

He worked to keep a straight face. "Sorry, but that information's privileged."

She brushed her blond hair back from her face. "Don't I have any privileges? As the mother?"

He shrugged, smiling now. "Hey, you created the situation."

She reached across the parking brake and placed her hand on top of his thigh. She moved it up and down, stroking the fabric of his jeans, her touch feathery.

"Tell me," she said.

He merged onto the 101 at Vine. He tried to concentrate on the road, the white lights of oncoming traffic sweeping past. He wondered where so many people could possibly be going at this hour of the night.

Her hand kept stroking his thigh, up and down. Their lovemaking had taken a turn over the past week or so, all for the better as far as he was concerned. There was an intensity that was there now, something he hadn't even noticed was missing, Laurie participating in a way that made him realize that she had been holding something back.

He couldn't figure out if it was the mental process she'd gone through in deciding to have the baby with him or something hormonal, but he wasn't about to argue.

She leaned over and whispered in his ear, her breath warm and moist. "Come on, just give me a name."

"I suppose I could do that," he said. "But just one."

"Okay."

Will waited, giving a pause for dramatic effect. "If it's a girl . . . Chantal."

"*Chantal?* That sounds like some hooker from Detroit."

Will shook his head. "Those are precisely the kinds of stereotypes our little girl will smash as she goes through life."

They held hands as they climbed up onto the small front porch of the house. The outdoor light was on, the sound of crickets coming from the darkness of the flower beds.

He began to reach into his pocket for the house keys, but she kissed him hard on the lips, her tongue thrusting inside his mouth. She tasted like the Red Vines they'd shared at the movie.

They stood there under the yellow glow of the porch light, making out like he was a teenager dropping her off at her parents' after the prom.

She reached her hand down into the front pocket of his jeans, fumbling around for the keys. He heard them jangle, but her fingers kept moving, dancing across his thigh, then taking hold of him in the warmth of her hand.

She looked into his eyes, what he saw there more erotic than her touch. Then she pulled her hand out and handed him the keys.

He fumbled with the lock, anxious to get her inside. When he finally managed to slip the key into the cylinder, he realized the dead bolt was already unlocked. He thought he remembered locking it, but they'd been in a big rush to make it to the movie.

He opened the door, and they pushed each other into the living room, her arms wrapped around his neck. He didn't bother to turn on the lights, his hands on her bottom, pulling her tight, their bodies grinding together as they kissed.

He could smell something, faint and dissonant, not part of the house's familiar smells.

"What?" she said.

"Nothing."

He opened the top button of her shirt, gentle as he slid his hand over the smooth fabric of her bra. Her breasts were bigger now, more than a handful, her nipple stiffening against his palm.

"Careful with those," she said.

"I know."

They held on to each other as he moved her backward, waltzing through the dark living room. He laid her down on the couch and started working at the rest of the buttons on her shirt.

"Don't you want to go in the bedroom?" she asked.

"We'll get there. Eventually."

The strange smell was stronger now. Metallic. Familiar, yet impossible for him to identify.

He kissed the fine and soft blond hair that grew along the nape of her neck, reached down and unbuckled her belt. He unzipped the fly of her jeans, worked his hand down, slipping it under the elastic waistband of her panties.

"*Stop,*" she said. Her whole body going rigid.

He looked down at her. "Did I hurt you?"

She pushed him off. "Turn on the light."

He was confused. "What for?"

"Something's wrong." The pitch of her voice rose. "Just turn on the *light.*"

He fumbled around in the darkness until he'd found the metal base of the lamp on the end table, feeling his way up to the pull chain.

He yanked it, but nothing happened.

"*Turn it on.*" She was almost screaming now.

"I'm trying." He pulled the chain again, but the light didn't come on. "Bulb's out."

"Come *on.*"

He jumped up and found his way over to the wall switch for the recessed lights. He hit the switch. The lights came on full blast, the light too bright after all the darkness.

Will blinked, momentarily blinded.

He saw Laurie lying on her back on the white couch. He looked at her, his heart beginning to hammer in his chest, his palms becoming slick with perspiration.

He blinked some more, not quite able to believe what he was seeing. "What happened?"

She was sitting up now, redness smeared on her hands and shirt, the white upholstery of the couch soaked with dark blood.

Her voice was shaky. "It's not from me."

FIFTEEN

The soapy water turned crimson as Will wrung the sponge out into the bucket.

He blotted the sponge against the white canvas fabric of a couch cushion, the stain lifting a little, fading to a dull pink. He wore yellow dishwashing gloves but still felt a sense of unease, not knowing whose blood had been dumped on the couch, or where it had come from.

The police had left just a few minutes ago, a couple of disposable coffee cups on the fireplace mantel the only sign that they'd ever been there. Laurie moved about the living room, trying to clean up. She was humming to herself as she worked, a song that he couldn't recognize.

Will rubbed harder at the cushion. "I don't think this's going to come out."

She came over and looked over his shoulder. "I'll try calling one of those upholstery cleaning services."

"I don't think they'll be able to do anything," he said. "It's blood."

She looked down at him. "I'm aware of that."

She hadn't said much since the cops had left. She hadn't said much when they were there, either, letting him take them through what happened. Listening as he told them about Crandall, what had happened the other day at the ballpark. How Will was positive this must have been his doing.

She put the coffee cups she was carrying down on the end table. "Why didn't you tell me? About this guy threatening you?"

"I didn't want to get you worried."

"And what about now? Do I not look worried?"

"I'm sorry, I thought I had it under control."

She looked down at the stained couch, not needing to say anything to get across her accusation.

He looked at his watch. Four ten. He had that curious feeling that came with staying up all night, bone-deep exhaustion combined with an adrenaline-fueled sense of being wired.

"This guy," she said. "What's his name again?"

"Crandall. Erik Crandall."

"Those things he told you. About his drugs being stolen. Why would he be saying that?"

"I don't know, maybe because he's crazy?"

"So you're saying he's just making the whole thing up?"

He ran his palm across his cheek, the stubble like sandpaper. "The things that happened back then? The things I did? They're all pretty hazy. But I'm pretty sure I'd remember stealing a pound of fentanyl, don't you think?"

She brought her arms up and hugged herself, looking around the living room. "This is just such a creepy feeling. Knowing he was in here."

They'd already gone through the rest of the house, but there was no evidence that anything else had been touched. Fortunately, they'd left Buddy out in the fenced backyard when they went to the movie, or no telling what might have happened.

"What're you thinking?" she asked.

"Nothing."

"Don't tell me *nothing*. What are you thinking?"

"That I need to find this guy. Make him understand that he better not pull a stunt like this again."

"And how are you going to do that?"

Will opened his mouth, then closed it again. He hadn't worked things through that far. In his mind's eye, he saw himself sticking his gun into Crandall's face. He could see that this plan had several flaws, not the least of which was the fact that he no longer owned a gun.

He stood up and threw the bloody sponge into the bucket, soapy red water splashing out onto the hardwood floor.

"You need to calm down," Laurie said.

He wheeled around, about to snap, then started to smile.

"What?"

"That's what I said to Crandall. It didn't work on him, either."

"Thich Nhat Hanh says that every time you act on your anger, you only make it stronger."

He smiled. "And Bobby Kennedy said don't get mad, get even."

He used a paper towel to wipe up the floor. She came over to him, put her hand on his shoulder, and looked into his eyes. "You're not a cop anymore."

"I know that."

"You're a citizen now," she said. "Let the police take care of it."

SIXTEEN

Los Alamitos Race Course was all the way out in the OC, west of Anaheim.

Crandall was afraid that he'd be violating the conditions of his parole by driving here, since he wasn't allowed to travel outside a fifty-mile radius of his listed place of residence. But he'd zeroed the odometer when he left work, surprised to see that it was only thirty miles. He'd made it in less than an hour, the traffic light this late on a Sunday night.

The Town Car was parked in a far-off corner of the racetrack's parking lot, away from the overhead lights. He was slumped low in the driver's seat, finishing off the last bite from his second order of mu shu pork. It came with some kind of rubbery Chinese pancakes, but he preferred to just eat straight from the takeout container.

He checked the clock on the dashboard, 1:45 glowing in green LEDs. The last car had driven out of the lot close to an hour ago.

Crandall lifted his fortune cookie from where he'd left it on the armrest, brought it up to his nose, and inhaled, silently praying to let there be something good waiting inside. He cracked it open with his right hand and extracted his fortune:

IF YOU WANT THE RAINBOW, YOU MUST TO
PUT UP WITH THE RAIN.
D. PARTON

He read it through twice, wanting to commit it to memory. He tucked the slip of paper into the pocket of his pants and used the grab handle to pull himself out of the car. He walked around to get the bolt cutters from the trunk.

He walked in the opposite direction from the entrance to the race-track, heading over to where a tall hurricane fence topped with razor wire ran along the southern edge of the facility.

A narrow concrete walkway ran beside the fence, the ugly yellow glare from security lights shining down on it. Crandall had planned for this, wore a black windbreaker he'd just bought over his black track pants. He'd even considered wearing a black ski mask but figured he might as well just put on a sign that read I'M A CRIMINAL.

He reached into his back pocket and pulled out the folded Google satellite map he'd printed out at the library, checking it to make sure he was heading in the right direction.

He went along the walkway until he saw a group of low-slung buildings lined up on the other side of the fence, then kept going until he came to a gate.

The padlock was a maximum-security job, a thick chromed-steel hasp arching over the heavy body. Crandall put the jaws of the bolt cut-ter on it, then squeezed the handles together. He grunted as he felt his triceps and pecs go hard, then the padlock popped open.

Crandall rolled the gate open and went through, closing it behind him. He put the padlock back, arranging it so that if someone gave it a casual glance it would look like it was still locked.

He found a building with a painted wood sign that read ART VAN-DELAY RACING STABLES. Crandall walked up to the front door and kicked it in.

It was pitch black inside the stable. He gave his eyes some time to adjust, inhaling the smell of hay and the tang of manure. Large animals rustled inside stalls.

He set the bolt cutters down against the wall, reached into the pocket of the windbreaker, and pulled out a folding knife. It was a Spyderco with a serrated blade. Carrying the knife was a violation of his parole, but so was everything else he was about to do.

The stalls had Dutch doors, the tops open. Crandall crept up to one of them and peered inside. In the darkness he could make out the massive shape of an animal. The horse was sound asleep on its feet, its tail switching to an erratic rhythm.

Crandall wondered how it could fall asleep without its muscles going soft, what kept it from just crashing to the ground. The dumb horse wasn't even aware of him standing there. He ran his thumb over the serrations of the knife blade, thinking now of the cop, the blood he'd left back there. He would let the man stew in it a little longer, then make his next move.

A canvas feedbag hung from the bottom of the stall door. Crandall stuck his hand down into it, pulled out a piece of hay. He stuck it into the corner of his mouth and chewed, something he'd seen Jack Palance do once in an old movie.

Crandall took a short metal flashlight from the other pocket of his windbreaker. He switched it on and went down a long corridor with stalls along both sides. Just a dirt floor with yellow pieces of hay pressed down into it. The walls were rough wood, bridles and ropes hanging from hooks.

At the far end of the corridor were three doors. He opened the first one, shining his light around the room. Only a metal desk, a computer, some file cabinets.

He shut the door behind him and tried the next one. Locked. He figured this must be it, took one step back, raised his right foot, and smashed the sole of his shoe just below the door handle.

The door exploded inward, pieces of wood like daggers flying from the frame. The noise echoed around up in the rafters of the stable, the horses moving now, blowing air out through their noses, their hooves stomping against the ground.

A huge sling hung down from a set of pulleys attached to the ceiling of the room. One wall was covered by built-in cabinets. A Formica counter held jars of cotton balls and bottles of rubbing alcohol.

Crandall went over to the cabinets, opened the upper set of doors, found bandages, packages of instant ice, and the biggest rectal thermometer he'd ever seen. He tossed it all out onto the floor. Outside the door, the horses began to whinny, joining together in a dissonant chorus.

He flung open the door to the bottom cabinets and found a box of syringes, the needles sheathed inside plastic protective caps. They looked enormous, but he figured he could make them work and shoved a handful into the pocket of his windbreaker.

He froze when he heard a noise outside the window and killed the flashlight. He crossed the room, up on the balls of his feet, pressing himself against the wall next to the window.

He craned his head to look through the glass. A man walked past, maybe a foot away from Crandall, the pane of glass all that was separating them. Crandall held his breath. The man looked like a Mexican, the sleeve of his shirt embroidered with the logo of a security company, an automatic holstered on his hip.

Crandall looked around the room for a weapon, then remembered the Spyderco. He'd left it open inside the pocket of the windbreaker. He wrapped his fingers around the plastic handle, raising it up in line with the front of his shoulder, waiting for the guard to turn and see him standing there.

Waiting. The feeling like being back in the yard, some poor bastard about to get shanked, everyone knowing it except for the poor bastard.

White wires hung down from the guard's ears. He bobbed his head, listening to music that Crandall couldn't hear. The guard kept walking, moving on to the next building, his tuneless whistling coming in through the glass.

Crandall let his breath out. He thought about bailing but figured that as long as he'd come this far, he might as well get what he came for.

He went back over to the cabinets and opened the door to the last one. Saw glass vials, his heart starting to race. He pulled one out, shined a flashlight onto the label: PHENYLBUTAZONE. Not what he was looking for. He grabbed another vial, some kind of antibiotic, tossed it out onto the floor.

He pulled the bottles out one by one, glancing at the labels, then hurling them onto the floor. Smashing them. Knowing he needed to be quiet, but his fury and disappointment now too much to control.

He'd felt sure this was the place to find what he needed. He couldn't deny the certainty that he was growing weaker with each passing day, becoming desperate to get his power back. He'd tried asking around at the gym, but everyone there told him they never touched the stuff. Judging from their puny biceps, he believed them.

He kicked shut the door of the cabinet and was starting to leave the room when he noticed the desk.

It was old, made from steel, like something the government would issue. He went around it and saw that the bottom drawer had a lock on it. He pulled on the handle, but it wouldn't open. He thought about using the knife but didn't want to risk ruining the blade.

He took a letter opener from the desktop and jammed it into the space between the bottom drawer and the one above it. He applied leverage, worried the blade would snap, but the drawer popped open.

Crandall shined the flashlight inside, saw close to a dozen white cardboard boxes. He grabbed one, ripping open the flap to pull out a glass vial. He looked at the familiar label:

Equipoise®
Boldenone Undecylenate Injection
50 mg/mL

And below that, in smaller letters:

Long Acting Anabolic Steroid for Horses

Crandall was gentle with the vials as he pulled them from the boxes, precious cargo, taking them out one at a time until he had filled all of his pockets.

SEVENTEEN

The Van Nuys Community Police Station of the Los Angeles Police Department is located in a complex of government buildings on Sylmar.

Will sat on a wooden bench in front of the station, sipping coffee from a steel travel mug. The late morning sunlight fell on the business card he was holding.

The card belonged to Richard Ryder, the detective who'd come out to the house in the aftermath of the blood-dumping incident. Will had already called the station's Detective Desk and been told that Ryder was out at a court appearance.

Will had been sitting there for almost an hour now, hoping to catch Ryder when he returned from the courthouse on the other side of the plaza. He wanted to see what kind of progress the police were making with Erik Crandall.

The air held the particular smell he'd come to associate with Los Angeles. It was something he could instantly recognize but could not describe, a mixture of brine from the Pacific and dust baked dry by the sun, rustling pepper trees and the mentholated scent of eucalyptus, *refritos* simmering inside taco trucks, chlorinated water evaporating from thousands of backyard swimming pools, wild sage flowering on the brown hills.

Will spotted Ryder making his way across the plaza and got up from the bench to head the detective off.

Ryder carried a battered leather briefcase in his right hand. An unlit cigarette stuck out from the corner of his mouth.

He stopped when he recognized Will. "Mr. Magowan? What brings you down here?"

"Just thought I'd check in."

Ryder nodded. "You could have just called."

"I did," Will said. "Three times."

Ryder looked at his watch. "I apologize for that. Things are absolutely bat shit around here."

"What kind of progress are you making?"

Ryder looked at him. "You mean with your thing?"

Will tried to keep his voice even. "Yes. With my *thing*."

Ryder glanced around the parking lot as if looking for someone to rescue him. "Like I told you and your wife, you need to be patient."

"It's been over a week. We haven't heard anything."

"We're working on it."

"Have you interviewed Crandall?"

"Not yet."

Will took a breath. "Why not?"

"We referred it to Parole."

Will shut his eyes, then opened them again. "And what did they say?"

"His parole officer was out. I left a voice mail."

Will pinched the bridge of his nose. "I'm handing you a collar on a silver platter here."

"It's not that simple. Look at it from my point of view. You say it's this guy, what's his name?"

"Crandall. Erik Crandall."

Ryder nodded. "Right. You say it's this Crandall guy, but you should know that's not enough. We've got no corroborating evidence."

"Then why don't you guys go out and *get* some?"

Ryder stared at Will. The cigarette was still in his mouth, but he made no move to light it. "I can see you're upset, but the only thing that got hurt here was a couch."

Will shook his head. "He threatened me."

"We've already been through that." Ryder picked up his briefcase. "Listen to me. You were a cop once. You know how things work, right? Even if we did have evidence to file charges, what would they be? Trespass? *Vandalism?* Those are misdemeanors."

"It would be enough to violate his parole."

Ryder jammed a finger at him, like Will was a star pupil who'd just given the correct answer in class. *"Exactly,"* he said. "That's why we punted it over to the Parole guys. Let them play out the string."

EIGHTEEN

Crandall felt like Superman.

He'd been into his stash of Equipoise, 150 milligrams a day for the last week, trying to make up for lost time. It felt like coming home, the first he'd felt like himself since leaving Quentin, confident he could do anything, free of physical limits.

He'd had a constant hard-on since he'd woken up this morning, like something they warned about in those commercials for Viagra, but he knew it was from the 'roids coursing through his bloodstream. He'd tucked it sideways inside the tight Jockey shorts he was wearing, the front of his cargo shorts like a pup tent.

He walked up to the ticket window at Dodger Stadium, bent down, and spoke into the small circular opening set into the Plexiglas window. He asked the woman on the other side for the cheapest ticket they had.

The seat was all the way up in the top deck of the stadium, but Crandall didn't care. He wasn't there to watch the game. He pushed some folded bills through the slot at the bottom of the window. He didn't have any credit cards.

He went through the security check without a problem, squeezing the stress ball in his left hand. The game was about to start, but lots of people were still milling around the concourse, buying food and plastic cups of beer. Many of them wore replica jerseys with the names of players on the back.

He walked past the concession stands, the smell of frying meat making him salivate. He thought about buying himself a cheeseburger, but thought he'd hold off for a little while. He'd just eaten some Chinese out in the car.

He came to a stand that sold souvenirs: miniature wooden bats, T-shirts, and giant blue foam fingers that you could stick on your hand. Against the back wall was a display of baseball caps. The Dodgers, of course, but also a small assortment of other teams.

When the guy behind the counter asked if he wanted anything, Crandall pointed at a black and orange San Francisco Giants cap. Not that he was a fan, but he knew that the Giants were the nemesis of the Dodgers. He figured he would wear it as a taunt, see if any of the Dodgers fans were actually foolish enough to give him any shit.

Crandall paid for it and walked away. The cap had a strap on the back to adjust the size, but even at the loosest setting it was a tight fit on his head. He knew that all the 'roids had been making his skull grow bigger but hadn't realized how much, since he didn't usually wear a hat. He left the strap undone and tugged on the brim to force the cap farther down onto the crown of his bald head.

His section was in the upper level, the diamond far down below, the players looking as small as ants.

A group of black kids was gathered in front of home plate, wearing matching yellow T-shirts, singing "The Star-Spangled Banner." Their high-pitched voices played over the PA system, the part about stuff gallantly streaming, people down below him all standing up with their caps pulled to their hearts.

He went down the concrete stairs to his row. The section was deserted, Crandall the only one up here in the Nosebleed. But he checked the numbers on the arms of the seats, moving along the empty row until he found the one he'd paid for.

NINETEEN

Will stood in the Dodgers dugout, watching one of the Diamondbacks players stride up to home plate. Will was amazed how different things looked when you were this close up, the way details stood out. The stitching that attached the number to the back of a jersey, the crisp white chalk line of the batter's box, the smoothness of grass the color of an emerald.

Will struggled to look serious but still couldn't quite believe that he was actually getting paid to be here.

The batter used his cleats to dig in at the plate, the stands rising up all around, dwarfing him. It was a strange ritual, tens of thousands of people sitting there, looking down to watch one man act alone.

It was a Wednesday night game, the crowd light, the upper deck of the stadium mostly unoccupied. A warm breeze fluttered the pennants lined up along the top of the stands. The stadium lights came on, the artificial white glow blending with the dying twilight.

He was a rover tonight, his assignment to move around the stadium and be ready to respond to any radio calls.

He took an elevator up to the press box, went inside to grab some popcorn from the machine. Most of the seats inside the box were filled, writers with laptops set out on the long white counter. They talked to one another, ignoring the game being played outside the open windows.

Will's radio had a coiled wire that ran underneath his uniform shirt, feeding the earpiece, like something a Secret Service agent might wear.

He listened to the radio chatter, heard his supervisor's voice asking for coverage on the upper deck. Will pressed the button to transmit, said that he was on it.

He took the elevator up, sharing the cab with a vendor clutching a metal pole topped with dangling plastic bags of cotton candy, like bales of human hair dyed blue and pink.

He wasn't all that surprised at how empty the upper sections were. It was only the bottom of the second inning, Dodgers fans notorious for showing up late and leaving before the end of the game, attempting to get a jump on the traffic.

He walked around the first-base side of the upper concourse, the night air now turning cool.

A man wearing a San Francisco Giants cap sat alone in the front row of section 36, down the right field line, the rest of the section empty. The man had his feet propped up on the tubular metal railing at the front of the section.

Far down below in the field level seats, fans batted around a beach ball, its primary colors spinning as it floated from one set of out-stretched hands to the next.

Will was about to move on when the man removed his cap. His head was bald, and two eyes stared out from the back of his skull. Will froze, his heartbeat accelerating.

He took a step down the staircase, unsure of what he was about to do, knowing only that he needed to take care of the situation once and for all. To impress upon this flaming asshole that he had made a big mistake.

He grabbed the back of a seat for balance as he went down the steep concrete stairs. The sensation was unsettling, like walking down the face of a cliff. He'd never liked it up here; the whole setup made him feel slightly dizzy from the height. Beyond the railing the section dropped off into thin air, fans moving around far down below. Over the PA system the organ played a series of notes, and then the crowd yelled out the word "Charge."

Erik Crandall brought a bag of sunflower seeds up to his mouth. Will was a couple of rows away when Crandall's bald head swiveled around on his neck, as if he'd been able to see him coming through the pair of tattooed eyes.

The big man stayed in his seat, his sneakers still propped up on the railing. He spit the sunflower shells out, the ground surrounding him already covered with them.

Crandall smiled. "I was hoping I'd run into you."

Will was having a hard time catching his breath. "I know it was you that dumped the blood. In my *house*."

"That's on you." Crandall spread his hands apart. "I told you you didn't want me in your life."

Will had been expecting him to lie. Now that Crandall had simply admitted to the act, he found himself unsure of what to say next.

Crandall tipped some more of the seeds into his mouth. "Calm down," he said. "No use crying over spilt blood."

"Did you enjoy your time in prison? Because I'm going to make sure you get sent back."

Crandall shook his huge head, as if Will had somehow disappointed him. "I was really hoping you'd come to your senses. That you'd do the right thing."

"You're delusional," Will said. "I told you I didn't take your drugs."

"And I know you're lying. I've been checking up on you."

Crandall grabbed hold of the metal railing and used it to pull himself to his feet. Will had forgotten just how enormous the man was, a head taller than him, his upper torso as wide as a refrigerator.

Crandall brought his face close to Will's, thick veins standing out from his bald skull. "I went to the library, read some old newspaper articles about you. I found out why you were shit-canned from the police."

"What does that have to do with anything?"

Crandall placed his index finger against the cleft in his chin and looked upward, acting as if he were pondering something. "Let's see, a cop who's addicted to heroin busts me with a pound of fentanyl, which then mysteriously goes missing. Gee, what's that say to you?"

"That your logic's flawed."

Crandall's face reddened. "You don't want me as your enemy."

"I don't want you as my *friend*," Will said. "Just stay the fuck away from me."

Crandall's right hand shot forward, his fingers clamping around Will's neck. Will's feet came off the ground. He felt himself rising up into the air, looking down now into Crandall's red eyes.

Crandall stepped forward, carrying Will out in front of him.

Will felt the metal bar of the railing bang against his calves. Then his body tilted backward, the stadium lights shining into his eyes. Crandall held him suspended over the rail by his neck, nothing but the cool night air beneath him. The next level was several stories down, the people below a sea of swimming dots.

Will thought about jabbing his thumb into Crandall's eye but was afraid that would only make him drop him. He reached up and grabbed on to the front of Crandall's shirt, just to hold on to something.

Crandall looked down at him. "Get me my money."

It was hard for Will to speak, Crandall's hand around his throat. "I don't have it."

"Like I said, I've been checking up on you. I got your property records."

From far below came the crack of a wooden bat making contact with a cowhide ball, the crowd cheering. Will reached his hand down to his waist, feeling for the radio on his belt. He found the TRANSMIT button and held it down.

Crandall didn't seem to notice. "Your house is worth five fifty, six hundred grand easy."

Will tried to stall for time, keeping his thumb pressed down on the TRANSMIT button. "What's your point?"

"My dope disappeared in September of 2003. Three months later, you pay cash for your house. That's quite the coincidence."

Will and Laurie had been renting the house for years, with an option to purchase. After Sean had died, they decided to buy it, using the money Laurie's mother had left them in her will. His wishful thinking at the time was that the house would somehow help to hold the two of them together.

Will heard footsteps on concrete. Over Crandall's left shoulder he saw two security guards he didn't recognize coming down the stairs.

"Stop right there," one of them said.

Crandall's head swiveled around. Will reached behind him and tried to grab hold of the railing, sure he was going to drop.

The other guard was talking into his radio. "We need backup in section thirty-six."

Crandall turned and looked into Will's eyes. He leaned forward, Will canting backward, his feet kicking at nothing but air. "Just get me my money."

Then he pivoted and tossed Will down on top of the row of seats. An armrest caught Will in the rib cage, making him gasp.

Crandall went up the steps two at a time.

Will pointed. "Stop him."

The two guards watched Crandall come, holding their ground.

Crandall reached out his left hand and stiff-armed one of the guards, knocking him to the concrete. The second guard jumped aside, letting the big man pass by.

Will climbed to his feet, but by the time he reached the aisle, Crandall was already cresting the top of the stairs.

Crandall paused, his bald head swiveling from side to side. His enormous frame was silhouetted in the whiteness of the stadium lighting. Then he turned into an archway and disappeared from sight.

TWENTY

"Are you okay?" Joe Gibbs shut his office door, then went around the desk and sat down.

Will rubbed his neck, his skin crawling with the sense memory of Crandall's hands around his throat. What he wanted more than anything was to just go home and take a long, hot shower.

"I'm fine," he said.

Gibbs picked up a gold-plated fountain pen and posted the cap on the end. "Take me through what happened. Start at the beginning."

Gibbs's cologne was overpowering inside the closed-up office, making Will feel a little dizzy. The situation with Crandall had gotten way out of hand, surpassing anything he'd envisioned. But after what the ex-con had just done, in a public place, at least there would be enough for the police to nail him.

"I spotted this guy sitting alone in section thirty-six." Will's throat hurt when he talked, his voice hoarse. "I approached him."

Gibbs made a note with the pen. "For what reason? Was he doing something wrong?"

"No, he already had. He vandalized my house."

Gibbs stopped writing and looked at him. "Wait a sec. You *knew* this guy?"

Will nodded. "His name's Erik Crandall. He came up to me a month ago, tried to threaten me."

Gibbs made another note. "Why would he have cause to threaten you?"

"It's a long story."

"I bet that it is." Gibbs reached up and tugged at the knot of his tie. "You see this shit? This is how come I didn't want to hire you in the first place."

Will's face felt hot. "He came after *me*."

"I don't want to hear it. You got some kind of beef with this guy, don't bring it into my ballpark." Gibbs picked up the incident report from his desk and shook it in the air. "What happens if the owner hears about this, what the hell am I supposed to tell him?"

Will looked at his watch, conscious of the time that was being wasted while he sat here. "The other two guards are eyewitnesses. I need to file a report with the LAPD."

"Not if you want to keep your job."

Will wasn't sure that he'd heard right. "What're you talking about?"

"You press charges, the *Times* will have a field day. That's exactly the kind of publicity we can't afford."

Will rubbed his neck. "I have the right to go to the police."

"And since you're a provisional employee, I have the right to fire you without cause. You go to the police, you go as an ex-employee."

Will raised his voice, his ribs hurting from where they'd slammed into the armrest of the stadium seats. "This lunatic needs to be arrested, not walking around out on the street."

"Then let him be arrested out on the *street*." Gibbs put down his pen. "It's just fortunate none of our guests were aware of what happened. I aim to keep it that way."

Gibbs put the cap back on his pen, clipped it to the inside pocket of his suit jacket. "Now, I understand this has been a rough night for you.

But I need to know if you want to stay a member of the Dodgers family. Or if you're gonna go off and cause some kind of a scene."

Will looked down at the floor, studying the carpet, a rubber band lying there by the toe of his right shoe. He imagined sitting down with Laurie on the living room couch, taking her hand and telling her that he'd been fired. Trying to explain how he didn't have a choice, how it was the right thing to do. If this was the first time, he could expect her to be sympathetic, but this was beginning to look like a pattern now, as if he were some kind of fuckup.

How would it look that he couldn't even manage to hold down a job as a security guard? With the baby on the way, they needed the paycheck. And Gibbs aside, he liked the job.

He spoke without making eye contact with Gibbs. "I want to keep my job."

Gibbs rapped his knuckles twice against the desktop. "Good answer."

TWENTY-ONE

Ray Miller lived on a leafy street in Encino, a few blocks from the El Caballero Country Club.

Miller had been Will's partner in LAPD Narcotics for almost eight years, up until the time Will left the department. The older man had showed him the ropes of working undercover, teaching him almost everything he knew about narcotics investigation.

The two men had been tight, but when Will was fired he'd felt Ray's disapproval, Ray like a father to him. After that, Will had felt awkward around the other man, and they'd simply drifted apart. They still sent each other cards every year around the holidays, but they hadn't gotten together in years.

Miller had bought the Encino house right after Sean had died, and Will had only been out there once before. It was a sprawling ranch with a deep front lawn, white clapboard siding, and trim that was painted loden green.

Will rang the doorbell. The air was perfumed from the jasmine that clung to the porch railing.

Miller's second wife, Suzie, opened the door. She stood framed in the doorway with her hands on her hips, dressed in a pink velour track-suit. "Talk about your blast from the past."

She'd moved out from Brooklyn after marrying Miller ten years ago, but her accent was still pure Bensonhurst.

Will took a step forward and hugged her. Her dark brown hair was stiff and smelled like perm chemicals. "Good to see you, Suzie."

"What's the matter, you too good for us now or something?"

"No." Will didn't know what to say. "Things have just been kind of crazy."

Over her shoulder he saw Ray come into the foyer.

"Hey, quit dry humping my wife." He looked the same as Will remembered, except his hair had all gone white. He was a big man, a yellow polo shirt stretched over a medicine ball stomach.

Will extricated himself from Suzie's embrace, then held out his hand to shake with Ray. Miller ignored it and swept Will up in a bear hug, his whiskers rough against Will's cheek.

Ray squeezed his shoulder. "It's been a coon's age."

"Yeah," Will said. "Whatever that means."

The two men sat out on the back patio, beside the in-ground swimming pool. The late June sun was strong, but a blue umbrella rose above the round table, white fringe hanging down from the edges.

Ray used a bottle opener to snap the cap off a bottle of Heineken. He held out the green bottle toward Will.

Will took it. "Why not."

Ray opened a beer for himself and extended it toward Will. "To the good old days."

Will clinked the base of his bottle against Ray's. "The good old days," he said. "When exactly were they, again?"

Ray smiled and took a long slug of his beer. "Ever miss it?"

Will remembered the adrenaline-fueled rush of walking unarmed into a darkened room all alone, paranoid and dangerous men packing guns and blades; nothing but his wits to carry him through.

"Parts," Will said.

"We put a lot of dope on the table. You were some kind of hot shit."

"I had a good teacher."

"I mean it. You were the best."

"Until I wasn't."

Ray wiped his mouth with the back of his hand. "It was a shame. The way they did you."

Will took a sip of the beer, his first in almost a year. It tasted a little skunky, but it still blew the fake stuff away. "The thing I'll always wonder about, till the day they put me in the ground?"

"Why you can't screw as long as guys in porn movies?"

Will smiled. It was a typical Ray line. "Why they did it. I mean, I expected to get a suspension, mandatory time in a treatment facility, something like that. But I could never figure out why they fired me."

"You should have fought it. The union would've backed you."

"By that point? I just didn't give enough of a shit."

"You need to stop worrying about it. Take some advice from your old partner. They call it the past for a reason. Nothing but pain's gonna come from you picking at it."

The glass patio door slid open on its track, and Suzie came outside carrying a wooden tray. "You boys hungry?"

She set down a platter of sliced turkey, seeded rye bread, lettuce, tomatoes, and dill pickles. "It's from Canter's," she said.

The two men took red plastic plates and assembled sandwiches. Ray took a bite from his and chewed, watching Suzie go back inside the house. "How's the food?"

Will nodded, his mouth full. "Good."

"You really think so?"

"Yeah, why?"

Ray shook his head. "It's goddamned *turkey*. She could go down the corner and buy it at Ralph's. But no, she's got to drive all the way into Hollywood."

They continued to eat, the silence awkward, just the sound of a lawn mower coming from the far side of the backyard's bougainvillea-covered fence.

"So. I haven't seen you in close to five years. You come all the way out here just to reminisce?"

"In a sense," Will said. "You remember a guy we busted just before I left the department, named Erik Crandall?"

Ray shook his head. "Not ringing any bells."

"We took him down for selling you a bunch of fentanyl."

Ray took a bite from his pickle. "Why're you bringing it up now?"

Will told him about his encounters with Crandall.

"You try sticking a gun in his face?" Ray asked when he'd finished.

Will shook his head.

"How come?"

"Don't have one."

"Why the fuck *not*?"

"Laurie."

Ray raised an eyebrow but didn't say anything.

Will felt his face go warm, sweating in the airless heat of the Valley.

"You tried going to LAPD?" Ray asked.

Will nodded. "They're not doing *jack*."

"Don't you have any friends left over there?"

Will shook his head. "No."

Ray scratched at his bare forearm, a tattoo there of a faded green mermaid. "Don't tell me you're actually taking this guy seriously."

"I don't know. It's just that he seems so certain about his dope being stolen. I mean, why would he be making that up?"

Ray shrugged. "Why do tornadoes always touch down in trailer parks? You're forgetting the first thing I ever taught you about the bad guys."

"They're all liars."

Ray nodded. "So why're you letting this hump yank your chain?"

Will looked at him. "You remember the way things were back then. I mean, it's not like it's completely outside the realm of possibilities."

"You were there when we booked him, Will. Do you remember seeing that much dope?"

Will shook his head. "I can't really remember." His memory from those days was shot; he'd been using so heavily at the time that it was a miracle he could even function.

"A pound of fentanyl," Ray said. "Surely you'd remember *that*."

They'd gotten turned on to Crandall by one of their confidential informants, but Ray had been the primary on the bust, had done the work to set up and make the buy.

"I was inside the car, listening on the wire," Will said. "When you made the bust I moved in. But I only took care of searching and hand-cuffing Crandall. You were the one who dealt with all the rest."

Ray looked at him. "We go back a long way. And that counts for a lot. But I'm not sure I like where you're going with this."

Will shook his head. "No, it's not like that, Ray. That's not what I'm saying here. It could have disappeared after we turned it in. Out of the evidence locker."

"What about our report?" Ray asked. "It would've listed the amount of dope we seized."

Will thought about it. In those days they'd had an arrangement, taking turns on who got saddled with typing the report. Since Miller had been the primary, he would have handled it.

"I didn't read it, I just signed it."

"I thought you said you couldn't remember?"

"You're taking this the wrong way."

"So what way am I supposed to take it?"

"I just thought you should know. I mean, if he tracked me down, he could come after you."

"Let him. He steps to me, he's gonna wish he hadn't." Ray pushed his plate away. "So where do things stand now?"

"I tried getting rid of Crandall, but he keeps coming back."

Ray looked out at the blue water of the swimming pool. An auto-mated vacuum machine worked its way out into the deep end.

Will waited, studying the tattoo inked across Ray's beefy forearm. The mermaid's iridescent, scale-covered tail curving upward to meet the ends of her long yellow hair.

Ray picked up his beer bottle and finished it off. "Why don't you let your old partner take care of this? I guarantee you'll never hear from this asshole again."

"What're you going to do?"

"I'm still tight with a lot of people inside the department. Trust me, you won't have to worry about it anymore."

TWENTY-TWO

Laurie's obstetrician's office was in a modern office building on Burbank Boulevard.

Will ran through the lobby and took the stairs two at a time, figuring it would be faster than waiting for the elevator. He was already fifteen minutes late; a big rig had jackknifed on the 101, and it had taken him forever to make it back from Ray Miller's place in Encino.

He pushed open the door to the doctor's waiting room but saw only empty chairs. He checked his watch, wondering if he'd gotten the time wrong.

He rapped his knuckles against the glass window at the reception desk. A young woman slid it open, and Will told her he was there for Laurie's sonogram. She said that Laurie had already gone in.

The receptionist led him down a hallway to an examination room. The room was windowless and had pink wallpaper. Laurie lay on her back on top of an exam table. A stout African American woman wearing hospital scrubs patterned with balloons stood beside her, writing something down on a clipboard. A plastic tag on her breast spelled out the name CLARICE.

She frowned. "You must be the father."

Will nodded. "I am."

He bent over the table and kissed Laurie on the cheek. "I'm really sorry," he said.

She continued to look up at the dropped ceiling, as if Michelangelo had painted a lost masterpiece up there.

Her lips were pursed. "We'll talk about it later."

The technician put her clipboard down on a laminate countertop built into the wall. "We were getting worried you weren't going to show up." She looked at him over the top of her gold-framed eyeglasses. "It happens more often than you'd think."

Will shook his head. "There was just something I needed to take care of."

The technician turned away and began to press keys on the ultrasound machine that sat on a rolling steel cart in the corner of the room. It looked like a personal computer, a CRT monitor perched on the top.

A plastic chair stood next to the examination table. Will sat down in it, his eyes level with the tabletop. Laurie's shirt was pulled up to expose her belly, and for the first time he noticed that her navel was protruding because of the pregnancy.

Will burped, the gassy taste of hops rising from his stomach. He inhaled through his mouth, trying to suck the smell back in before Laurie could smell it.

The technician took a probe from its holder on the side of the sonogram machine. "If you two lovebirds are ready, I need to get the show on the road."

She squeezed a plastic bottle, and a translucent blue gel oozed out onto Laurie's skin with an obscene sound. She began to move the plastic wand around in the gel.

On the screen of the monitor, a grainy black-and-white image shaped like an inverted funnel appeared. Inside the funnel, grainy and abstract shapes began to form, along with white ribbons of static. For some reason he thought of an old World War II movie, a naval officer wearing a big headset staring at a monitor, searching for a German submarine.

The technician stopped moving the probe, the shapes now becoming more concrete. He could make out the profile of a face, a miniature nose joining a forehead that swept upward in an arc rimmed with a halo of light.

The baby lay on its back, the white ribbons of static swirling all around it, as if it were floating in a blackened sky wreathed with broken clouds.

The technician tapped a long pink fingernail against the glass screen. "Here's the heart."

Will watched as it beat, then beat again.

He blinked his eyelids, trying to hold back his tears, not wanting to let the technician see. He reached out and took hold of Laurie's hand. Her fingers closed around his and squeezed, her skin smooth and dry.

"Everything looks just fine," the technician said. "Do you want to know the sex?"

"I do," Laurie said. "But my husband doesn't."

The technician looked at him. "Why not?"

"I like surprises," Will said.

"And I don't," Laurie said.

The technician looked back and forth between the two of them. "So how're we gonna break this logjam?"

"You can tell us," Will said.

Laurie turned her head on top of the pillow and stared at him. "Really?"

Will nodded.

The technician pointed at a tiny shape on the screen. "You see that? There's the penis."

Will looked at the screen. "So it's a boy?"

The technician looked at him over the top of her glasses. "I certainly hope so."

Will stood up and kissed Laurie on the mouth. Her arm moved around his neck, pulling him closer.

A son. It really was as if they were being given a second chance, another try to get it right.

He straightened up and stood staring at the image of his son that was frozen on the monitor. Laurie lay there, gazing up at him.

"What?" he asked.

She shook her head. "I wish you could see the smile on your face. I haven't seen you this happy in a long time."

"Don't I have a lot to be happy about?"

"Yeah, you do. But you've been so preoccupied. About that guy."

Will looked down into her blue eyes. "We don't have to worry about that anymore," he said. "It's being taken care of."

TWENTY-THREE

On the first Thursday in July, Will and Laurie drove over to Burbank and ate lunch at a Thai restaurant on Magnolia.

They sat at a metal table set out on the sidewalk, shaded from the summer sun by the spreading canopy of a mimosa. Will was wearing shorts, and he leaned back in his chair as he sipped an iced tea. There had been no sign of Erik Crandall in over three weeks.

"So how are the names coming?" Laurie asked.

"It's a big job, but I'm dealing with it."

"I would think it would be easier, now that we know it's a boy."

"Why's that?"

"Half the work. You can just focus on boy's names."

"Except all the best stuff I had was for girls. Now I'm back to square one."

She chewed on a skewer of chicken satay. "You need some help?"

"I think I can handle it. Worst case, I'll just use one of the girls' names."

She put the wooden skewer down on her plate. "Excuse me?"

"It'll help build his character. You know, like in that Johnny Cash song."

" 'A Boy Named Sue'?"

"Exactly."

She looked at him. "The way I remember it, the boy in that song hates his name so much he murders his father."

Will shook his head, trying to keep a straight face. "No, he only *tries* to kill him. But before he can, the father cuts off the kid's ear."

Laurie looked at him. "Lovely."

When they arrived back home, a car was parked at the curb in front of the house. The white Crown Victoria had a long whip antenna mounted to the lid of the trunk. Will never understood why they couldn't use unmarked cars that didn't look so obvious.

He pulled the Volvo into the driveway.

The front doors of the Crown Vic opened, and two men wearing sport coats and dress slacks climbed out. One was white and tall, a fringe of blond hair ringing a balding head. The other was Hispanic and overweight.

Will stood in the driveway and slipped one arm around Laurie, the other holding on to the paper doggie bag of leftovers.

The white cop fished a badge holder from the inside pocket of his sport coat and opened it up for Will to see. "Detective Denslowe, LAPD. We'd like to talk to you."

Will felt himself smiling: Ray really had come through.

"This is about Erik Crandall?" Will asked.

The two detectives exchanged a look.

"We were hoping you might come with us," Denslowe said.

Will pulled his arm from around Laurie's back and took the badge case. He held it up, examining the identification card. Ed Denslowe was a homicide detective out of the West Valley Division.

"We just need to ask you a few questions," Denslowe said. "Thought maybe you could help us out with something."

Will could feel grease coming through the paper bag, leaking out onto the bare skin of his left arm. "Can you be a little more specific?"

The two detectives traded another look, the silent communication between them impossible to decipher. A breeze picked up from the west, the branches of the jacaranda swaying overhead, flowers from it drifting down like purple snow.

Denslowe pointed at the Crown Vic. "Hop in. We'll have plenty of time to talk on the way."

The viewing room of the Los Angeles County Coroner's Office was located in the subbasement of a brick and stone building in Boyle Heights.

The room had cinder-block walls painted pale yellow, several vinyl upholstered armchairs, and a green sofa pushed against the wall.

Will sat in one of the armchairs facing a plate glass window set in the front wall. White curtains were drawn across the far side of the glass. Denslowe rapped his knuckles against the glass, and then the curtains slid apart.

It was brightly lit on the other side of the glass. A man wearing a white Tyvek jumpsuit stood at the head of a metal gurney. A large form in the shape of a human body lay on top of the gurney, draped with a white sheet.

Denslowe gave a nod to the man in the suit, who reached out and lowered the sheet.

The big man had been cleaned up for the viewing, but there was only so much that could be done. His mouth was still intact, but everything above it was destroyed, a mass of raw tissue and congealed blood. One eye remained in place, but that lid was closed.

Will used the arms of the chair to push himself to his feet. He went toward the window, as if he were being drawn forward on a conveyor belt. Up close, he could see a small hole surrounded by blackened skin above the left ear.

There wasn't much to go on to make the identification, but Will was sure from the body type who it was.

"It's him," he said.

Denslowe looked at him. "You're positive?"

Will shut his eyes, then opened them again. "Pull the sheet down more."

The detective gestured to the morgue technician.

The technician folded the sheet, exposing the naked body down to the navel.

Will ran his eyes along the left bicep and down to the massive forearm. Under the fluorescent lights the mermaid tattoo looked green, her scale-covered tail curving upward, almost reaching the locks of golden hair.

"It's definitely him." Will reached out and leaned against the cinderblock wall. "It's Ray Miller."

Denslowe nodded toward the glass, and the curtains shut.

Denslowe watched him. "You all right?"

Will nodded.

"At least you spared the widow from having to make the ID." Denslowe took a pocket notebook and a ballpoint pen from his jacket and started writing. "According to her, you were one of the last people to see him alive. You up for answering a few questions?"

"I can do better than that," Will said. "I can tell you who murdered him."

Denslowe stopped writing and stared at him.

"Who said anything about *murder*?" he said. "It was suicide. Poor bastard shot himself."

TWENTY-FOUR

Denslowe handed Will a Styrofoam cup filled with water and shut the steel door to the interview room.

"Do I need a lawyer?" Will asked.

Denslowe set a steaming cup of coffee down on the other side of the table. "I already told you Ray Miller committed suicide. So why would you need a lawyer?"

After they'd left the coroner's, Denslowe and his partner had driven Will to the West Valley police station in Reseda. The room was a small box with a two-way mirror set into the far wall. The Formica tabletop was scarred with cigarette burns.

Denslowe sat down across from him. "Last time you saw him, how did he seem?"

"Not like he was on the verge of blowing his brains out, if that's what you're asking."

"Didn't act like he was depressed?"

"No," Will said. "Not at all."

Denslowe slid a legal yellow pad in front of him and clicked open a ballpoint pen. "No mention of anything that in retrospect might indicate he was thinking about taking his own life?"

"No." Will stared at the detective. "Because he didn't. He was murdered."

Denslowe drank some of his coffee. "I don't know why it is you keep saying that. Every piece of evidence points to suicide."

"Such as?"

Denslowe held up his left hand and extended his thumb. "One, there was no sign of forced entry at his house. No sign that anyone else was there after his wife went out." The detective extended his index finger. "Two, he was shot with his own gun."

Will caught his reflection in the two-way mirror behind the detective and wondered if Denslowe's partner was back there, watching.

Denslowe extended another finger. "Three, in the days immediately preceding his death he was acting depressed—"

"Where'd you get that?"

"This was according to the man's *wife*. Who knows, maybe he was putting on a happy face for you. Maybe the depression kicked in after you left. But she says he was drinking heavily, having trouble sleeping. She asked what was wrong, but he wouldn't talk to her."

"Where was Suzie? When it happened?"

"She went out for a couple of hours. Shopping. When she came back, she found him dead in the study."

Denslowe picked up a large plastic evidence bag from the table, then extended his ring finger. "Plus, four, we found this."

Denslowe pushed it across the table toward Will. Inside the bag was a piece of plain white paper, cursive lettering scrawled across the page in blue ink. Will recognized Ray Miller's handwriting.

> Suzie,
> Please forgive me for taking the easy way out, but I just can't take it anymore. It hurts so much that it burns.

Please tell the kids I love them.
Love,
Ray

Will read through the note a second time, feeling as though someone had pulled the chair out from under him.

Denslowe took back the note. "According to the wife, he was in good physical health, so we're assuming the pain he's referring to there is psychological."

Will's stomach began to churn. He wished he hadn't eaten so much of the Thai food at lunch. "I don't buy it."

"The widow says it's his handwriting."

Will stood up and walked over to Denslowe. He made his hand into the shape of a pistol and put the tip of his forefinger up to the detective's temple. "If I put a gun to your head and told you to write a note, would you do it?"

Denslowe pushed his chair back, moving himself away from Will. "Are you listening to anything I'm saying? The bullet came from Miller's own gun."

"The killer could have taken it away from him, used it against him."

"That wouldn't be easy. Ray Miller was a pretty big man."

"You should see Crandall."

"Who?"

"The guy that killed him. Ray and I busted him five years ago. He got released from San Quentin back in April. He showed up and started hassling me, he's got this obsession that Ray and I stole his dope."

Denslowe ran his palm over the bald spot on top of his head. "You say this guy, Crandall, was hassling you. Was he hassling Ray?"

Will shook his head. "Not that I know of."

"You have any reason to think this guy had any contact with him?"

"No, but the last time I talked to Ray, he said he was going to take care of Crandall."

"Take care how?"

"He told me he was going to reach out to his contacts in LAPD. But knowing Ray, he probably went after Crandall himself."

Denslowe took a slow sip of the coffee. There were dark rings beneath his eyes. "I can understand why you're thinking what you're thinking. I was the man's partner, I'd like to believe I'd be doing the same. But you're grasping at straws here."

"Bring in Crandall, give him a test for GSR."

Denslowe shook his head. "It's a little late for that. Even if we did find residue, the defense would just claim contamination from another source."

"Crandall doesn't know that. You put him in this room, tell him his only shot at a deal is if he confesses before the test comes back."

"All due respect? I really don't need you telling me how to do my job."

"Then why don't you *do* it?"

Denslowe put his cup of coffee down on the table. Brown liquid sloshed over the rim and ran out onto the Formica. "I checked you out," he said. "You were tossed from the department because you were using. And you're actually going to sit there and talk to me about how to do my job?"

The room felt too small now, not enough air inside it.

I'm sorry," Will said. "I was out of line."

Denslowe nodded. "You need to understand that unless the lab work comes back with something unexpected, the coroner's going to rule this a suicide."

"If you let that happen, it means Ray's killer is walking around free."

Denslowe ripped a blank sheet of paper from the legal pad and used it to wipe up the spilled coffee. "You know how this works. My job is to close cases, not to turn suicides into open homicides."

"It won't be open. I'm handing you the killer."

Denslowe held Will's eyes. "You're sure about this."

"One hundred percent."

Denslowe clicked the ballpoint pen, over and over, not speaking.

Then he picked up the pad. "I should have my head examined for doing this, but I'll check it out. Where do I find this asshole?"

TWENTY-FIVE

Crandall stood inside the pink-tiled bathroom of his studio apartment. His cargo shorts and underwear were pulled down, bunched around his ankles.

He held the syringe up to the light fixture above the medicine cabinet and slowly pushed in the plunger to remove any air, being careful not to waste any of the liquid.

The apartment was on South Virgil, just north of Wilshire in Koreatown. The building had been a motel before being converted into apartments, small balconies with metal railings hanging from the blue stucco facade.

The place was cheap, and it had come furnished. The old Korean guy who managed the building hadn't even run a credit check after Crandall had offered to pay his rent up front in cash.

Crandall reached behind him with his left hand and pinched the skin on his ass. Then he leaned over and drove in the needle.

He sucked in air through his clenched teeth. It stung like hell, the needles on the stolen syringes intended for horses. He pressed the plunger with his thumb. The liquid burned like acid.

His head jerked to the side when he heard the sound—someone pounding on the door to the apartment. He froze, bent over the toilet, the syringe still sticking out of his ass.

The pounding started up again. Could it be his parole officer making a visit, after all this time? He didn't have any friends, and nobody at work knew where he lived.

He pulled out the syringe and picked up the half-full vial of Equipoise from the lid of the toilet tank.

Right after he'd moved in, Crandall had removed the porcelain soap dish from the tiled wall of the shower and dug a hiding place out of the mortar bed.

He put the syringe and the vial inside the hiding place with the rest of the stuff he'd stolen from the racetrack and fitted the soap dish back in place.

He pulled up his shorts and buttoned the waistband but didn't bother to put on a shirt.

The pounding started again as he walked through the living room. A rectangular mirror hung on the wall. He did a double take as he went past, catching a glimpse of his naked torso. He was always surprised to see how huge he'd become, like looking at a stranger in the mirror.

He pressed his face against the inside surface of the door and looked through the peephole. Through the fisheye lens he saw a big brass badge in some kind of wallet, an arm stretching backward away from it, attached to a man dressed in a brown suit.

Crandall pulled his face back, adrenaline coursing through his veins, going into full-blown fight or flight. He spun around, looking for a way out. The only other exit from the apartment was the sliding glass doors that went out onto the balcony, but the apartment was five stories above the street.

From behind him, the pounding started up again, louder now, plates and glasses rattling inside the kitchen cabinets.

"*Police,* open up."

Crandall opened the door a few inches. He peered out into the hall-way through the gap. "Yes?"

There were two of them out there in the hallway. A tall guy wear-ing the suit, his head balding up on top, and a Mexican.

The white cop continued to hold up his badge. "Erik Crandall?"

Crandall's whole body went stiff. His butt cheek still stung from the injection. "Yeah?"

The detective reached inside his suit jacket and pulled out some papers. "You're coming with us."

The hallway smelled of garbage and kimchi. "What for?"

The cop ignored him. "Open the door. We need to take a look around."

"You got a search warrant?"

"You're on parole, asshole. We don't need one."

Crandall started to shut the door, but the cop managed to get his shoe inside before he could do it. Crandall's heart began to hammer inside his chest, the edges of his vision turning red. He was really feel-ing the 'roids now, pumping through his veins, thumping in his skull. His hand was still on the doorknob, and he thought about putting some muscle into it, crushing the man's foot.

But instead he forced himself to smile as he opened the door all the way. "I didn't do anything."

"You can tell us all about it later." The detective took a set of hand-cuffs from a leather case on his belt. "Right now I need for you to turn around and grab some wall."

Crandall could hear the television of the old lady who lived next door coming through the paper-thin walls, the voices speaking Ko-rean, fast and angry.

Crandall stood in the doorway, looking out into the hall. The Mexican cop had made a mistake. He was standing too close. Crandall realized that he could reach out and grab him, throw him into the other cop, then beat feet. Or, even better, pound the living crap out of both of them, grab their guns, then take off.

"We can do this easy or hard," the detective said. "Your choice."

Crandall had heard the stories when he was inside. How if you hurt a cop they'd do anything to find you, how they'd never stop hunting you down. He wasn't ready to blow the country just yet. Not until he got back what he'd come for.

He smiled at the cop and raised his hands into the air.

If you want the rainbow, you must to put up with the rain.

Then he stepped out into the hallway, turned around, and put his palms against the wallpaper.

TWENTY-SIX

Ray Miller's funeral was held at a synagogue in Woodland Hills. The next day, Will and Laurie drove out to the house in Encino to pay a shivah call.

The living room was filled with people Will didn't know. The big mirror that hung over the fireplace was covered with a bedsheet in an observance of mourning. A folding table set up in the corner of the room held Tupperware containers filled with food.

Laurie squeezed his hand. When he looked at her, she raised her chin, pointing toward the far end of the room where Suzie Miller sat cross-legged on the floor.

Will went over to her, still holding on to Laurie's hand. "I'm sorry, Suzie."

She looked up at him. Her eyes were puffy, buried deep inside shadowed sockets. A torn black ribbon was pinned to the front of her blouse.

The cadence of her voice was mechanical. "Thanks for coming."

He tried to think of what to say next. He squatted down, feeling awkward standing over her. He wondered if he should get down on the floor with her.

Laurie tugged on his hand. He turned his head and saw that a line of people had built up behind them, waiting to pay their condolences. Will reached out and patted Suzie on the top of her shoulder, then stepped past her.

Will looked around the room. A small crowd had gathered around a tall man who stood in front of a set of sliding glass patio doors. The man turned, and Will saw that it was Dennis Byrnes.

Byrnes was the current chair of the Los Angeles Board of Supervisors. The Board of Supes was where the real power was at in L.A.; the five supervisors were some of the most powerful politicians in the entire state, holding the purse strings to enormous budgets.

Will was a little surprised to see him there, but it made sense. Byrnes had been the commanding officer of the LAPD Gangs and Narcotics Division when he and Ray Miller had been partners there. After Will left the department, Byrnes had briefly served as chief of police before making his successful run for supervisor.

Laurie squeezed his hand. "I'm going in the kitchen, see if I can help."

Will went over to a table that held bottles of liquor and wine, cans of soda, and a galvanized steel tub filled with ice cubes.

He filled a clear plastic cup with cranberry juice and club soda. As he took a sip, he felt a hand on his back.

Will turned and saw Dennis Byrnes standing there, holding out his hand. "Will the Thrill."

"Dennis." Will shook his hand. It was the first time he'd seen Byrnes in person since he left the department. "Or now do I need to call you *Your Honor?*"

"I'm good with Dennis. The *Times* usually calls me a lot worse."

"Nice to see you here. I didn't realize you and Ray were that close."

"We grew up in the same neighborhood. My family moved away when I started junior high."

Dennis had a head of silver hair and a patrician bearing. Will was never able to picture the man starting out as a young cop, walking a beat.

He held out a cup filled with dark liquid toward Will. "To Ray."

Will tapped his cup against the other man's. His mind flashed on clinking his beer bottle against Ray's. Not that long ago, but he couldn't remember what it was they had toasted to.

Dennis drained half of his cup, studying Will's drink. "What is it you're drinking there?"

"Club soda and Ocean Spray."

Dennis smiled. "Good to see you're finally on the straight and narrow."

Will swallowed, the drink too sweet.

Dennis crunched a piece of ice between his molars, then held the cup out again. "To us."

Will looked at him. "What for?"

"The Last of the Mohicans. Hernandez, Fenske, now Ray. Everyone from the old days, gone. We're all that's left."

Will touched cups again, feeling a little ridiculous. "For some reason, I never figured on being the last man standing."

"You were always a great detective, Will. You just needed to exercise a little more self-control."

Dennis looked around the room. "These shivahs, I always feel like I'm getting ripped off." He raised an eyebrow and smiled. "I mean, you don't even get to see the body."

"Not funny. Take it from me, you wouldn't want to see it."

Dennis shook his head. "What a dumbshit. Guy has it all, but he goes and eats his gun."

"He didn't."

Dennis looked at him.

"Ray was murdered."

"What are you talking about?"

Will told him about Crandall.

"Jesus," Dennis said. "You told all this to the police?"

Will nodded.

"What did they say?"

"That they were going to arrest him."

"Good work. I'll check in with the chief, make sure the department's all over this."

A female aide with a cell phone headset clipped to her ear came up behind Dennis and whispered something to him. He nodded his head once, then thrust his hand out toward Will. "Gotta move on. Let me know if I can help with anything."

Will went down the hallway that led to the back of the house, needing to use the bathroom. Ray's study was on the right, the door standing half open. The room was deep in shadow, the wooden slats of the venetian blinds tilted shut.

Suzie sat on the brown leather couch beneath the windows, alone, holding a wineglass.

At first Will thought she was looking at him, then realized she was just staring off into space. He entered the room and sat down beside her.

"It's all going to be okay," he said. His voice sounded too loud inside the room.

She turned to look at him. "Is it?"

"He was a good man."

She nodded. "He loved you, you know that? Ray always said the two of you were like father and son, except without all the baggage."

"I'm sorry I didn't come around to see him more, the last few years."

Suzie took a sip of her wine. "When they kicked you out of the department? It broke his heart."

"I didn't mean to let him down. It wasn't his fault."

"He always acted like it was. He never said anything, but it was like he felt guilty or something."

A large leather-covered album was open on Suzie's lap, color photographs sealed beneath a shiny sheet of plastic.

Will pointed a finger at one of them. A young blond woman sitting on the hood of a red sports car. "Cathy? Hard to believe how much she's grown up."

Suzie nodded. "She's doing great. Sophomore at Brown."

"Good school."

"No UC for Ray Miller's kids. All three of them, they went to school back east."

He looked back down at the photo album. Ray, Suzie, and the kids, all dressed in pastel ski outfits, standing on the porch of a cedar-shingled house, virgin snow layered on top of the porch railing.

"Where was this?"

"That's our house. Up in Mammoth."

"You guys own it?"

Suzie smiled. "We bought it right before Ray retired."

The room smelled like Pine-Sol. The surface of Ray's dark oak desk was empty. The desk chair was gone, and there were faint rust-colored stains visible on the beige carpeting.

Suzie stared down at the photo album. One of Ray alone, tan and smiling, a powder blue cable-knit sweater draped across his shoulders like a shawl. Below it was another shot of the whole family, standing on the deck of a large power boat.

Will tapped his finger on it. "How about this one?"

Suzie smiled. "On our boat."

Will took a closer look at the photograph. He wasn't sure if you'd call it a yacht, but it was close. "You have a boat?"

"Ray wanted to rename it *The Money Pit*."

Will licked his lips, his mouth dry. "You don't have to answer this, but are you going to be all right? I mean financially?"

"It doesn't seem right talking about it, time like this." She nodded her head. "But, yeah. That's one thing I don't have to worry about."

"Did your family leave you money? Or Ray's?"

She looked up. "What kind of a question is that?"

Will shook his head. Ray had left the department with a full pension, but still. "I was just wondering."

"Well, the answer's no."

Will looked away, his face growing warm.

Suzie slammed the photo album shut. "One thing *I'm* wondering about? What is it you said to him, anyway?"

"What do you mean?"

"That day you showed up here, out of the blue? What is it that you two talked about?"

Will blinked. "Nothing. Just old times."

She held his eyes. "Whatever it was, when you left here he was all worked up." She looked over at Ray's desk. "Then he goes and does *that*."

He looked her in the eye. "He didn't kill himself, Suzie."

"What the hell are you talking about?"

"You're going to hear from the police. They're bringing in the guy who murdered him."

"Why would someone want to murder Ray?"

"It was somebody we arrested years ago, back when we were partners. This guy was convinced Ray and I stole his drugs."

She looked at him. "Stole his *drugs*? What the hell did you get Ray involved in?"

"What?" Will shook his head. "*No,* this guy just *thinks* we stole them."

She chewed her bottom lip, her eyes becoming wet. "What the fuck is this? This is supposed to make me feel *better*? You telling me that instead of my husband committing suicide, he got killed over drugs?"

"It wasn't over drugs. This guy is crazy. When I saw Ray, he said he was going to take care of it."

"You made him do this? That's what you came here for that day?" Her New York accent was more pronounced now that she was growing upset. "He was retired, Will. He played *golf*. And then you show up here and get him killed?"

Will held up his hands. "You're taking this all wrong."

"*No.* Get the fuck out of my house."

"Suzie, I'm—"

She jumped up from the couch. "Don't make a scene." She pointed her finger at the door. "Just get the fuck out."

TWENTY-SEVEN

A giant bird of paradise grew along the redwood boards of the fence in the front yard.

The plant towered over Will as he squeezed the handle of the pruning shears to cut the stem of a dead leaf. He pulled the enormous leaf free and tossed it onto the freshly mown grass.

The Dodgers were out of town, so even though it was a Sunday he had the day off from work. Buddy slept in the redwood chips at the base of the plant, his head resting on one of his front legs. Charcoal smoke rose up from the neighbor's backyard.

Earlier that morning, he'd called Suzie to apologize for what had happened at the shivah. He shouldn't have grilled her about Ray's money, but his ingrained detective's curiosity had gotten the better of him. He'd only reached her voice mail and left a message.

Even if Ray had been dirty, what difference did it make now? Nothing Ray might have done could justify Crandall killing him. That was the important thing here, the thing he needed to focus on.

Let Crandall ride the needle, then let everyone get on with their lives.

The sound of a ball slapping into the leather pocket of a baseball glove came from across the street. He turned and saw his neighbor playing catch with his young son, the boy wearing a blue Dodgers cap. Will stopped to watch them, the father laughing as the boy jumped into the air, his glove extended, the ball sailing over his head.

Will went over to the front of the house and turned on the hose bib. He held his hands under the cold water, scrubbing the dirt from his fingers.

A car horn blared behind him, shattering the quiet of the afternoon. Will shut off the water. The car horn blasted again, a single and continuous note reverberating off the houses.

Will turned to see the neighbor's boy frozen in the middle of the street. His baseball lay a few feet in front of a black Lincoln Town Car that had come to a stop.

The driver's side of the car was facing Will, but he couldn't see the face of the driver because of the sun glaring off the glass. The car's horn continued to blare, not stopping, the sound only serving to terrify the young boy.

Buddy was up on his feet now, his body rigid, his tail down between his back legs.

Will started toward the street, still holding the hooked pruning shears in his right hand. He cut across the green lawn, the soles of his running shoes crushing purple petals that had fallen from the jacaranda.

The boy's father went out into the street and snatched up the baseball. He glared at the driver of the Lincoln, then took his son's hand and pulled him back into the safety of their front yard.

The Lincoln's horn finally stopped, the noise of the crows up on the telephone wires rising up to fill in the sudden silence.

Will stepped off the curb and into the road.

The Lincoln's engine revved, its tires squealing as the car shot forward. He jumped back, the fender of the big car just missing his hip as it blew past.

Will swiveled his head, trying to get a look at the driver. He had the sense that it was Erik Crandall, but he told himself that it was just his imagination, that Crandall was locked up in jail.

The sedan sped away down the residential street, fishtailing as it hung a left turn at the corner.

Will stood there in the street, breathing in the smell of exhaust and burned clutch, unable to convince himself, certain now that the driver of the car was Erik Crandall.

TWENTY-EIGHT

Crandall leaned back against the bar and picked up his longneck bottle of Bud. The music was too loud, coming through the nightclub's sound system, the bass swirling and throbbing.

He took a swig of the beer, wondering whether the cop had recognized him this afternoon. Did the asshole really think he could get rid of him that easily, just by getting him arrested? He bobbed his head in time with the music, trying not to think about it. He'd have plenty of time to get even with the *lying-thieving-conniving-asshole* cop later, but first things first.

The other drivers at work had been telling him about this place for weeks now, and he'd finally decided to give it a try. He was getting desperate, hadn't gotten laid since he'd been out of Quentin.

He added it up: the almost five years he'd been locked away, plus maybe three months or so before he'd been arrested. No matter how you sliced it, it was a long time. He'd never paid for sex in his life, but he was starting to think about it now.

He stared out at the dance floor, trying not to let his jaw hang open at what he saw. An ocean of bodies writhing beneath a hot white light that strobed in time with the beat. Flashes of bare skin, breasts straining inside push-up bras, round ass cheeks packed into skintight denim.

He gulped more of the beer, trying to get his courage up. He squeezed the stress ball in his left hand. He remembered when he'd first started shooting the 'roids, how horny he'd been all the time. He'd lie there in his bottom bunk and jerk off six times in a row, afraid his right arm was going to break.

He glanced over at a small round table against the wall. A blonde who was all alone now, her girlfriend out on the dance floor getting down with some yuppie in a shiny shirt.

She leaned forward to sip her drink through a cocktail straw. The back of her shirt rode up, revealing a tattoo of a butterfly on the small of her back. She wouldn't be half bad if she just lost some of the weight, rolls of baby fat bunching up above the waistband of her stonewashed jeans.

Crandall drained the rest of the beer and forced a burp, the spicy taste of the mu shu burning the back of his throat. His heart pounded as he walked toward her, like he was back in high school. He hadn't been with that many girls before he'd been sent away, could count them all on one hand. But even that seemed like it was in another lifetime, as if it'd happened to somebody else.

He stood next to her chair, looking down at her, not sure what he was supposed to do now. She kept staring out at the dance floor, watching her friend dance. Her V-neck pink shirt showed off the white tops of her enormous tits.

"How's it going?" He had to yell over the music.

She looked up at him. The black makeup around her eyes made her look like a raccoon. Her hair was parted down the center, pink scalp with black roots on each side.

"Can I buy you a drink?" he shouted.

She shook her head no, then looked back out at the dance floor, like she was hoping that her friend would come and rescue her.

Crandall pulled out the empty chair and sat down next to her. She smelled like strawberry air freshener.

"My friend's sitting there," she said.

"I'll just keep it warm for her." Crandall smiled. "My name's Erik."

"Whatever." Her voice was gravelly.

"What do you do? I mean when you're not here?"

"I work in a dialysis place." She looked bored.

"Dialysis? You mean for sick people?"

She nodded. "Their kidneys don't work. It's pretty sad."

Beneath the tabletop, Crandall worked the stress ball. "I'm a producer."

She eyed his dark suit. "Really, what kind?"

"Features, mostly."

She turned in her chair, facing him now.

Crandall was amazed that this bullshit would actually work. When he'd first started dealing coke, some of his regulars had been young agents, low-level guys at Morris and CAA. A bunch of nerds, but they were always bragging to him about how much trim they scored.

She reached up and brushed back her hair. "Anything I've seen?"

He named a movie that he'd watched on the small television he'd been allowed to have inside his prison cell.

She looked at him. "You produced that?"

"I was just an associate. But I'm an executive on this new one, with Leonardo. You like him?"

"*DiCaprio?* He's great."

Crandall squeezed the stress ball. "What about you? You ever do any acting?"

She sipped at the drink through the tiny straw. "Not for a while now."

"You should. You've got a good look."

She blushed. "That's nice of you to say."

"No, I really mean it." Crandall continued to work the stress ball. "I got an eye for talent."

*   *   *

Her apartment was in Los Feliz, just south of Griffith Park.

It was a studio, decorated with cheap Swedish furniture. Her bed stood in the corner, a colorful collection of stuffed animals piled on top. Kenny G played low on the stereo.

The apartment smelled like cinnamon from the candles she had burning inside little glasses.

She sat upright at the foot of the bed, naked, her clothes and underwear in a tangle on the carpet. She'd dimmed the track lights, but he could still see that she was older than he'd thought, thick makeup crinkling in the corner of her eyes.

He reached down with his right hand, grabbed hold of one of her big boobs and squeezed.

"*Ouch,*" she said. "Gentle."

He bent over and put his mouth on her dark nipple, sucking. Her body stiffened, and she scooted backward on top of the pink chenille bedspread.

She turned onto her side, propping her head up on one hand. "Why don't you take off your clothes?"

He took a step back. He was already barefoot, since she'd made him take his shoes off at the door. He stripped down to his white Jockey shorts, careful to keep facing forward so she wouldn't see the rash of acne that wrapped across his upper back.

She looked up at his body, checking him out. "Wow, you have a personal trainer or something?"

He shook his head. "Just work out a lot."

She lifted her chin. "Take off your panties."

His palms were wet. He felt nervous, her sitting there watching him with the raccoon eyes. He wondered if he should ask her to turn off the lights.

He hooked his thumbs into the elastic waistband and slid his underwear down over his bulging thighs. He'd started shaving his pubic hair with a beard trimmer to make his package look bigger, but all the 'roids had shrunken his testicles down to the size of raisins.

He stepped forward, his dick level with her face, rising up as it got hard.

Inside the prison, everybody had his personal stash of porn. Guys would barter pages cut from skin magazines and color printouts from the Internet. Crandall's own collection was dominated by close-up shots of chicks' faces dripping with come, like they'd been standing next to a blender of vanilla milkshakes when it exploded.

The other inmates had a specific name for this kind of porn, some Japanese word, Kabuki or Bukake, something like that. He didn't care what it was called, all he knew was that he couldn't stop thinking about it. Every time he looked at a girl's face, even the ugly old lady at the Chinese, he would picture it covered with jizz.

More than anything, he wanted to make it happen right here and now, with this one. The only thing, he wasn't sure how to go about making it happen.

He took hold of himself and began to rub his dick against her cheek. Her makeup felt like lard.

She jerked her head back. "What're you doing?"

He stuttered. "I don't know."

"Well, stop," she said. "It's gross."

Some of her makeup had rubbed off on the head of his cock. He stood there, looking down at it. For some reason it reminded him of a clown.

She rolled over on the mattress, reached out, and opened the drawer of her night table. She handed him a foil-wrapped Trojan and gave him the raccoon eyes as he fumbled it on. His fingers were coated with lube from the rubber, so he wiped them against the bedspread.

She pushed aside some of the stuffed animals and laid back on the bed, opening her thighs a little. Her pussy was shaved, like a Girl Scout.

He climbed on top of her, the bed sagging under his weight. He kissed her on the cheek, trying to thrust inside her.

She was looking up at him. "What's the matter?"

He looked down. He'd gone soft, not able to push himself inside.

The saxophone music stopped playing, the room going quiet. He waited for the next song to start, but the CD had ended. He tried to conjure images inside his mind but couldn't do it. Not with her lying there underneath him, breathing and staring.

He reached down, grabbed the crest of her hip, and flipped her over. "Not so rough."

He pushed down on her upper back and climbed between her legs, forcing them apart with his knees. He grabbed hold of the cheeks of her ass with both hands and pulled them apart. She tried to reach a hand behind her, but he grabbed her wrists and leaned his weight down on them.

He looked down at the colorful wings of her butterfly tattoo, feeling himself grow stiff again, fitting himself against her.

"Not there," she said.

She tried to turn over, but he held her down and forced his way inside her, clamping his hand over her mouth so that the neighbors couldn't hear her.

TWENTY-NINE

"Can you please tell me what the hell Erik Crandall's doing out on the street?"

Will sat in front of Detective Ed Denslowe's desk in the West Valley police station. His desktop was covered with leaning stacks of file folders, most of them crowned with Styrofoam coffee cups. A framed photograph stood beside his telephone, Denslowe posing with a wife and two small boys.

Denslowe's pale olive summer suit set off the dark rings beneath his eyes. "Who told you that?"

"I saw him. Why'd you cut him loose?"

"You used to be a cop. You might remember the law tends to frown on us detaining someone unless we can charge them with a crime."

"What's wrong with murder?"

"He's no good for it."

"Why *not*?"

"Because there's no way he could have done it."

Will's stomach was starting to burn from his morning coffee. "What are you saying?"

"That you fucked me. You told me you were positive. One hundred percent, remember? And I trusted you, because you used to be a cop. You have any idea how many favors I burned up on this one?"

"What makes you so sure he couldn't have done it?"

"His alibi."

"Big deal."

Denslowe nodded. "Yeah, it is," he said. "It's iron-fucking-clad."

He leaned to his left and slid a black automatic out of a pancake holster on his hip. He opened a desk drawer and placed the holstered gun inside. "He was at a mandatory NA meeting. Condition of his parole."

"How do you know he was even really there?"

"Counselor takes attendance."

"How long was this meeting?"

"Four hours."

"He could have left early."

Denslowe shook his head. "They take attendance after every break, and at the end."

"Maybe it wasn't even Crandall who was there. He could have sent someone to go for him."

"I'm not stupid. I showed the counselor Crandall's photograph. It was him."

Will felt pressure building inside his skull, the flicker from the fluorescents giving him a headache. "You know as well as I do that the coroner can't nail down the time of death that precisely."

"But Ray's wife can. She left him alive in the house at 1:00 P.M., comes home at three and finds him deceased. That's a pretty tight window."

"She's under a lot of stress. Maybe she got the times mixed up."

"I checked with her credit card company. The times of the transactions match."

"Crandall's gaming this somehow. You're still working it, right?"

Denslowe shook his head. "I've wasted enough time."

Will tried to keep his voice from shaking. "He's a suspect in a murder case."

"Except there isn't any murder. Coroner came back with a final report. Cause and manner are suicide by gunshot." He looked at his wristwatch. "Anything else I can do for you?"

Will shook his head. "How hard can it be? Give me a week with a badge and gun, I could bring this guy in."

Denslowe's smile wasn't friendly. "Maybe you should have thought about that before you went and got yourself kicked off the force."

THIRTY

On a Wednesday evening toward the end of July, the Dodgers played Colorado in a game that went eleven innings. By the time it finally ended, Will was dead on his feet. He wanted to just head home and crawl into bed beside Laurie, but there was something else he needed to take care of.

He changed out of his uniform and drove over to Silver Lake. The club was on North Hoover, on the fringe of Filipinotown.

Inside it was dim, colored lights washing over the musicians that were playing on the elevated stage. Will sat down at a table a few rows back, the club half empty. The band's name was silk-screened onto the head of the kick drum.

The Grievous Angels.

Will had first noticed the ads for the band about a year ago, tucked in the back of *LA Weekly*. They were a Gram Parsons tribute band, playing covers of songs by the country-rock pioneer who'd died of a drug overdose in the early seventies.

Will had done a double take when he'd spotted the ad, staring at the face of the lead singer, positive that it was Gary Ackerman.

Ackerman had worked as a confidential informant for Will and Ray when they were partners in Narcotics. He'd been the one who'd first tipped Ray off to Erik Crandall and worked with him to set up the buy that resulted in Crandall's arrest and imprisonment.

Now Ackerman stood strumming a Gibson Hummingbird, singing into a microphone mounted on a chromed stand. His hairstyle was straight out of the seventies, parted in the center, hanging down to his shoulders.

He wore a pure white Western-style suit. The jacket was cut high on the waist, showing off a hand-tooled leather belt. The suit was covered with sequins that formed colorful images.

Red flames sprouted from the bell-bottomed pant legs, licking their way upward toward the crotch. Kelly green marijuana leaves decorated the lapels of the jacket, and pink opium poppies stood out at the front of each shoulder.

Gary turned to signal the drummer, revealing a dramatic pachuco cross covering the back of the jacket, like an enormous prison tattoo, sequined rays of light radiating out from it.

A waitress wearing a straw cowboy hat came over to the table. Will decided to order a bottle of Heineken.

His gut was telling him that Ray didn't commit suicide. It was just too much of a coincidence: Ray says that he's going to take care of Crandall, then turns up dead?

But his gut had been wrong before. He'd see if Gary could give him anything useful. If not, he'd let it go.

The band finished the song and left the stage to scattered applause from the audience. Will started to get up, but then the band came back and began to play an encore. Will had heard the song before, was pretty sure the name of it was "Sin City."

Will drank some of the beer. Two middle-aged women wearing cowboy boots and long skirts got up and started to dance together near the apron of the stage. The pedal steel player tore into a descending run, the notes falling like teardrops.

Gary didn't just look like Gram Parsons, he sounded like him, his singing slightly off-key in a way that was bittersweet, filled with a desperate and aching beauty.

After the show ended, Gary stood at the bar, still dressed in the sequined suit. Will went over and put his hand on his shoulder.

Gary's eyes widened with recognition. "Will the Thrill," he said. "Holy shit, man, I figured you were dead."

Will smiled. "Apparently not."

Gary drained the amber liquid from his highball glass and set it down on the bar. "Good to see you again, Detective."

"I'm not a detective anymore."

"You got promoted?"

Will shook his head. "Fired."

Gary shrugged. "Bummer."

The waitress poured a stream of Maker's Mark into Gary's glass. "So what brings you around here?"

"I wanted to catch your act." Will pointed his chin toward the empty stage. "Nicely done."

"Thanks, bro."

"Also, I wanted to talk to you about something."

Gary held up his hands. "I'm not a snitch anymore."

"Like I said, I'm not a cop anymore."

"So what's this about?"

"Some things that happened, back in the old days."

Gary picked up his glass and sipped. "Do I have to?"

Will looked at him. "It's not like I can force you."

"Then I'd rather not."

"How come?"

"I'm sorry, man. But all that shit, it happened a long time ago. Things are different now. I got a kid."

"Congratulations. But I'm only asking to talk."

Gary stared down into his glass. "Some things I'd rather forget."

Will finished what was left of his beer and set the bottle down. "Ray's dead, Gary. I think he was murdered."

Gary turned and looked at him.

"I could really use your help."

Gary's eyes swept the room, as if checking to be sure no one was watching.

"Not here," he said. "Let's take a ride."

THIRTY-ONE

Gary drove east on Temple. The night air was warm and rushed in through the open windows. Lights streamed by in neon trails of pink and blue and green.

Gary's car was a dark blue Crown Victoria. It was obvious that it had once been an unmarked police car, a spotlight still mounted to the driver's door.

"Nice car," Will said.

"Yeah, pretty cool, isn't it?"

"I was being sarcastic," Will said. "I feel like we're going on a stakeout."

"I got it at a sheriff's department auction."

The car smelled of old marijuana smoke trapped in the upholstery.

"You staying clean?" Will asked.

Gary nodded. "Yeah. I was on methadone for a while, but I stopped. That shit got frustrating. It kept me well, but I was never really high. What about you, you clean?"

Will didn't remember ever telling Gary that he was using, but he guessed it had probably been common knowledge. "Yeah."

"Ever miss it?"

"Which *it* are you referring to?"

"You know, getting high."

Will could still remember the sensations even now, the flooding warmth. "No."

They went past the Rampart police station, soon to be retired in favor of a new building that was being built nearby. Gary drove into Elysian Park and turned into the parking lot of the old Barlow Sanitarium. He pulled into a space and killed the engine.

The moon was almost full. Gary's car was the only vehicle in the dark lot. Some old stucco buildings stood behind them, a light showing in one of the windows.

Barlow Sanitarium had been built in the early 1900s to serve indigent tuberculosis patients. The facility had been established in the days when this part of L.A. was still country, prized for its clean air. At some point in the recent past it had been turned into a treatment center for respiratory diseases.

Gary pushed in the dashboard lighter. When it popped out, he used the glowing coils to light a joint. He blew out a cloud of smoke that swirled blue in the moonlight.

Gary held the burning joint out toward Will.

Will shook him off. "Aren't you worried about the cops? You're like fifty yards away from the police academy."

Gary took a hit and held it deep in his lungs. His words came out as puffs of smoke. "This is my *spot*. I come here every night on my way home. Never been hassled once."

Will looked out through the windshield. Across the road, small bungalows climbed their way up a scrub-covered hillside. They'd once been used to house tuberculosis patients but were now deserted. Sheets of plywood covered the windows, strands of ivy growing up the crumbling stucco walls.

Gary sucked in smoke. "This is what my life's come to," he said. "My wife won't let me smoke in the house, because of the kid."

Will turned on the bench seat, facing him. "You remember a dealer named Erik Crandall?"

Gary shrugged. "I'm not sure. My brain's like a piece of Swiss cheese."

"Young, skinny kid. At least he was back then. Ray and I took him down for dealing fentanyl."

Gary reached up and tapped a key that was hanging from the rear-view mirror, attached to a plastic fob. White letters printed on the maroon fob read:

JOSHUA TREE INN
ROOM #8

"That's the room Gram died in," Gary said. "His manager stole his corpse, took it out into Joshua Tree, and burned it."

"What for?"

Gary let out a stream of smoke and stared at the dark windshield. "I'm not really sure."

"Quit stalling," Will said. "What about Crandall?"

Gary nodded. "Yeah, I remember the dude."

"What can you tell me about him?"

"I don't know. His dope was always super clean. Dependable, never tried to short you on the weight."

"How'd you meet him?"

Gary sat there. He was still wearing the sequined white suit, the knees of his long legs poking up on each side of the steering wheel. "I don't remember."

"Just tell me."

"I'm being straight with you, bro. I swear. All the shit I've done? I'm glad I can remember my own name."

"He was dealing heroin? Coke? What else?"

Gary shook his head. "The fentanyl. He had a connect with some kind of lab."

"How did you get Ray hooked up with him?"

"The usual. I introduced Ray to the dude, told him he was good people. Ray started copping from him, then told Crandall he was interested in scoring weight."

"You were there? When Ray set up the deal we ended up busting Crandall for?"

Gary stubbed the roach out in the ashtray. "Yeah, I was there."

Will felt like he was getting a contact high from the smoke. "What makes you so sure? I mean, given the Swiss cheese and all."

Gary dropped the roach into a small ziplock bag. "Because it's something I've always been wondering about, all these years."

Will looked at him through the haze. "How come?"

"Because I could never figure out what the fuck happened. I mean, it was all set up to be this big deal. I mean, we're talking a *pound* of fentanyl. But when you guys busted him, there wasn't hardly jack shit."

THIRTY-TWO

Morning light leaked in around the edges of the window shade.

Laurie lay on her back, snoring softly through her open mouth. She'd kicked off the comforter cover sometime during the night. She was really showing now, a white T-shirt stretched taut over the curve of her belly.

Will slid toward her and placed his head sideways on top of her stomach. He held his breath, trying to hear the sound of his son moving inside her, but could only hear her stomach gurgling.

Laurie reached down and began to stroke his hair. "Where were you last night?"

"At work."

Her hand stopped moving. "Until two in the morning?"

"There was something I had to do after."

He kept his head on her belly, his face turned away from hers. It was like balancing his head atop a miniature basketball. A trail of fine yellow hair led downward, disappearing into the waistband of her pajama bottoms.

"Am I just supposed to leave it at that?" she asked. "Or are you going to tell me?"

He lifted his head and looked at her face, her hair fanned out on top of the pillowcase. "That story Crandall gave me, about his drugs getting stolen? I'm starting to think he's not lying."

"What do you mean?"

"That they really might have been stolen."

"By who?"

"I think Ray Miller might've had something to do with it," he said. "But I don't get it. I mean, a pound of fentanyl? What would Ray have done with that?"

"You're not a cop anymore, Will."

"Meaning?"

"You don't have to get sucked into this."

"We already *are* in this, Laurie. What about Crandall?"

"If he bothers us any more, we'll deal with it then."

Outside the window he could hear the sound of children's voices, playing. "It's not that simple."

"Yes, it is. There are enough problems in life as it is, Will. You don't have to go looking for them."

He let out his breath. "I didn't go looking for this. Crandall walked up to me. Ray Miller turned up dead. Those weren't *choices* I made."

"But now you do have a choice. Not to let this take over our lives."

"What is it you want me to do? Just pretend none of this happened, go back to leading a normal life?"

She looked at him. "Isn't that what you said you wanted?"

She rolled over and started to climb out of bed. He reached out and took hold of her hand. "Hang on."

She turned. "Why can't you see what you're doing? You've got a job you like. We're about to have a son." She paused, tears building up in her eyes. "There's *us*. Why is it that every time things are going good in your life, you feel the burning need to fuck it up?"

He shook his head. "I won't let that happen."

He was still holding on to her hand. He gave it a soft squeeze. "I need to try and find out what's going on. Just talk to some people, you won't even know I'm doing it. Then I'll turn over what I've got to the police and we'll be done with it."

"That's all?" She looked at him. "Just talk?"

He nodded. "I promise."

THIRTY-THREE

The *lying-thieving-conniving-asshole* cop's wife had a mighty fine ass.

Crandall stared at it as he trailed along in her wake as she walked along the path. She was wearing expensive-looking workout pants, the material stretched tight over her butt cheeks as they rose and fell.

Crandall had to hand it to the cop. If he had an old lady looked like this, he didn't think he'd ever be able to leave the house. Shit, he'd never even want to get out of bed.

He'd been following her since she'd left home. She'd driven over to this park, climbed out of her car with the dog and gone off on a walk.

The dog was clipped to a leather leash, its metal choke collar jangling as it trotted along the asphalt path. Crandall kept a safe distance behind, but the wife had headphones stuck into her ears, a white cord dangling down to the player clipped to her waist. She hummed along to the music, oblivious to his presence.

The park was deserted. He hadn't seen anyone else since they'd gotten here.

It was time for a new plan of attack, show the cop he was done playing.

He thought he'd been getting somewhere with the cop's old partner. That one had looked like he was about to shit his pants when he'd seen Crandall, got a look at what he'd become. It seemed like he was actually taking Crandall seriously, not trying to bullshit him. Telling him he needed a few days to see what he could do. Crandall believing that he was going to come through.

But now he was dead.

Crandall struggled to keep pace with the wife, short of breath. His muscles were sore, but it was a *good* sore. He'd spent two hours at the gym this morning, back up to five hundred on the bench press.

The wife was healthy looking. Like somebody you'd see in a TV commercial for yogurt or whole-wheat crackers. She wore a blue tank top, her naked arms pumping as she walked. Her long blond hair was in a ponytail, a pendulum swinging from side to side.

He wondered if she knew the truth about her husband, whether he'd ever told her about his conniving and thieving ways. He'd have to remember to ask her.

Crandall panicked when he heard the cell phone start to ring. He patted the pocket of his suit jacket, trying to remember where he'd put it. But then he saw that it was hers. She stopped walking, pulled out one of her earphones, and held the phone up to the side of her head.

Crandall stopped in his tracks and stepped off the path. He tried to think of something he could do to look busy, in case she glanced over at him.

She was maybe ten yards ahead of him, her back still turned to him, talking into the phone.

He reached inside the pocket of his suit jacket and pulled out the fortune cookie he'd saved from lunch. He looked at it, trying to act like he was there having a picnic or something. He cracked the cookie open in his palm and popped it into his mouth.

Then he unfolded the strip of paper and read it:

YOU WILL INHERIT SOME MONEY OR A SMALL PIECE OF LAND.

He heard her saying good-bye to whoever it was she was talking to on the phone, then click off. He kept staring at the fortune cookie, telling himself not to look at her.

He waited until she started up again with the dog and then fell into step behind her. The trees were thicker here, crowding the path.

Crandall hated walking. It made his knees ache. They'd been bothering him for a while now. He thought it might have something to do with the 'roids.

Up ahead the path turned off to the right. He slowed down. As she went around the curve, he caught a glimpse of her profile.

He did a double take, staring at her. At first he thought that she had some kind of weight problem, but that didn't make any sense given how fit the rest of her body looked.

Then he got it, all at once: *She's got a bun in the oven.*

He wondered what *that* would be like. He'd known guys inside the prison who got off on that, kept pictures of chicks with babies on board, down on all fours while they took it from behind.

He walked faster now, closing the gap between them. He worked his stress ball in his left hand, squeezing it over and over. It was hot out, and he was sweating like crazy inside the dark wool suit.

Then the path turned again, and he blinked as she walked into a clearing that was filled with sunlight. There was a small pond with some benches set around it. Another girl wearing workout clothes got up from one of the benches and waved to the cop's wife.

Crandall stopped, hanging back as the cop's wife walked up to the other one and threw her arms around her. The dog started to jump up on the other babe, but the cop's wife made it stop.

Crandall stood there, watching, as the two of them set off walking along the path together.

Crandall started to follow but then thought better of it. He needed to get her when she was alone. He turned around and started to make the long, hot walk back to the Town Car.

To be continued, he thought.

THIRTY-FOUR

Will heard the phone ringing as he got out of the shower. Laurie was out teaching a class, so there was no one else home to answer.

He wrapped a towel around his waist as he crossed the living room. He grabbed the cordless off the tiled kitchen counter.

It was Ray Miller's wife, Suzie.

"I got the message you left," she said.

"I meant it, Suzie. I still feel bad," Will said.

"No, I'm the one who should be apologizing to you, the things I said. I shouldn't have flown off the handle like that."

"You're going through a lot."

He stood there in the kitchen, dripping water onto the hardwood floor, not sure what to say next.

"I need to talk to you," she said. "Something's come up."

"What's wrong?" he asked.

"Not on the phone. Can you come out to the house?"

Will glanced at the digital clock on the stove. "I'm late for work."

"On a *Sunday?*"

"I'm working for the Dodgers. There's a game."

"How about after?"

"I wouldn't be able to make it out there until six, six thirty."

"I'm not going anywhere," she said.

The Dodgers lost to the Rockies. Even late on a Sunday afternoon the traffic was heavy heading north on the 101. Families were packed into SUVs and minivans filled with folding beach chairs and mountain bikes and plastic coolers, everyone working their way back home.

The Griffith Observatory perched high up on a bleached hillside, the western sun gleaming off the domed metal roof.

The traffic lightened up as he went over the Cahuenga Pass and entered the Valley. Cars started to change lanes, frantically jockeying for position as they picked up speed. Off to the east side of the freeway was Universal Studios; on the other was the headquarters for the world's largest producer of pornographic videos.

He pulled up in front of Ray's house. The front lawn had turned dry and yellow, the flowers wilting from lack of water.

Will rang the doorbell, listening to the chimes echoing inside the big house.

Suzie Miller opened the door dressed in a navy velour warm-up suit. It looked like she wasn't wearing any makeup, dark circles visible beneath her eyes. He put his arms around her shoulders and tried to hug her, but she just stood there, her body rigid.

When he let go, Suzie went over to the living room couch and sat down. She picked up a glass of red wine and took a sip. The bottle was open on the coffee table.

She pointed toward it. "Want some?"

"No, thanks."

Will started heading for the easy chair, but then changed his mind and sat down beside her on the couch. The room smelled the way someone's breath does after drinking wine. A flat-screen television was mounted on the room's opposite wall. It was tuned to a home improvement show but the sound was muted.

"How're you holding up?" It was the best he could come up with.

She shrugged. "I went through this when my first husband died. Now Ray. Maybe I'm just not lucky."

He realized he'd never been with her when Ray wasn't around. The television screen cut to black, her face reflected in the glass, as if she were trapped inside it.

"Thanks for coming," she said.

He looked at her. "Why don't you just tell me what's up, Suzie."

She sipped some of the wine. The glass was smudged with fingerprints. "I've been trying to deal with things." She waved her arm in the general direction of the back of the house. "Stuff that Ray's always taken care of."

"Do you need some help?"

She shook her head. "There was a charge from the bank. For a safe deposit box."

He waited.

"I didn't know we even had a safe deposit box."

"You need to get them to open it up."

"I did. I went down there yesterday."

"How much?" His mouth was dry.

She looked at him. "How much what?"

"How much money was inside the box?"

She shook her head "No, it wasn't that." She leaned forward and picked something up from the coffee table. It had been sitting there the whole time. "There was just this."

She gave it to him. He turned it over in his hand: a red pocket notebook with a fake leather cover. He opened it and flipped through the pages. The front two-thirds of the book was filled with neat handwriting in black ink, the rest of the pages still blank. Each page was set up the same way, almost like an accounting ledger. Three vertical columns of writing ran down each of the pages. The left column was a series of random numbers. The center column held letters that didn't form words. In the right column were more numbers.

Will stared down, trying to comprehend what it was about. But none of it meant anything to him.

What the hell were you up to, Ray?

Suzie was watching him. "I want you to take it."

He looked at her. "What do you want me to do with it?"

"Whatever you think is right. Isn't that what Ray would have wanted?"

He closed the notebook and tapped the cover against his knee. "You need to understand something, Suzie. If I follow up on this, things could get messy."

"Messy?"

"For Ray. He might not come out looking so good."

"Do whatever you feel you need to. I know you seem to think that Ray was up to something bad. But you didn't know him like I did. He was a good man."

"I know he was."

Outside the picture window it was growing dark.

"He really cared. You remember all those people who died?" she asked. "It was like he took it personally."

"What people who died?"

"You don't remember? It was all over the news. All those people who overdosed from heroin. It was horrible, Ray was depressed for weeks. He would never talk about it, but I think he blamed himself. For not being able to keep the drugs off the street."

Will was confused. "When was this?"

"Right around the time you got fired. You don't remember?"

He shook his head.

"I had a lot going on back then," he said.

THIRTY-FIVE

Will sat at the desk in the home office and watched through the window as Laurie drove off to work in her convertible.

He slid open the bottom drawer and took out the red ledger.

He opened it to the first page and stared down at the three columns holding their random collection of numbers and letters.

He took a sip of his still-warm coffee and focused his attention on the first column. The string of numbers stretched down the left side of the page.

9402
9402
9402
10202
10302
10302
11302

He flipped through the ledger, concentrating only on the first column. He thought that he could detect a pattern, but he kept turning the pages, until he felt sure that what he was looking at was a list of dates, the slashes that would divide the day, date, and month missing. The first entry was for 9/4/02, the final one on 10/14/03.

He took another sip of the coffee and stared at the middle column.

MF
AB
RM

He leafed through the entire ledger, but there were only three pairs of letters: MF, AB, and RM, repeated over and over.

What if the letters were sets of initials? If that were the case, then it made sense that RM was Ray Miller. But what about the other two?

He froze when he heard something moving outside the office door. He went over and opened it. Buddy came into the room, his plumed tail wagging. The dog went inside the kneehole of the desk, turned in a tight circle, then lay down.

Will got back in his chair and studied the ledger.

MF

There'd been a detective named Mike Fenske working Narcotics out of Rampart at the same time Will and Ray had been there. He'd been killed in the line of duty not long after Will had left the department.

It added up. Will had always suspected that Fenske was dirty.

Which left AB. He closed his eyes and tried to remember someone who had those initials.

The room's window was shut, but sounds came in through the panes of glass. Car tires moving along the street, blue jays screeching in the trees, the neighbor's window air conditioner laboring against the stifling Valley heat.

He couldn't think of anyone he'd worked with at LAPD whose initials were AB. It was possible the initials belonged to someone he didn't know or wasn't remembering. Maybe even someone outside the department.

He turned to the last column, more numbers.

15
15
15
25
30
30
50

The amounts grew larger with the passage of time. The smallest number was 15. The largest was 150.

He wondered if the numbers represented dollars, and if they were each missing the trailing three zeros, as in a financial statement. Then the amounts he was looking at would range from $15,000 up to $150,000.

It seemed obvious to him that the ledger had been used to keep track of payouts. Given what Will already suspected about Ray, and given that Fenske was also working Narcotics, it wasn't that big a leap to assume that the payoffs had something to do with drugs.

The dates inside the ledger spanned a period of fourteen months. The largest amounts were identical payments of $150,000 paid to each person on 10/13/03 and 10/14/03.

$450,000.

He and Ray had busted Crandall in September '03. If Crandall really had been holding a pound of fentanyl, it would have wholesaled for roughly that amount on the street.

Right around the time you got fired. You don't remember?

Will had been suspended pending an IAG investigation at the beginning of October '03, then been officially terminated that December.

He drained what was left in the mug, the coffee now cold. Will looked down at the dates for the big payments again. The payments stopped after that, no entries in the ledger after October.

It was horrible, Ray was depressed for weeks.

He tried to concentrate, to remember things from that time, but it was pointless.

It wasn't as if he had complete amnesia, because there were certain things he could remember, events that emerged from the drug-fueled haze. Random images that came back to him now with detailed and stunning clarity.

A stain on the velvet-covered bier at Sean's funeral. Laurie seated on the edge of the bed, trapped inside the perpetual darkness of the bedroom. An abscess in the crook of his left arm.

He could sense something else pulling at him, something dancing at the ragged edge of his memory, just out of reach. It felt relevant, important. But the harder he struggled to remember, the more distant and elusive it became.

THIRTY-SIX

The central branch of the Los Angeles Public Library is housed in an Egyptian-influenced building capped by a pyramidal roof covered with a tile mosaic depicting a blazing sun.

Will would have preferred to avoid having to make the trip downtown, but the branch libraries didn't have full text editions of the *Los Angeles Times*.

He ditched his car in the Flower Street Garage and took the library's escalator down to the History room. The modern space was lit with overhead fluorescents but had no windows, since it was below ground level.

He went over to the reference desk and filled out a form requesting the materials he wanted. The back issues of the *Times* were kept on microfilm. The librarian told him that it would take at least twenty minutes for the reels he wanted to be brought up.

He killed the time by looking at a display of historic photographs on the wall.

The framed pictures were rendered in silvery tones of black and white: klieg lights beaming up at the marquee of the old Carthay Circle theater; long-shuttered Central Avenue jazz clubs; a Studebaker idling at the curb in front of Chasen's. Images of a Los Angeles that was now gone.

When enough time had passed, he went back to the desk and picked up a plastic tote filled with reels of microfilm. He carried it over to a carrel that contained a battered viewer and sat down in the wooden chair.

He loaded the first reel and switched on the lamp of the machine. He started with June of 2002, three months before the first entry in the red ledger.

The LAPD was all over the front pages, news that the Civil Grand Jury had declined to release any report on their probe into the Rampart Scandal. The foreperson had directed that the grand jury transcripts remain sealed in perpetuity.

He turned the dial on the machine, pages of the newspaper marching by on the screen. He stuck to the front and local news sections, skipping sports, business, and entertainment. He wasn't sure of exactly what he was looking for but was hoping that something would jump out at him.

You don't remember? It was all over the news.

He put up a new reel and turned the dial, the old newspaper pages stirring his own memories, like kicking up dust inside an attic. Halftone photographs and headlines in bold letters flashed on the ground glass, advertisements for stores and restaurants now out of business.

He stopped turning the dial when he spotted an article in the paper dated October 7, 2002. Will knew what it said, remembered it almost verbatim. He knew that he shouldn't let himself look at it, but he couldn't stop himself.

The article had run the morning after Sean's death. The department's PR people had tried to kill it, but the paper had run it anyway, the death of the child of a prominent LAPD detective and the strange circumstances of the death too good a story to pass up.

The reporter had spun the incident as a cautionary tale about a young boy stung by a wasp while alone with his mother in a remote area of Griffith Park. How the resulting anaphylactic reaction had killed the child before the EMTs arrived and pronounced him dead at the scene.

Will spun the dial of the viewer without enthusiasm, the gray type gone blurry, as if both he and the machine were now submerged in seawater. When the reel ran out he sat and stared, dust particles blown up to gigantic proportions on the blank screen.

He remembered one night a few weeks after Sean's funeral. Staggering out of a downtown bar, trashed on Dilaudid and Jack Black. He'd somehow managed to get his car started, and the next thing he knew he found himself pulling into the darkened parking lot of the cemetery.

He hadn't brought a flashlight, so he staggered around in the feeble moonlight until he managed to find Sean's newly cut gravestone. He lay down on top of the grave and stared up at the night sky, trying to identify the constellations and inhaling the smell of the new sod. Finally falling asleep for the first time in days.

Sometime during the night the marine layer had come in, and he woke up with his clothing damp. His teeth were chattering, but he rolled over onto his stomach, dirt entering his ears and nostrils. He hugged himself as he tried to fall back asleep, not wanting to leave Sean there alone.

He fed a new reel into the machine. In February 2003, the LAPD was back on the front page with the kind of publicity money can't buy, or quash. An officer Will had known from Rampart had been sentenced to one year in prison and three years probation after pleading guilty to beating a gang member and filing false reports.

Will put up the last reel. He was thirsty, but they didn't allow drinks inside the library. There was a water fountain in the corner, but Will avoided them on general principle, always figuring they were pretty much petri dishes.

His hand froze on the dial when he saw the headline in the local section:

WAVE OF DRUG OVERDOSES KILLS 31

Will sat up in the chair, reading the headline again. The man in the next carrel began to cough.

You remember when all those people died? It was like he took it personally.

Will used the lever to zoom in on the page. He leaned forward and put his face close to the screen as he read the first paragraph:

> More than 31 people across the Los Angeles area have died over the last two weeks, including 19 over a four-day span beginning Columbus Day, according to investigators with the LAPD.

The article had run on October 31, 2003. Six weeks after Ray and Will had busted Crandall, a little over two weeks after the dates of the big payoffs that were recorded in the red ledger.

> The epidemic of overdoses was caused by an illegal version of the painkiller fentanyl. According to investigators, the victims apparently believed they were injecting heroin and were unaware of the greater potency of fentanyl, a powerful narcotic often prescribed to cancer patients that is exponentially more potent than heroin. Several of the victims were found dead with syringes still in their arms.

Will sat back in the wooden chair. He was sweating in spite of the building's air-conditioning. He stared at the image frozen on the screen, thinking about Ray.

Given the circumstances, it wasn't really all that surprising that he'd taken the deaths personally.

THIRTY-SEVEN

Will walked out of the Flower Street side of the library and into the late afternoon sunlight.

He started to head toward the parking garage but stopped when he realized that he might be able to save himself another trip downtown. He turned the other way, walked over to South Grand, then headed north.

He began to perspire as he walked up Bunker Hill. Skyscrapers rose from the street and blocked out the sun, leaving him in shadow. He glanced at his watch and saw that it was already almost four o'clock. He thought about calling Laurie, but she'd be in the middle of teaching her yoga class and never bothered to check her voice mail.

After he passed the courthouse, the view opened up and he could see the ziggurat at the top of City Hall peeking out from behind a tall acacia tree that grew in Civic Park.

It took him ten minutes to reach the Los Angeles Hall of Administration on West Temple. He took the elevator up to the eighth floor, where the county supervisors had their offices.

Dennis Byrnes had a suite of rooms with dark oak paneling on the walls and Oriental rugs laid on top of the wall-to-wall carpeting.

A woman with gray hair held back with a blue leather headband sat at a desk, typing into a computer. Will waited for her to look up.

"Is he in?" he asked.

"Do you have an appointment?"

"No, but I need to see him."

"What do you mean *see* him?"

"I mean go inside his office and talk to him. My name's Will Magowan."

"Would you care to tell me what this is about?"

"I'd rather not."

She was still smiling but spoke to him now as if he had some kind of learning disability. "Sir, you can't expect to just walk in off the street and see him."

"I used to work for him. I was a detective with LAPD."

"Are you still with the police department?"

"No, I—"

A heavy oak door behind her opened, and Dennis Byrnes walked out with the female aide who had been with him at Ray Miller's shivah.

Dennis did a double take when he saw him. "Will? What are you doing here?"

"We need to talk."

Dennis looked at his watch. "I'm swamped."

The receptionist smiled. "That's what I've been trying to tell him."

The female aide came toward him. "Mr. Magowan, is that right?"

Will nodded. He wondered how she'd been able to come up with his name.

"Why don't you come with me, tell me what this is all about."

She reached out her hand and placed it on his elbow. Dennis turned away and stepped back inside his office. He began to shut the door.

Will spoke to his back, not quite shouting. "It's about Ray Miller."

Dennis turned in the doorway.

"There are some things I found out," Will said. "I think you need to hear them."

The aide still had hold of Will's elbow.

Dennis looked at her and shook his head. Then he turned to Will. "This better be good."

Dozens of Dennis Byrneses smiled out from framed photographs that hung on the walls of the office. Dennis cutting ribbons and holding oversized checks and wearing yellow hard hats at construction sites.

The flesh-and-blood version stared at Will from the other side of his glass-topped desk. "So tell me, Will," he said. "What is it that's so goddamned important?"

Will leaned forward in his chair, then realized he didn't know where to begin. When he'd come up here he hadn't really expected to get this far.

"You remember that guy I told you about at the shivah, Erik Crandall?"

Dennis nodded. "I already spoke to the chief about him. They think you have some kind of hard-on for this guy, that you sent them on some kind of goose chase."

Will shook his head. "That's not—"

Dennis held up a hand to stop him. "Don't shoot the messenger," he said. "Just passing it on."

Will took a breath, then tried again. "Remember I told you how Crandall came to me with this crazy idea that Ray and I stole his drugs?"

"I remember."

Will looked at him. "It turns out he's not crazy."

"I'm listening."

"I think Crandall's drugs really were stolen. They were worth close to half a million dollars on the street. He was trying to shake Ray and me down for the money. Only Crandall ended up killing Ray."

Dennis loosened the knot of his necktie. His dress shirt was a pale blue color, but the collar and cuffs were white. "So why come to me?"

"Because the cops won't listen to me. But they'll sure as shit listen to you."

Dennis nodded.

"Plus, I figured that for you it would be personal."

"In what sense?"

"Because of what Crandall did to Ray."

Dennis's chair made a mechanical creaking noise as he leaned back. "Take me through it."

"The night Ray and I busted Crandall, he was supposed to be holding a pound of fentanyl. But only eighty grams of it got turned in to evidence. That's because Ray took it. Ray and other people inside the department were stealing dope from busts, then turning around and selling it on the street."

"How is it that you know all this?"

"I've talked to Suzie. Ray had money. Too much money. She found a ledger he was hiding in a safe deposit box."

Dennis looked at him. "What kind of ledger?"

"It's a record of payoff amounts, lists of dates and people's initials."

"Whose initials?"

"Ray's. Mike Fenske. A third set I haven't been able to figure out yet. Maybe it's someone outside the department, who knows?"

"You've seen this ledger yourself?"

Will nodded. "Suzie gave it to me. I've got it at home."

Dennis nodded. "Nice work."

"There are some big payoff amounts, the dates line up with the time frame when Crandall got busted."

Dennis brought his hands together on the desktop, his fingers forming the shape of a pyramid. "I've got to hand it to you, Will. You've done a yeoman's job here, gotten more police work done without a badge than the whole worthless department."

"So you believe me?"

Dennis looked at him. "I wish I didn't," he said. "But I do."

"Can you trust the department to take it from here?"

Dennis shook his head. "I better bring it to the DA, let them run the investigation. I want to be sure there's some adult supervision."

"Thanks."

Dennis nodded. "That's why they pay me the big bucks."

He picked up a pen from his desk and wrote something down on a legal pad.

Will waited for him to finish. "There's something else."

Dennis looked up at him.

"You remember all those people who overdosed from fentanyl, about five years back?"

"Vaguely."

"That was the fentanyl Ray stole from Crandall."

"How can you possibly know that?"

"It's all in the ledger. The dates, the amounts, it all works."

Dennis ran a hand through his silver hair. "Jesus. What a fucking mess."

He swiveled his chair around toward the big double-hung windows and looked out at the Times Building and the Civic Center. The sounds of buses and cars rose up from Hill Street.

Dennis shook his head, still staring out the window. "Can you just imagine the shit storm that's going to rain down on the city when this comes out? We finally get Rodney King behind us, Rampart. Now we're going to reopen the wound."

He swiveled around in his chair to face Will. A happier version of Dennis smiled out from an election poster that hung on the wall behind him. "We go back a long way, Will. And I'm willing to play this any way you want. But I want you to go home and think this through."

Will looked at him. "In what sense?"

"Think about the greater good. About whether you want to take the lid off this particular Pandora's box. We need to stop and consider what we're about to do here. The fallout."

"I already have."

"No, I want you to really think about what will happen if and when this goes public. How it's going to affect the department. Ray." He looked at him. "And you."

"Me?"

Dennis nodded. "Once I turn this over to the DA, the thing takes on a life of its own. I won't be able to control it."

"What does that have to do with me?"

"The political theater of this situation will require a villain. I seem to remember a lot of speculation that you were the one using the evidence locker as your personal stash."

Will felt his face growing warm. "They were never able to prove—"

"I understand, but how's it going to look? You need to understand that once the witch hunt starts, you never know who's going to get burned at the stake. You need to go home and think about this, what else they might turn up."

Will shook his head. "I don't need time to think."

"Just sleep on it. For your own sake. Nothing's going to happen today, in any event. In the cold light of morning, if you still want me to take this to the DA, I'll do it. Either way, I'm good with it."

"I don't understand," Will said. "You'd be willing to just cover it up?"

Dennis shook his head. "There's nothing to cover up. Given your history, you aren't exactly the most credible source. The police department's already written you off. So you came barging in here with a load of crazy theories. Who could blame me for not taking you seriously?"

THIRTY-EIGHT

By the time he got the car out of the parking garage, Will found himself snared in the heart of rush hour traffic. It was close to seven thirty when he finally made it out to Van Nuys.

When he walked inside the house he found Laurie seated in a perfect lotus position on the living room rug. An instruction manual was spread open on her lap, the floor around her covered with the unassembled parts of a white wooden crib, hand tools, and an opened cardboard shipping carton.

"The crib came?" Even as he spoke the words, he realized how stupid the question was.

She picked up a screwdriver without bothering to answer him. Her belly was large and round inside her yoga top. She looked like a female Buddha.

"Sorry I'm late," he said.

She looked up at him. Her eyes were puffy, as if she'd been crying. "Do you even know what tonight was?"

Shit. He knew there'd been something important that he needed to get back home for. He was supposed to have met her at the Lamaze class, but he'd gotten so caught up in the events of the day that he'd forgotten.

"I'm really sorry," he said. "I tried to call you."

"I didn't get a message."

He climbed down onto the floor with her. "I really wanted to be there." His knees popped as he tried to sit cross-legged. "It won't happen again."

She picked up one of the crib pieces, a side panel with wooden bars. "They all had their partners there. That's what the instructor calls the men. Partners. I was the only one who was alone. But you know what? I'm all right with it. Because it just drove home the truth."

She was trying to fit a bolt into the piece of the crib. He reached out to hold it steady for her, but she turned her body away, so that it was out of his reach.

She looked at him, her eyes moist. "The truth is, I don't *have* a partner."

"What're you—"

She managed to get the bolt fitted into the crib piece and then looked at him. "No, really. It made me realize that I can't count on you."

"Could you at least listen to me for a second, so I can tell you where I was?"

She put her hand on her belly. "What could be more important than *this*?"

He opened his mouth, then closed it again.

He pushed himself to his feet and went into the kitchen. He opened the cabinet above the refrigerator and pushed aside serving bowls and empty vases until he located a bottle that was covered with a coating of gray dust.

He poured two fingers of the dark liquid into a glass, then took the glass back out into the living room.

"What's that?" she asked.

"Cognac," he said.

"I believe it's customary to drink that *after* dinner."

"We don't have anything else."

"That's because you're not supposed to be drinking."

He took a sip of it, like liquid fire against the back of his throat, his first taste of hard alcohol in close to two years.

"I was with Dennis Byrnes."

"The politician?" She looked up at him. "What for?"

He sat back down on the floor and told her everything, in order, starting with the ledger and ending with the newspaper story.

"But why go to Byrnes?" she asked.

He reached out and took hold of her hand. "I figured if he took it to the police, then they'd have to take it seriously."

She didn't try to take her hand away. "So what did he say? Byrnes?"

"He's going to turn my information over to the district attorney. Let him oversee the investigation. To make sure LAPD doesn't try to cover anything up."

She smiled at him. "You should feel really good."

He nodded. "I guess."

She studied his face. "You *guess*? What's wrong?"

"Nothing."

The windows in the front of the house were all open and the scent of the Spanish jasmine that grew on the porch came in through the opened windows.

Laurie shook her head. "You just can't stand for it to be over, is that it? You liked having this, and now you just don't want to let it go."

He shook his head. "No—"

"Then what is it?"

"It was just the way we left it, is all."

She raised an eyebrow. "How *did* you leave it?"

"He told me to go home and sleep on it. He said he'd take it to the DA, if that's what I really wanted, but he thought I should think it through first."

"I don't understand. What is there to think about?"

Will nodded. "He said I needed to think about what an investigation might turn up on me."

"Why? You didn't have anything to do with what happened."

"There were some allegations. About how I was stealing drugs from the department back then."

She looked at him. "Were you?"

He took another sip of the cognac. He could feel it working already, like a giant hand pressing down on him.

"You need to understand how it was. How crazy things were back then. There wasn't any black or white, just a million shades of gray. I was a junkie, there was a lot of dope lying around. It's no big surprise I may have taken some now and then."

"Now and then."

"It was only small stuff. Nothing anyone would ever miss. Never anything that would jeopardize a case."

She looked him in the eyes. "The important thing is you didn't steal Crandall's dope. What we're talking about here, the dope that killed all those people, you didn't have anything to do with *that*."

He looked down into the liquid glowing at the bottom of his glass.

She watched him. "Right?"

"That night Ray and I busted Crandall, I was in the car. Listening in on the wire. I remember hearing Ray identify himself as a cop and telling Crandall that he was under arrest. That was my cue to move in. When I did, Ray told me to take Crandall into custody while he took care of the evidence."

"Did you see what he did with it?"

Will shook his head. "I was too busy with Crandall."

She smiled. "So you don't have anything to worry about."

He drained what was left in the glass. "I took it."

"Took what?"

"I took Crandall's dope."

He could remember frisking Crandall, telling him to grab the wall of a store. Kicking his feet apart, running his hands up and down his spindly legs.

Finding the bindle in the back pocket of Crandall's Levi's, the dope folded up inside a lottery ticket.

Laurie was staring at him. "I don't understand. You just said that you never even saw it."

"He had some in his pants. Not much. An eighth, maybe not even. But I took it. I didn't think it would make any difference."

"What did you do with it?"

He looked at her. "What do you *think*?"

"But you said that it made people OD. How come you didn't?"

"I cut it. I guess I'm just smarter than your average junkie."

"But you didn't steal the rest of it?"

He shook his head no.

"You're positive?"

"Yes."

She nodded her head once. "So you're okay then."

"No, Laurie, I'm not. I mean, just think about how ridiculous that sounds: *Yes, I stole some of the drugs, but I didn't steal all of them.*"

"No one has to find out."

"I'm not going to lie, Laurie. If Byrnes goes to the DA, I'm going to have to give a statement, minimum. Maybe even get sworn in front of a grand jury. We're talking about perjury."

"Like you said, everyone was up to something back then. But you never did anything like Ray did. Byrnes will be able to see that."

"They'll need a scapegoat. Ray's dead. So is Fenske. There's no one else for them to throw overboard."

She blinked but didn't say anything.

"You need to understand something, Laurie. I could end up going to prison over this. You ever hear what it's like for a cop in there?"

"So what're you going to do?"

He rubbed his forehead.

"I guess I'll just have to figure something out."

THIRTY-NINE

Crandall was beginning to feel like he was back in prison.

He'd been sitting here inside the Town Car since lunchtime, waiting for the cop's wife to come home. The sun had already set, but the car's interior was still broiling and reeked to high heaven of takeout Chinese and his body odor.

He stared across the street at the cop's perfect house. Just the sight of it ticked him off, seeing the life the cop had built for himself at Crandall's expense. The way everything was arranged just so, the manicured green lawn and the clipped hedges and the pink and yellow flowers blooming in the flower beds.

He finished the last dregs of mu shu that were left at the bottom of the cardboard container. It was cold and the sauce had congealed, but he didn't want the protein to go to waste. He needed to keep feeding the Equipoise a steady supply of protein so that it could work its magic.

Crandall always got the mu shu to go. He didn't feel comfortable eating in restaurants because he couldn't stand to have people looking at him when he ate. Even back inside the apartment, he would always close the curtains on the patio doors before sitting down to eat.

152

He remembered what it was like trying to eat in prison, the big mural on the walls of the chow hall at Quentin.

The mural was a visual history of the twentieth century. In the middle there was a big picture of Charlie Chaplin wearing that funny little hat he used to wear, surrounded by some old-time actresses whose names Crandall didn't know.

The inmate who had painted the mural had used some kind of trick when he'd painted the faces, so that no matter where Crandall sat in the cavernous room the painted eyes of the mural would always be looking right at him, watching him from high up on the wall.

He heard a car engine coming from behind him. He looked up at the headlights in the rearview mirror, hoping it was the Volkswagen convertible that the cop's wife drove. He slid down in the driver's seat, but it was only a Ford Taurus that looked like a rental car.

The car slowed as it went past. Crandall slid all the way down in his seat and tried to make himself disappear. The Taurus kept going, turning left at the corner.

Crandall sat up and reached his fortune cookie from the dashboard. He broke open the cookie and held the strip of white paper so that it would catch some of the glow from the streetlight:

MANY A FALSE STEP IS MADE BY STANDING STILL.

He stared at the fortune as he crunched the cookie, wondering if it was trying to tell him that he should just hang it up for the day. The cop and his wife must have gone out for the evening, maybe met up for dinner somewhere after they finished work.

He heard the sound of another car. He looked up at the mirror, surprised to see the Taurus coming down the street again.

He slid down, listening to the metallic squeal of the other car's brakes as it came to a stop. The engine shut off. Crandall peeked out over the dashboard and saw the Taurus parked at the curb just past the cop's house.

The driver of the car sat there for a minute. Then the door opened without the dome light inside the car coming on. The man climbed out and shut the door but didn't bother to lock the car. He was wearing a pair of wraparound sunglasses even though it was dark out.

The man started to walk up the sidewalk toward Crandall. Crandall reached for the keys dangling from the Town Car's ignition, thinking the guy was headed for him.

But then he turned down the cop's front walk and went up onto the front porch.

The guy rang the doorbell. He was white and was wearing a Dodgers cap, a dark polo shirt, and jeans. It was hard to make out his face in the dark, but Crandall had the feeling he knew this dude from somewhere. He thought maybe it was someone he'd jailed with but couldn't be sure.

No one answered the door, which Crandall already knew was going to happen, since no one was inside the house. The guy rang the bell again, then cupped his hands around his eyes and looked inside through the little window next to the door.

After a few seconds, the guy reached out and tried the latch on the front door, but it must've been locked because it didn't open. The man came down off the porch and went along the front of the house to a wooden gate that led into the backyard.

He pushed on the latch, and the gate swung inward. The cop's dog was back there, and it came running up to the guy. The dog started to bark, but the man dropped down into a squat and petted the dog, then shut the gate behind him.

Crandall sat in the car and waited for the guy to come back out, but he didn't. Crandall figured he must have gotten inside the house through a back door. Maybe the guy was a friend of the cop's. He thought about taking off, that he'd missed his chance to get the wife alone. But he was curious now.

Another forty minutes went by on the dashboard clock before the gate opened and the man came back out into the front yard. He shut the gate and walked across the front lawn, looking from side to side, still wearing the dark glasses.

Crandall slid down in the seat. He waited until he heard the car door shut, then looked over the dash to see the headlights of the Taurus come on as it started to drive away.

He thought about following, but he had a pickup at LAX in less than an hour and was worried about the traffic.

FORTY

His first thought was that there was an earthquake.

Will felt himself shaking as he came awake in the bed. He opened his eyes to see Laurie's face floating above him. Her hand was on his shoulder, shaking it.

"What's wrong?" he asked.

"Someone's been in the house."

He sat up against the headboard and looked around the bedroom. Everything looked normal, the same way it always did.

"What do you mean?"

"Just what I said." She was already dressed, wearing a tank top and yoga pants. "You've got to get up."

He was still half asleep. He'd worked last night and the game had gone extra innings. He hadn't gotten home until after midnight.

He threw off the comforter cover and followed her out of the bedroom dressed only in his pajama bottoms. He checked his watch and saw that it was just after seven.

The living room was filled with bright sunlight, the sky outside the sliding glass doors tinged with smog. He looked around the room but didn't see anything that looked out of place.

"I could just tell," she said. "I had this *feeling* as soon as I got up."

"Is anything missing?"

"No. But things have been moved. I can tell."

"Why would someone break into the house and not steal anything?"

"Maybe they took something we haven't noticed yet."

Will went into the office and looked at the things on top of the desk. He couldn't be positive, but everything looked the way he remembered leaving it. He pulled out the middle drawer of the desk, wobbling it up and down until it pulled free.

Laurie watched from the doorway. "What're you doing?"

"Checking something."

He turned his body to block her view and then flipped the drawer over. The red ledger was still duct-taped to the bottom of the drawer, just as he'd left it. He slid the drawer back into place.

He walked through the living room to the front door. Everything looked normal. He checked the door, flipping the dead bolt off. He opened it and knelt down to inspect the lock cylinder, strike, and door frame.

"There's no sign that anyone broke in."

"What about the patio doors? When I came home last night, they were unlocked."

He stood up. "That could have been from me. I'm not sure if I locked them when I left for work."

"Dammit, Will. We talked about this. You promised you were going to be more careful."

"I'm sorry," he said. "But even if I did forget, I doubt anyone would come in."

She put her hands on her hips. "How do you know?"

"Buddy was back there."

She shook her head. "What's he going to do? Lick them to death?"

She had a point, but still. "He's a pretty big dog. I think just the sight of him back there would be enough to scare someone off."

"Well, it obviously wasn't."

He yawned. He needed a cup of coffee bad, get his brain kick-started. He headed for the kitchen.

"Where are you going?"

"Make some coffee."

"Don't you think this is a little more important?"

He stopped walking and turned around. "Laurie, I'm telling you, no one broke in."

"What about that Crandall guy?"

Will shook his head. "C'mon, you saw this place the last time. It was like a bull in a china shop."

She grabbed hold of his wrist. "All I know is someone's been in here."

He spoke to her in what he still thought of as his cop voice, calm and soothing. "Look, I don't blame you for thinking this. After all we've been through. But I think you're being a little bit paranoid."

She licked her lips. "Paranoid."

"Like I said, I don't blame you. Maybe it's hormonal, because of the pregnancy."

Tears came into her eyes. "Fuck you, Will."

She turned and went over to the wooden bookcase. She slid out a blue linen-covered box that she stored photographs in. "When was the last time you looked at the pictures of Sean?"

He wasn't sure what she was asking him. Was she angry that he wasn't looking at them enough? "I don't remember."

"So you haven't looked at them since Saturday?"

"No."

"Well, that's when I looked at them. Saturday." She lifted the lid and held out the box so that he could see the photograph at the front of the stack.

The picture showed Sean at maybe six months old. He was in the kitchen sink, naked, the sink filled with soapy water. Will's bare arms entered the frame from the left side, his skin slick with bubble bath.

Will blinked. He made himself stop looking, the picture transporting him back to another time.

Laurie took a different photograph out of the stack. "I keep these in chronological order." She held it up to Will. "*This* is the one that goes in front."

It was one he had taken at the hospital, Laurie holding Sean minutes after he'd been born, the baby swaddled so tightly in the receiving blanket that it looked larval, no arms or legs.

"Maybe you just put them away in the wrong order."

She stared at him. "First I'm paranoid. Now I'm careless."

"I mean, who knows. Maybe you were interrupted, the phone rang or something."

When she shook her head a tear traced a path down her cheek.

"I would never do that. I always keep them in order. A *specific* order. So I won't lose them."

The look on her face filled him with self-loathing. He took the box from her hands and hugged her against his naked torso. Her body shook with her sobs.

"I'm sorry," he said. "I shouldn't have doubted you."

She pulled away from him and looked into his face. "So you believe me?"

He nodded.

"Then what are you waiting for?" she asked. "You need to call the police."

FORTY-ONE

Richard Ryder, the detective who'd investigated the blood-dumping incident, sat on the living room couch. An unlit cigarette was stuck in the corner of his mouth as he used a ballpoint pen to write something down in a pocket notebook.

Will faced him across the coffee table. The sound of breaking glass came from the kitchen, Laurie throwing away open containers of food. She was afraid Crandall might have been trying to poison them. She'd only grown more freaked out since Will had called the police.

He'd dialed the phone number from the business card Ryder had left at the house the night Crandall dumped the blood. Will thought it would be a good thing to have some continuity, instead of having to start over at square one with someone new. He was pleasantly surprised when Ryder agreed to come right over.

Will and Laurie had already taken the detective on a tour of the house, Laurie showing him the box of photographs and explaining how she knew they'd been tampered with.

Ryder flipped shut his notebook. "I think that should do it."

Will looked at him. "So what're you going to do?"

"I don't know that there's all that much we *can* do. I'll write up a report."

"A report."

"What is it you're expecting, Mr. Magowan? There's no evidence of a break-in. Nothing's been stolen. There's no sign that anyone was even inside the house."

"What about the photographs?"

Ryder's cell phone vibrated from where it lay on top of the wooden coffee table.

He picked it up and read a text message off the screen, then looked back at Will. "We don't have the manpower to follow up on this Goldilocks stuff."

"Come again?"

"You know, 'Someone's been sleeping in my bed.' "

Will took a breath. He knew what they had was pretty thin, but he'd expected better than this. "It seems like you could at least have someone check for prints."

Ryder took the unlit cigarette from his mouth. "They call them crime scene technicians for a reason. I can't get one out here unless there's evidence of a *crime*."

"So you're saying we just imagined it?"

"I'm saying I don't know."

Ryder was dressed in a cotton suit and a maroon tie that had a pattern of old-time golfers wearing knickers and knee socks. A dried yellow stain sat just below the knot.

He tapped his ballpoint pen on the cover of the closed notebook. "Let me ask you: Is there maybe another reason somebody would want to break in?"

"Like what?"

"A lot of times, these home invasions are related to . . ." His voice trailed off.

"Related to *what*?"

Ryder looked at him. "Do you keep any illegal drugs in the house?"

Will blinked, caught off guard by the question. *"No."*

"I'm not Narcotics," Ryder said. "You can tell me."

"I just did."

Ryder nodded but didn't look entirely convinced.

"This's got to be Crandall," Will said. "Why don't you at least bring him in, see where he was last night."

Ryder shook his head. "We don't have PC."

"He's on *parole*."

Ryder picked up a mug of coffee from the table. "I'd still have to clear it with my captain."

"What for?"

"Department's got to be careful of a civil suit, for harassment. We already pulled this guy in for nothing."

Will looked at him and waited.

"I talked to Denslowe, in Homicide," Ryder said. "He told me how you wasted his time."

"I wasn't wasting his time. Crandall did it."

Ryder sipped some of the coffee. "You need to start being a little more careful. I'm on your side, but word's starting to get around the department about you."

"Like *what?*"

Ryder looked down at his lap.

"Just tell me."

"That you're not reliable," Ryder said. "That all the drugs fried your brain."

"That's *bullshit*."

Ryder held up his hands. "Don't get pissed at me. You were the one who asked what it is they're saying." He took another sip of the coffee. "Here's an idea for you, if you and your wife are really worried about this Crandall guy."

Will couldn't stop staring at the stain on Ryder's tie. "Let's hear it."

"You could probably get a restraining order."

"You mean go to court?"

Ryder nodded. "That's right."

"Let me get this straight. You want me to spend my own money to hire a lawyer, so I can solve a problem my tax dollars are already paying you to take care of?"

He must have raised his voice, because it suddenly grew quiet inside the kitchen.

Ryder put down the coffee cup. "I think I'm done here."

"Funny, I didn't notice that you ever got started."

Ryder's face flushed with color. "I came out here because you called me. Because you asked me to," he said. "What is it you want from me?"

Will looked him in the eye.

"I thought you could help," he said. "I guess I was wrong."

FORTY-TWO

The gun shop was in Burbank, on a busy strip of Magnolia across the street from a health food store. Will had been driving past it for years, but had never gone inside. The small windows in front were covered with black iron security bars.

An electronic chime sounded when he pushed open the door.

The store was long and narrow and had glass display cases along one side that were filled with handguns. Racks that hung on the wall held shotguns and assault rifles.

A clerk stood behind the cases, talking into a cell phone. He was wearing a black polo shirt with the name of the store embroidered on the chest in red thread. He looked like he was fresh out of high school. There was no one else inside the store.

Will looked down into the glass cases. The guns were laid out side by side on the glass shelves, each one set at the same slight angle, as in a tableau. He knelt down for a closer look but didn't see what he wanted.

He'd owned the same personal weapon since making detective. A Browning Hi-Power. It had served him well, and he'd grown used to it, the feel of its trigger pull, the way the thumb safety and trigger fell naturally to hand.

Laurie had talked him into getting rid of the gun when he moved back in with her. At first he'd thought about selling it, but then got too worried about what some idiot might do with it. In the end, he'd turned it in at a program run by the police department.

He hadn't picked up a gun in almost two years; had never regretted not having one until now.

The salesman finally wrapped up his call and slid the cell phone inside the front pocket of his jeans. "Can I help you?"

"I'd like a Browning," Will said. "The gun, not the poet."

He was paraphrasing a line he remembered reading in a Raymond Chandler novel, but the reference seemed to be lost on the kid.

"We don't carry Browning."

"Can you order one?"

"Which model are you looking for?"

"Hi-Power," Will said. "Nine mil."

"I'd have to check with the owner." The kid reached down and slid open the glass doors at the back of the display case. "But let me show you the gun I personally carry."

He came up holding a matte black automatic. "Heckler & Koch P-2000. Polymer frame, so it's like half the weight of the Browning, which believe me you'll appreciate at the end of the day."

He released the magazine and showed it to Will. "Higher capacity, too. Ten in the mag and one in the chamber."

He laid the gun down on a black velvet pad, then pulled out the slide release and broke the gun down into five pieces. "Plus, you can field-strip it in less than ten seconds, with your eyes closed."

Will looked at him. "I can't really see having the need for that."

"No matter," the kid said. "It's still pretty cool."

"I want something I can carry cocked and locked, like the Browning."

"You mean a 1911 type?"

Will nodded. He'd never really been into guns. He'd always thought that anyone that was a gun enthusiast was someone who'd never had to use one on another human being.

"I've got Smith & Wessons, Kimber, Wilson Combat. What is it you'd like to see?"

Will shrugged. He didn't need this turning into some kind of shopping spree, just wanted to get it over with. "I don't know. What would you recommend?"

The kid reached back inside the display case. "If you like the Hi-Power, I think you'll love this."

He placed a gray steel automatic down on the black velvet pad. "Kimber Tactical Custom. Comes with night sights, ambi safety, match-grade trigger."

Will looked down at it. "It's a nine?"

The kid shook his head. ".45."

"I'm used to a nine."

"You should really think about stepping up to a .45. I've heard stories, dude. Where a nine just couldn't get it done."

Will remembered the last time he'd had to fire a gun, when he'd been chief of police in Haydenville. A tweaker had attacked him inside a bar, and he'd had to empty almost an entire clip into the guy's chest before he'd finally gone down.

An image of Erik Crandall came into his mind, his massive torso, the bulging pectorals that were like slabs of meat.

The kid was holding the gun out toward him. Will took it, the metal greasy with a coating of Cosmoline.

He wrapped his palm around the checkered grip, the pad of his index finger falling onto the curve of the trigger.

He racked back the slide and checked that the chamber was empty. He brought the gun up with both hands and came into a Weaver stance. He thumbed off the safety and sighted the gun on a combat target that hung on the back wall.

"May I?" Will asked.

"Go for it."

Will squeezed the trigger to dry fire the gun. He focused on the front sight, the target going slightly soft, the line drawing of the bad guy morphing into Erik Crandall. The trigger pull was smooth, with a clean break, like a sheet of glass.

Will turned back to the kid, the gun still in his right hand, hanging down at his side.

"Sold," he said.

FORTY-THREE

The top of the dining room table was covered with sheets of old news-papers.

The new gun was fieldstripped, the parts laid out on the newspaper along with some cleaning tools, a small bottle of Hoppe's No. 9, and gun oil. Buddy slept beneath the table, his head resting on top of Will's bare feet. Laurie was gone, out teaching an evening class.

California had a ten-day waiting period, so the pistol had been sitting in the gun shop until he'd finally been able to pick it up that morning.

He used a nylon brush to scrub out the barrel. The gun was brand-new, but he didn't like to leave anything to chance, wanted to be sure there weren't any metal shavings inside the bore. Then he used the brush on the breech face and slide rails.

In the morning he would take the gun down to the range and run some rounds through it to break it in.

The gun had set him back $1,250. With the cleaning supplies, three boxes of Hydra-Shoks, and tax, it had come to almost $1,500 on the MasterCard.

He worried what Laurie would have to say when she saw the charge, but the statement didn't come until the beginning of the month. He'd deal with it then. Besides, he was doing this for her safety.

He soaked a patch in some Hoppe's No. 9 and used a rod to run it through the bore. He had the exhaust fan over the stove running, but the solvent smell was dizzying. Buddy moved beneath the table in the instant before he heard the front door open behind him.

He turned around to see Laurie come into the house carrying a paper shopping bag from the baby store at the mall. Buddy trotted up to her and licked the back of her hand.

"You're home early," he said.

"My class was canceled."

She set down the shopping bag and petted Buddy on top of his head. "My god," she said. "What's that *smell?*"

He screwed the cap back onto the bottle of solvent. "Nothing."

She walked over and stood behind him, looking over his shoulder. "Is that a *gun?*"

He gave her his best smile. "I'm just happy to see you."

She walked around the corner of the table and looked down at him. "I'm serious," she said. "What's that doing in here?"

"I bought it." He was feeling a little light-headed from inhaling the solvent fumes.

"We've talked about this, Will. I don't want that inside my house."

"Do I need to remind you that *our* house has been broken into twice already?"

She pulled out a chair and sat down. Buddy came over and rested his head on her lap, against the rise of her pregnant belly. "I thought we agreed, no more guns. We're about to have a child."

"He's only a fetus, Laurie. I don't really think there's much danger of him getting his hands on it."

"I'm *serious*. I want it out of here. Now."

"What am I supposed to do with it?"

"I don't care."

He looked at her. "Did you forget? What Crandall just did?"

"Guns don't solve problems, Will. They create them."

"This isn't some bumper sticker, Laurie. It isn't theoretical. This guy's dangerous, we don't know what he's capable of."

"You know how I feel about guns. Just because we're worried about this guy doesn't mean I'm suddenly going to join the NRA."

He picked up the frame and slide, trying to figure out how to put the gun back together. "I don't like it any better than you do. But the situation's gone way too far."

"This isn't the Wild West. You can't just go and solve your problems with a gun."

"You have a better idea?"

"We need to leave it to the police."

He let out his breath. "You were here. You heard what Ryder said."

He looked at the darkness outside the sliding glass doors, the two of them reflected in the big panes of glass, the vertical piece of the wooden frame separating their images.

"Crandall's been in the house twice," he said. "What if he comes again, while we're home?"

"What if you point the gun at him and he doesn't want to listen? You'd just shoot him in cold blood?"

He looked away.

"*Jesus*, Will."

He fitted the recoil spring back inside the slide. "You really think the world would be a worse place if a guy like Crandall wasn't in it anymore?"

"I don't think it's for you to decide."

He had the gun back together now. He racked back the slide, then pressed the release. The slide shot forward, the dog jerking his head from Laurie's lap at the sound.

Laurie pushed her chair back from the table.

"I'm not going to argue with you anymore," she said. "You can have a gun in the house. Or you can have me. Pick one."

FORTY-FOUR

The cop's wife was a creature of habit.

Crandall had followed her back to the same park as the other day, the same dog pulling ahead of her on the same leather leash. It even looked like she was wearing the same clothes, her ass cheeks rising and falling inside the stretch fabric of her yoga pants, déjà vu all over again.

It was late morning, already hot as hell out here in the Valley, the park deserted. He trolled along a few yards behind her, his gait stiff. His butt was sore from where he'd injected himself back at the apartment.

At least he was dressed for it this time, wearing his red stretch top and a pair of black track pants that had white racing stripes down the sides.

He squeezed the stress ball in his left hand.

The headphones were stuck inside her ears. She sang along to the music, her voice high and soft, like a little girl's.

He followed her around a bend in the trail, almost there now. He wanted to let her get a little farther away from the parking lot but didn't want her to make it all the way to the open area with the little pond.

He was glad for the shade from the surrounding trees because his head was throbbing. He'd been getting some bad headaches lately, thought it might be from all the Equipoise he'd been shotgunning.

The dog stopped walking and sniffed at the base of a bush. The cop's wife waited while the dog lifted its back leg and took a whiz.

Crandall saw that this was his chance and kept moving toward her, trying to act casual. She glanced at him, still listening to her music through the earphones.

When he came up next to her on the path, he stopped and stood in front of her. Her breasts were full and round inside her tight top, so close now that he could reach out and give them a squeeze.

He smiled down at her.

"Hey, there," he said.

FORTY-FIVE

The man was talking to her, but Laurie couldn't hear anything he was saying because of the music from the iPod.

She reached up and pulled the earphones out. "Sorry?"

"I was just saying hello."

He reminded her of someone, but she couldn't think of who. "Do I know you?"

"I'm a friend of your husband."

"Will?"

The man nodded his bald head. "That's right."

He was checking out her swollen breasts. She wrapped her arms around her chest, hugging herself. She realized who the man reminded her of.

Mr. Clean. He looks like the guy on the bottle of cleanser. Only somehow scarier.

The man held out his hand. "My name's Erik."

Buddy began to bark at the man. She tugged on his leash to make him stop.

"Erik what?" she asked.

Buddy continued to bark.

"Erik Crandall," he said.

The name sounded familiar, but at first she didn't know why. Then it hit her, and she took a step back.

"Hold up." The man smiled. "I just want to talk to you."

She glanced around, thinking she should run away.

Then the man's right hand shot forward and snatched the leash away from her. The metal choke collar made a jangling sound as it tightened around Buddy's neck. The dog's claws scraped against the asphalt as the man dragged Buddy toward him.

"What are you *doing*?"

Buddy tried to bark, but the sound was strangled by the choke collar. The man looped the end of the leather leash around his hand a few times and then lifted his arm. Buddy rose up into the air, his back legs coming off the ground.

"*Stop it.*" She couldn't think of anything else to say.

The man looked at her, broken blood vessels webbing the whites of his eyes. He extended his arm to the side. Buddy hung from the leash, the paws on his rear legs scrabbling against the surface of the path.

"Put him *down*." She made a grab for the leash, but the man reached out with his empty hand and caught hold of her forearm. He pressed his thumb into the flesh on the inside of her arm, just above the wrist.

She gasped, the pain like fracturing bone.

Crandall lifted the dog higher up in the air. Buddy's eyes bulged out.

"Please," she said. "He's only a dog—"

"Blame your husband, this is all because of him. Do you have any idea what a lying sack of shit he is?"

The dog's legs kicked at the air, as if he were trying to run. The strangled barking had stopped, replaced by a guttural choking sound.

"*Answer* me."

She jumped, so much fury in his voice. "Answer you what?"

"Do you know what a lying sack of shit your husband is?"

She looked at Buddy, his mouth hanging open as he struggled to gasp for air. "I don't know what you want me to say. Please, just put him down."

The flesh below Crandall's eye twitched. "Lady, you need to stop worrying so much about the fucking dog."

Laurie looked at the man. "Please. You can do whatever you want to me. Just stop hurting him."

The man's grin split his face. "You really mean that?"

His eyes crawled over her tits again, nothing subtle about it.

"Lady, I'd love to, *believe* me. But I got a game plan and I need to stick to it."

She tried to remember something her meditation teacher had once said during a dharma talk. Something about dealing with fear.

Then she charged him, grabbing for his extended arm.

He tried to step back, but she'd already gotten hold of his wrist. The one that was holding Buddy's leash.

She used both of her hands to claw at his skin, trying to make him loosen his grip on the leash. She wished she hadn't been keeping her fingernails so short.

She felt the fabric at the neck of her shirt move against her skin, and then she was all of a sudden lifted up into the air. She looked down to see his fist bunched up in the front of her shirt.

He shook her. "There's a baby inside you. You really want me to hurt you?"

She reached down and touched her belly, then stopped struggling.

He smiled. "I didn't think so."

"What do you want?"

"For you to listen to me. When I'm done talking, I'll put the dog down, *deal*?"

She looked over at Buddy, then nodded.

He lowered her to the ground but continued holding on to the front of her shirt. "I know your husband's probably tried to make me out as some kind of bad guy. But believe me, I'm not."

She found it hard to focus on his words, worried that he was taking too long, not sure how much longer Buddy could survive. Buddy wasn't kicking so much anymore. He just dangled from the end of the leash, fighting to breathe.

The man shook her again. "Stop looking at the fucking dog," he said. "Look at me."

She did it, her vision blurring as she fought to keep herself from crying.

The man moved his face closer to hers. His skin had an unhealthy greenish hue. "All I want is to get back what's mine, then get the fuck away from here. I never wanted to hurt anybody. But your husband had to be a greedy pig. I mean, how much money do you fucking people need?"

She tried to act like she was listening, just wanting him to hurry up and finish already.

The man lifted Buddy higher into the air. The dog weighed close to eighty pounds, but the act of holding him up didn't seem to be requiring much effort from the man.

He just continued to talk. "I want you to deliver a message for me. You tell your husband that I will take away everything in his life. Everything that he cares about. Unless he gives me back what he stole."

"He can't."

Crandall cocked his head, studying her.

"There's been a misunderstanding," she said.

"Misunderstanding."

She nodded. "Just put the dog down and I'll tell you the truth. I'll tell you everything."

"You tell me first. Then I'll put him down."

She stole a glance at Buddy. He was still breathing, but his head lolled to one side and a thread of drool hung down from his open mouth.

"Will did steal some of your drugs. But it's not what you think. He didn't steal all of them."

He squinted, veins standing out against his bald skull. "You honestly expect me to believe that?"

She started to answer, but then the man swiveled his head to the side. His eyes narrowed, as if listening to something.

Then she heard it, too. The sound of male voices coming toward them along the path, running shoes slapping against asphalt.

She turned, but they were out of view, around the bend in the path.

Crandall looked at her, still holding on to the front of her shirt. "You tell your husband I'm done playing around."

He opened his left hand and let go of the leash. Buddy dropped to the ground, letting out a grunt when his body landed on the asphalt path.

Crandall reached down into the pocket of his track pants. She gasped, sure he was going to come out holding a knife.

But it was only a business card. He pressed it into her hand. "When he has my money, he can get in touch with me here."

He let go of her shirt and ran off into the woods, his gait as stiff and lurching as a monster from a black-and-white movie.

FORTY-SIX

Every light inside the house seemed to be burning. Laurie wasn't in the living room or dining room. Will went into the kitchen, but it was empty, no sign that she'd started to make dinner.

He opened the bathroom door. The air was thick with steam. Buddy lay on the floor next to the bathtub, his head resting against the porcelain base of the toilet.

Laurie was inside the tub. The curve of her belly rose up above the surface of the soapy bathwater like an island. He was surprised, since she didn't normally take baths.

"Are you okay?" he asked.

She looked up at him. The look on her face made the breath catch in his throat.

He knelt down on the tile floor.

"What's wrong?"

She told him what had happened in the park. He leaned forward and wrapped her up in his arms. She was trembling. Warm bathwater soaked through the fabric of his shirt.

Will struggled to keep the lid on his anger. "Did he hurt you?"

She shook her head. "Not really. I tried to hurt *him*. He just grabbed my shirt and told me to stop. That he didn't want to hurt me, because of the baby."

He closed his eyes, knowing that this was all because of him, no one's fault but his own.

"I'm so sorry," he said.

She pulled away from his embrace and sat up in the tub, hugging her knees against her chest. Goose bumps stood out along the flesh of her arms.

He looked over at the dog. "How is he?"

"Still pretty freaked, but it seems like he's okay."

Will reached out and petted the dog's back. Buddy lifted his head and began to lick Will's hand with his rough tongue.

The dog's choke collar was off. Will gently parted the fur around the dog's neck. The skin there looked irritated where the collar had been, but it wasn't broken.

Will leaned over and kissed Laurie on top of the head. "Did you call the police?"

She nodded.

"What happened?"

"Not much. He took a report."

"*He?* They only sent out one cop?"

She nodded.

Water dripped from the tub spout, like the ticking of a clock, echoing inside the tiled room.

"When Crandall was talking to you, did he make any specific threats?"

"Not really. He wanted me to tell you that he was done playing around."

Will thought about it. Maybe Crandall was smarter than he'd given him credit for. He hadn't left the cops much to work with.

"Were there any witnesses?"

"What do you mean?"

"Did anyone see Crandall with you?"

She shook her head. "Some joggers came along at the end, but he took off before they got there."

Laurie lifted her arm from the bathwater and pointed at the top of the toilet tank. "He wanted me to give that to you."

Will picked up the business card lying on the tank lid.

"He said that when you had his money, you'd be able to find him there."

The card was from a health club on Santa Monica Boulevard. Will slid it into the back pocket of his jeans.

He used the edge of the tub to climb to his feet. "I'll be back soon."

"Where're you going?"

"Where do you think?"

She shook her head. "We need to let the police take care of this."

"You really think they're going to do anything, Laurie?" He took a breath, the moist air infused with the lavender smell of her bath salts. "There are no witnesses, so Crandall will just deny everything. He didn't hurt you, didn't directly threaten you. Buddy's going to be okay. Trust me, they aren't going to do shit."

"You need to at least give them a chance."

"We already have."

FORTY-SEVEN

A red neon sign hung above the front door of the gym, the glowing silhouette of a chambered nautilus.

The gym's plate glass windows were fogged with condensation from people working out inside beneath the greenish glow of fluorescent lights.

Will watched from across the street, then opened the Volvo's glove compartment. He reached inside and took out the Kimber. He'd been keeping the gun there since Laurie told him to get it out of the house. His rationalization was that, strictly speaking, he was doing what she asked.

He racked back the slide to feed a round into the chamber and cock back the hammer, then thumbed on the safety.

He climbed from the car and slid the gun down into the waistband of his jeans at the small of his back. He put on a blue nylon windbreaker to cover the gun. He tapped the jacket's left front pocket, checking to make sure the pair of handcuffs was still there.

A dark-skinned woman wearing a colorful sari sat behind the gym's reception desk. She looked up when he came through the door.

"May I see your card?" she asked.

Will pretended that he hadn't heard her and walked straight into the weight room. The air-conditioning was blasting, his shirt still damp from Laurie's bathwater. The room smelled of sweat-soaked carpeting.

The entire rear wall was covered with a mirror. Weight machines were arranged in stations on the gray industrial carpeting. A handful of men were inside the room, using the machines.

Erik Crandall was off by himself at the far end of the room, using a bench press machine that sat just in front of the mirrored wall. He lay on his back on the padded bench, working the machine's handle so that an enormous stack of iron plates moved up and down at the end of a braided steel cable.

Crandall wore a pair of shiny basketball shorts and a white T-shirt that had the sleeves cut off. His skin glistened with perspiration.

Will walked across the dirty carpeting, feeling like he was moving in slow motion, his heart hammering inside his chest. Crandall must have somehow sensed his presence, because he let go of the handle of the machine and sat up on the bench.

The stack of weights crashed down.

Will forced a big smile onto his face, as if he were there to greet an old friend. He extended his right hand to shake with Crandall.

Crandall looked confused, but he reached out to take it, which was what Will was hoping he'd do. Will wrapped his fingers around the other man's hand and squeezed. Then he brought up the handcuffs with his other hand and snapped the bracelet around Crandall's wrist.

The big man's eyes went wide with surprise. Will seized the moment, took the other bracelet and locked it to the metal frame of the weight machine.

Crandall grunted and pulled at the cuffs, the muscles of his arms writhing. The bracelet rattled against the frame of the machine, Crandall trapped on the bench.

"What is this?" he said.

Will's anger made it difficult for him to speak. "You keep the fuck away from my wife."

Crandall smiled. "That's asking a lot, don't you think? I mean, she's quite the piece of ass."

It was the smile, more than anything else, that sent Will over the edge. He'd come here thinking that he only wanted to scare Crandall off, to end this once and for all, but realized now that what he really craved was to hurt him.

The gun was all of a sudden there in his hand. He whipped it forward, the muzzle lashing across Crandall's cheekbone.

A long gash opened along the side of his face and then the gash welled up and began to bleed.

Crandall pulled at the handcuffs, his face straining with effort, the powerful muscles of his arms moving like snakes inside a burlap sack.

Will watched with growing horror as the steel frame of the weight machine began to bend. The metal bowed outward an inch or two but held.

Crandall let out his breath through his nostrils and stopped pulling at the cuff. "This your idea of a fair fight? Take it off and we'll see how tough you really are."

Will hit him again with the gun, this time catching him in the mouth.

"That one was for my dog."

Will glanced at the mirrored wall and saw that the other men were coming up behind him.

He spun and leveled the pistol in one motion.

Will counted five of them. He sighted the gun on the chest of the one in the center. "Nobody do anything stupid. This is between me and him."

The men stopped coming.

Will raised his chin to indicate the other side of the room. "Get back over there."

The men glanced at each other, but then began to back away.

Will turned back to Crandall. He was sitting on the bench, straining at the cuffs, like an animal caught in a trap. He reached up and wiped blood from his split lip. He looked at his fingers, then wiped the blood off in a vertical smear down the front of his white shirt.

"You come down here to waste my time?" he asked. "Or did you bring me my money?"

"I'm not going to ask you again. You stay the hell away."

Crandall sat there on the bench, grinning up at him, implacable. "Or what?"

Will held the gun down at his side. How the hell was he supposed to get through to this moron?

"Or I kill you," he said.

Crandall's bloody lips stretched into a smile. "For some reason, I don't think you're cut out for it."

Will saw himself reflected in the mirror, his hair disheveled, the gun in his hand. The others watched from across the room, their eyes wide.

"Give me back what you stole," Crandall said. "Then I go in peace."

A clock on the wall ticked. "How many times do I have to tell you? I don't have your money."

"That's not the sense I got when I talked to your partner."

Will looked at him. *"Ray?"*

Crandall nodded.

"So you admit that you spoke to him?"

"Yeah, why?"

Will's heightened senses registered the sound of the gym's front door as it opened and closed, but he kept his attention focused on Crandall. "I don't know how you managed to work your alibi, but I know you killed him."

Crandall cocked his head to the side. "Why would I want to do *that*? He was going to get me back my money."

"Bullshit."

"I mean it," Crandall said. "I talked to him, but I didn't kill him."

"You expect me to believe that?"

"It's a lot better than your story."

"*My* story?"

Crandall smiled. "You stole some of my drugs, but you didn't steal *all* of them."

Will looked at him. "Who said that?"

"Your bride."

Will sensed movement behind him.

"*Police.* Drop the weapon."

He looked up at the mirror and saw two uniformed LAPD officers standing with their guns pointed at his back.

Will was careful not to make any sudden movements. He raised the gun into the air and used his thumb to flick on the safety. Then he opened the fingers of his right hand and let the pistol drop soundlessly down onto the carpet.

FORTY-EIGHT

The offices of Feingold & Anderson, Attorneys-at-Law, were located on the nineteenth floor of a high-rise building in Century City.

Barry Feingold was one of the top criminal defense lawyers in Los Angeles. When Will had been with LAPD, he'd spent years watching Feingold work his magic for the other side. The lawyer was the first person Will had called after Laurie had gotten him bailed out.

Will held Laurie's hand as they sat side by side in wooden armchairs on the other side of Feingold's marble-topped desk.

Feingold was a short man, dwarfed by the high back of his leather desk chair. His skin was deeply tanned, setting off a full head of gray hair. When he smiled his teeth were unnaturally white, making Will assume that they were caps.

"Let's get the housekeeping out of the way," Feingold said. "Like I told you on the phone, my retainer is one hundred thousand dollars up front, against an hourly rate of seven hundred and fifty. Did you bring a check?"

Laurie reached down into her bag and handed Will a cashier's check with the name of a large brokerage firm printed in the corner.

They'd had to liquidate both of their IRA accounts to come up with the money.

Will held up the check but didn't give it to Feingold. "I'm okay with the hourly rate. But I don't understand why we need to pay so much in advance."

Feingold continued to smile. "My line of work, if I happen to lose a case, it can be problematic to collect after the fact."

Will slid the check across the stone desktop. Feingold folded it in half without bothering to look at it and put it in his shirt pocket.

"Now that we've gotten that out of the way, why don't you tell me again what happened. Walk me through it."

Will cleared his throat. "The guy I told you about, Erik Crandall, he followed Laurie into the park. Then he threatened her—"

Feingold held up his hand to stop him. "Not that part. Tell me what happened prior to the arrest, what took place at this gymnasium."

Will nodded. "I went in and found Crandall there, doing bench presses on a weight machine. I went up to him, and he sat up."

Feingold nodded. "As if he was expecting you."

"I guess," Will said.

Feingold picked up a gold-plated ballpoint and made a note on a yellow legal pad. "Maybe that's because Crandall had set up the meeting in advance? He'd made some kind of threat to you, about your wife's safety, told you he intended to hurt her if you didn't come to the gymnasium?"

Will felt confused. "No."

Feingold's look communicated a subtle disappointment in Will's answer. "Go on."

"I acted like I wanted to shake Crandall's hand, then I cuffed him to the machine."

"Because you felt your life was in danger?"

Will shook his head. "No, because I needed to restrain him while I tried to talk some sense into him—"

"Hold on," Feingold said. "Maybe you're forgetting something here.

Perhaps you saw a gym bag lying there on the floor, you thought there was a gun inside?"

"No." Will shook his head. "There was no gym bag."

Feingold held the pen poised above the legal pad. "You're *positive*? Take a minute."

Will took a breath. It was apparent what Feingold was trying to do. Will had seen enough defendants take the stand and give testimony that had obviously been coached by their sleazebag lawyer.

"I'm sorry, but I'm not willing to lie."

Feingold's smile went away. "I'm not asking you to lie. I'm not trying to put words into your mouth. What I *am* trying to do is get you to think about what really happened, about the thoughts that might reasonably have been going through your mind at the time. Something that might justify your actions."

Will bit at his bottom lip. "This guy threatened my wife. He choked my dog."

"So why didn't you go to the police?" Feingold asked.

Laurie pulled her hand away from his, a silent accusation.

Will looked at the lawyer. "Come on, Barry. I've been on the other side of you in court. I've seen the miracles you can work."

"That's when I've got a client who's a little more motivated to try and save himself. And who hasn't done something so flat-out stupid."

Will forced himself to smile. "You'd think that for a hundred grand, your clients would get some better customer service."

Feingold laced his fingers together on top of the marble desk. "There's nothing humorous here. Perhaps I need to clarify the gravity of your situation. From what I'm gathering, I'm not going to win this case on the facts."

Will started to interrupt, but Laurie kicked his foot to shut him up.

"So my only shot is jury nullification," Feingold said. "That means I need to somehow get a jury to see your actions as reasonably justifiable under the circumstances. But even assuming I can paint this Crandall as the bogeyman you claim he is, I'm still up the creek. Because how the hell do I justify you turning the gun on five innocent bystanders? That's not something juries tend to admire."

"So you don't take it to a jury. You cut a deal."

Feingold shook his head. "I already spoke to my colleague in the district attorney's office."

"And?"

"He told me to batten down the hatches. That they're not inclined to deal on this one."

"How come?"

"Try to see it from their point of view. They see you as a rogue ex-cop with some kind of vendetta. They go soft on you, they'll end up with a public relations nightmare on their hands. And let's not forget we're in an election year."

"Of course not."

From the other side of the closed office came the sound of telephones ringing and people conversing. All of it hushed, as if they were inside a church.

"So what's the worst case?" Will asked.

Feingold shook his head. "Not a good question."

"Just tell me."

Feingold tapped the gold pen against the desk top. "Assuming I get the criminal threats charge thrown out, but they convict on the assault and unlawful imprisonment, you could be looking at ten years before you're eligible for parole."

Laurie's hand fluttered upward and came to rest on her face, covering her mouth.

Will looked at Feingold. "So let me get this straight," he said. "All the things Crandall did to us, and *I'm* the one who's going to prison?"

"You're the one who got caught. Unless we get some kind of pleasant surprise during discovery, we're in for some tough sledding."

Will sat back in the chair. None of this felt real. "What can I do? To help?"

Feingold shook his head. "Not much. Keep your nose clean. Not to state the obvious, but stay the hell away from this Crandall. You see him walking down the street, you cross to the other side."

Will let his breath out.

"I mean it," Feingold said. "You go anywhere near him, you're in violation of the terms of your bail agreement. The court will revoke your bail and you'll forfeit the bond."

Laurie gave him a panicked look. They'd signed over the deed to the house as collateral to the bail bond company.

Will nodded. "What else?"

Feingold slid open his desk drawer. He fumbled around inside, took out a business card, and passed it across to Will. "It's still early, but it couldn't hurt to give him a call."

Will read the card. It was for a prison consulting firm. He knew that prison consultants could help if you were convicted of a federal offense, could work the system to get you into the right penitentiary, but didn't really see what they could do for someone facing state time. Probably just some high-priced training on how to survive inside.

"I recommend them to all my clients," Feingold said. "But given your law enforcement background, they could make all the difference in the world."

FORTY-NINE

Will left the ballpark after working a night game against the Braves and drove through the darkness of Elysian Park.

He turned onto Stadium, the shadowy silhouettes of the palms going by outside the car's passenger window. He passed the Barlow Sanitarium on the left. Gary Ackerman's converted police car was parked in the deserted lot, the burning tip of a joint glowing from the Crown Victoria's dark interior. The windows of the car were down, the sound of Gram Parson's voice leaking out into the night.

Will flashed his lights in greeting as he passed by.

When he got home, it was almost eleven thirty. The living room was dark and empty. Laurie had probably gone to bed.

He started down the hallway that led to the bedrooms, trying his best to be quiet. As he passed the spare bedroom, he saw that the light was on inside it.

He stuck his head into the open doorway and saw Laurie kneeling on the floor. She was dressed in old clothes, using a paint roller to stencil a line of red teddy bears onto the pale blue wall. The white crib was set beneath the curtained window, a brand-new changing table standing next to it.

He didn't want to startle her, so he spoke in a soft voice. "It's looking really good. The room."

She turned and looked up at him. Her eyes were puffy. "Yeah, too bad we're going to end up losing the house."

"Stop," he said. "We're not going to lose the house."

"Really? Because some bail bondsman has the deed to it. And we just handed our life savings over to that lawyer."

"Is that all you can think about? *Money?*"

She dropped the paint roller down into the plastic tray. Droplets of red paint splashed out onto the wood floor.

"Don't make it like I'm being materialistic. Like I'm some trophy wife worrying about how much jewelry she can go out and buy. I'm freaking out because I'm about to have a baby and it looks like I'm going to be homeless."

He picked up a rag and used it to wipe the paint from the floor. "It's all going to work out. We'll be fine."

"How can you even say that? How can you possibly imagine that we'll be *fine?*"

"We're the good guys here, Laurie. We're the victims. There's no way the system can be that screwed up."

She sat back onto the floor and arranged herself into a lotus position. "Unbelievable. *Now* you believe in the system?"

He stood there but didn't say anything. The air in the room had the smell of baby powder from the supplies she'd already bought for the changing table.

"I didn't sign up for this," she said.

He looked at her. "You think I did? It just happened."

"Why can't you at least take some responsibility? It didn't just *happen*. Crandall didn't just suddenly become manacled to a weight machine. The gun didn't magically materialize and start hitting him. *You* did that."

He concentrated on not raising his voice. "I did it because of what he did to you. What he did to Buddy."

"What that man did was horrible. But your response was totally inappropriate."

He was still wearing his security guard uniform. He felt stupid standing there in it, like a boy playing a dress-up game. "I'm sorry, I screwed up."

He reached out to touch the top of her shoulder.

She pushed his hand away. "I don't think I can do this anymore."

He stared at her. He didn't need this. Not now. It was enough of a struggle trying to keep it together with what he already had on his plate.

"Don't," he said. "Please."

"I'm about to have a child, Will. That has to be my priority now."

"What does that mean?"

"I'm worried, about what all this stress might be doing to him."

He swallowed. "I know things have been hard. But you can handle it. What about all that stuff you're always talking about from yoga? About not getting caught up in worrying, about learning to accept things as they *are?*"

She pulled her knees up against her pregnant belly and wrapped her arms around her shins. "It's a lot easier to do when things aren't so completely screwed up."

The room was only lit by the lamp on the night table. It had originally been in Sean's room, Laurie refusing to get rid of it. The lamp was made to look like a miniature hot air balloon, the figures of two small children standing inside the wicker basket, the bulb casting out light from inside the colorful balloon.

"I need you," he said. "I love you."

"I love you, too. I just don't see how this can work. We need to think about what's best for the baby."

"What's best for the baby is for him to have a family, a father."

"You heard the lawyer, Will. You're going to prison for like ten years. What am I supposed to do, bring your son along on conjugal visits?"

"What's the alternative, that you pretend that I don't exist? That he never knows who I am?"

She spoke without looking at him, her eyes wet. "It might be for the best, don't you think?"

He shut his eyes. He heard her moving on the floor, and then he felt her arms wrapping around him, her swollen breasts pressing against his upper back.

He reached up and took hold of her hand. "I see what you're saying. And I swear, I'll do whatever it is that's best for our son. But we're getting way ahead of ourselves here. I haven't been convicted yet. There's still a chance I can get out of it."

"I don't see how."

He turned around so that he was looking at her. It was uncomfortable sitting there on the wood floor, but he didn't want to move away from her. "I just need to figure out what really happened."

She looked at him, confusion on her face. "Happened to *what?*"

"The department stealing drugs, selling them. I need to find out who else was involved."

She shook her head. "You need to start thinking about how you can save yourself."

"I am. Don't you see it? I've already got the ledger. If I can just put it all together, then we can take it to the DA and work out some kind of deal on my case."

"You heard the lawyer, they're not interested in making a deal."

"They will be if I can give them something they can use."

She shook her head. "It seems like a long shot."

He put his hand on her knee and looked into her eyes. "Right now, it's the only one we've got."

FIFTY

Erik Crandall glanced up at the rearview mirror of the Town Car.

The client in the backseat was an older dude wearing a cowboy hat and one of those weird string ties with a big turquoise and silver clasp.

Crandall had picked him up at LAX arrivals and was running him out to the Convention Center.

The stereo played one of the classical music CDs. It wasn't the Vivaldi. This one had a clanging harpsichord that was making his migraine even worse.

The headaches had been more frequent lately. It seemed like he was getting one almost every day. He was sure now that they were from all the Equipoise. But at least the 'roids were doing their thing; as big as he was, he was continuing to become even bigger.

He had to buy a new suit because he couldn't fit his arms down inside the sleeves of the old one anymore. He hadn't been able to find anything that would fit on the rack at Goodwill, so he'd been forced to buy new at the big and tall shop on Wilshire.

"Man, it smells like a Chinese restaurant in here." The man in the backseat had some kind of a cracker accent.

Crandall met his eyes in the rearview. "I'm sorry, you want me to crack the windows?"

The man waved a hand in front of him. "It's fine. I'm just saying."

Just saying *what*? Crandall's hands tightened on the leather-wrapped steering wheel, feeling the familiar stirrings of his anger.

The traffic was backed up on the 110, so he got off and took Hill Street to Pico. A vinyl banner draped across the front of a liquor store promised THE COLDEST BEER IN TOWN. People stood on the sidewalk out front, waiting for the bus.

The client looked out through the tinted window. "I honestly don't understand how you people can live out here."

"How's that?"

"Just look at it. It's like a goddamned third world country. I mean, someone wants to serve me a Big Mac, they should learn to speak English. Am I right?"

Crandall remembered the Aryan Brotherhood guys inside the prison, how they'd tried to recruit him after he'd gotten big. But he could never get behind the whole racism thing. In his experience, white people could be just as fucked up as anyone else.

"So where is it you're from?" Crandall asked.

"San Angelo."

"Where's that?"

"Texas," the man said. "Ever been?"

Crandall shook his head.

"You should come on down. See the real America."

Crandall rubbed his cheek. He still had a bruise from where the *lying-thieving-conniving-asshole* cop had hit him with the gun. The lady lawyer from the district attorney's office had talked to him about how he should get a lawyer and file a civil suit. Said he could collect big money for the way the cop had done him.

Crandall had thought on it, but it seemed like it would take way too long before he saw any money.

Besides, it wasn't his style.

"What's going on at the Convention Center?" Crandall asked.

"Gun show."

Crandall glanced up at the rearview. "Is that what's in all those cases in the trunk? Guns?"

The man nodded. "Pistols, assault rifles, you name it."

Crandall stopped for the light at Figueroa. A gun could come in handy, some of the things he was going to have to do.

He stole some of your drugs. But he didn't steal all *of them.*

He couldn't stop thinking about what the cop's wife had said in the park. Did everyone in the world think he was stupid? Was there some big neon sign hanging over his head that said I'M AN IDIOT?

Crandall tried to focus on the positive: What she'd said meant that she *knew*. The cop must've told her about what he'd been up to, which meant she probably knew where he was stashing the money.

And something told him she'd be an easier nut to crack than the cop.

"I've been thinking about buying a gun," Crandall said.

"Living out here, I can't say as I blame you."

Crandall turned down the music. "You think you could sell me one?"

"Son," the man said, "that's what I do."

"I wouldn't want to hassle with a whole lot of paperwork."

"I'm not exactly a big fan of the government myself. ATF had its way, the only folks carrying guns would be the hajjis."

"So what would I need?"

The Texan pushed up the clasp on his string tie.

"Cash usually works."

Crandall steered the Town Car into a parking lot across the street from the Convention Center.

The Texan pointed out through the windshield. "Park up over yonder."

Crandall pulled the car into an open space at the far end of the lot. He popped the trunk, and they both got out and went around to the rear of the car.

The Texan was shorter than Crandall had thought, even though he was wearing fancy cowboy boots with high heels. The brim of his hat cast a semicircular shadow down onto the creases of his wrinkled face.

The man reached inside the trunk and popped the latches on a long black case. "I'm not sure what it is you're looking for, but have a look at these."

He opened the lid. Three machine guns nestled inside cutouts in the gray foam liner. The Texan pointed at them. "I got a real nice AK, a brand-new MP-5, and a Ruger Mini-14."

Crandall looked at the Ruger. It was the same machine gun that the guards carried up in the towers at San Quentin. He took hold of the gun with both hands and brought the stock up against his shoulder. He sighted it on people walking down the sidewalk in front of the Convention Center and pretended to pull the trigger.

Pop. Pop. Pop.

The Texan put his hand on the barrel and pushed it down. "You got to be cool, partner. There's police all around here."

Crandall set the machine gun back down in the case. As much as he wanted it, he could see that it wouldn't be practical.

"I need something smaller," he said. "That I can carry around."

"I hear you." The Texan grabbed a smaller case and opened it up. "This is what I've got for handguns."

Crandall bent over and looked down into the case. It was mostly filled with automatics, a few revolvers. There was one gun that was huge, bigger than anything else in the case.

Crandall pointed at it. "What's that?"

"You got an eye for quality, friend." The Texan smiled and picked up the gun. "This here's a Desert Eagle .50 caliber automatic."

It was enormous, the biggest gun Crandall had ever seen.

Crandall held out his hand. "Can I?"

The Texan handed him the big gun. "Just keep it low."

Crandall bounced it gently in his palm, the gun as heavy as a bar-bell.

The Texan watched him. "Ever see the movie *Dirty Harry?*"

Crandall nodded.

"You remember how Clint's always bragging on that .44 Magnum wheel gun he carries? How it's 'the most powerful handgun in the world'?"

"Yeah."

"Well that was *before* they invented the Desert Eagle. You shoot somebody with that thing, I guarantee they're going to have a bad day."

Crandall wrapped his hand around the grips, aiming the gun down into the darkness of the trunk. It felt good holding it in his hand, like it belonged there.

The Texan watched him. "Got it off a gunsmith. The trigger's been worked on."

Crandall squeezed. The pull was light, the hammer falling with a dry snap. "How much?"

"Fifteen hundred, and I'll throw in a box of ammo."

Crandall took the money from the cashbox he kept in the glove compartment. He counted out the bills into the Texan's hand.

The man folded up the bills and shoved them down into his cowboy boot. "Pleasure doing bidness with you," he said.

Crandall helped him get the cases out of the trunk. He watched the man walk away across the parking lot with his heavy load, shimmers of heat rising up off the blacktop.

He was halfway to Pasadena before he realized the man had never paid him for the ride.

FIFTY-ONE

Gary Ackerman's Crown Vic was parked in its usual spot in the empty parking lot of the Barlow Sanitarium.

Will turned into the lot and parked in the space next to the converted police car. The clock on the Volvo's dashboard stood at eleven thirty, but it felt even later. He was exhausted from work, but he wanted to follow up on a few things with Ackerman.

Will walked up to Gary's car. Gary extended his hand through the driver's window and gave Will a soul shake. The pungent smell of marijuana smoke seeped out into the cool night air.

Gary held up a glowing joint and offered it to Will.

"I'll pass," he said.

"Beer?"

Will thought about it. "Why not?"

Gary pointed toward the passenger door. "Climb aboard, brother."

Merle Haggard was playing on the car stereo. Will popped the top on an icy can of Coors and took a long sip.

Gary was dressed in the same white suit he'd been wearing when

Will had gone to see him at the club. In the dim glow of the dash lights, the sequined marijuana leaves on the front of the jacket took on a sinister aspect, as if the plants were overgrowing his body.

Gary took a hit off the joint. A clear plastic envelope filled with color photographs lay on his lap. Gary stared down at them as he sucked in smoke.

He held up the envelope for Will to see. There were sheets of school photographs inside, featuring a young girl who looked like she was in second or third grade.

"My daughter," Gary said. "Only good thing I've ever done."

"She's beautiful—but don't you think there's something that's just a little *wrong* about this?"

Gary looked at him. "What do you mean?"

"Shouldn't you be home with her, instead of sitting here in your car, smoking weed?"

Gary shook his head. "What would be wrong is if I got high at home, where she could see me."

"Ever thought about not getting high at all?"

Gary took another hit. "Is that why you're here? To give me that Partnership for a Drug-Free America crap?"

Will shook his head. "I need to talk to you about something."

Gary blew out smoke and shook his head. "Here we go."

"You remember that bust I was asking about? With the fentanyl?"

"I already told you everything I know about that."

"Just hear me out. You told me you were surprised that so little fentanyl had been turned in. That Crandall was supposed to be holding a pound."

"So?"

"So I think Ray Miller stole the dope, then turned around and sold it."

"Whatever."

Will looked at him. "That's all you have to say? It doesn't even surprise you?"

"Not really. Wouldn't be the first time it happened with LAPD."

"You knew about it?"

"No, I'm just saying that it doesn't surprise me that some narc would be stealing from the evidence room. You're gonna try and tell me you never did it?"

Will took a sip of his beer. "What I'm talking about here, it wasn't some isolated incident. It was organized and going on for years."

The song on the car stereo faded out, and then Merle began to sing "I'm a Lonesome Fugitive." Gary crushed his empty beer can against the top of his thigh and tossed it into the backseat.

"You don't have anything to add?" Will asked.

"It's good to see you, man. For real. But like I told you last time, all that shit that went down in the past? I don't want to go there."

"I could really use your help."

"You don't want to go dredging up the past. Let it go."

"I need to do this, Gary. I wouldn't be asking if it wasn't important."

Gary took the photos of his daughter and put them away inside the glove compartment. "That stuff you're talking about? I don't know anything about it, I swear. But I always figured something like that was going down."

"How come?"

"Because there was this *pattern*. There would be some big drug crackdown by LAPD. The streets would be dry, everyone would be getting sick. People would be willing to pay anything to score. But every time that happened? There'd be this one dealer, dude up in Angelino Heights, he'd always end up coming through. Ended up making a killing."

"And you figure LAPD was behind it?"

Gary nodded. "Too much of a coincidence any other way."

Will looked out through the windshield at the abandoned cottages climbing their way up the scrubby hillside.

He turned back to Gary. "You remember a batch of fentanyl that killed a whole bunch of people about five years back?"

"How could I forget? On the street they were calling it White Death. That shit was the bomb, long as you had the common sense to cut it."

"This dealer you were talking about, the one up in Angelino Heights? Was he selling it?"

"Big-time."

"This guy got a name?"

Gary brushed ashes from the front of his suit jacket, but didn't answer.

"The cops needed somebody to sell the drugs they were stealing," Will said. "It isn't like they could do it themselves. I think the guy you're talking about might have been working with them. Just tell me his name."

Gary looked at him. "I got a kid now. I can't take the chance of getting labeled a snitch."

"C'mon, Gary. I'm not even a cop anymore."

Gary spoke without looking at him, his hands gripping the steering wheel. "Dude's name was Victor Luna," he said. "But everyone called him Chongo."

"I need to talk to him."

"I don't think that's gonna happen."

Will looked at him. "Why not?"

"Cops shot his ass a while back," Gary said. "Killed him dead during a drug bust."

FIFTY-TWO

Thursday was a day game, the Dodgers fighting to hold on to first place in the National League West. After it ended, Will changed out of his uniform in the employee locker room and then walked out into the parking lot.

He tossed his backpack onto the passenger seat of the Volvo. He flipped open his cell phone and dialed the number for the Rampart police station. When the operator answered, he asked to be connected to the Detective Desk.

The day was warm, a blanket of smog obscuring the view of the skyscrapers downtown. He lifted a bottle of water from the cup holder and took a sip. It was warm from being inside the closed-up car, tasted of plastic.

A man's voice came through the phone. "Prickett."

"I'm looking for Detective Lorton," Will said.

Charlie Lorton had been Mike Fenske's partner. Out of the three sets of initials in the red ledger, two of the men, Ray Miller and Fenske, were now dead. He needed to find the identity of the third.

Even though there were no payments recorded to anyone with Lorton's initials in the ledger, Will figured that since he was partners with Fenske, chances were good he might know something.

"He's out," the voice on the phone said. "You want to leave a message?"

"I'll try him again. When's he due back?"

"Not till the morning."

Will thanked the man, then flipped the phone shut. He looked at his watch. Four fifteen.

Will remembered Charlie Lorton as a drinker. If Lorton's shift had just ended, and assuming that he hadn't gone and joined AA, Will had a pretty good idea of where he might find him.

The Dugout was on Sunset, a few blocks north of the Rampart police station.

Pink neon letters above the front door spelled out the word COCK-TAILS. The place was a sports bar that caught a crowd before Dodgers games but also served as a hangout for cops from the nearby station.

Will pushed through the front door. Men huddled at the bar turned to check him out. Charlie Lorton wasn't among them.

The back room had a checkered linoleum floor and was filled with scarred wooden tables. Will spotted Lorton sitting alone in a small booth back by the men's room.

Charlie Lorton was a beefy man with short yellow hair and pink skin. He was hunched over the sports section of the *Los Angeles Times,* the fabric of his short-sleeve dress shirt stretched tight across his broad upper back. The tabletop was patterned with rings of moisture from his half-empty glass of beer.

Will extended his hand to shake. "Hey, Charlie. Remember me?"

Lorton looked up at him but made no move to shake hands. "Sure."

Will took back his hand. "Mind if I sit?"

Lorton took a long sip of beer. Flecks of foam stuck to the bottom of his brush mustache. "What for?"

"You know, talk, have a drink."

Lorton's face was empty of expression. "I thought you liked taking yours from a spike."

Will dropped onto the vinyl-covered bench across from Lorton. "I've been clean for over four years."

The man stared at him with tired eyes. "Well, bully for you."

Will pointed at Lorton's glass. "Can I buy you a refill?"

Lorton signaled for the waitress and ordered another Bud. Will told her he'd have the same.

Lorton waited for her to walk away. "What is it you want?"

"I wanted to talk to you about Mike Fenske."

Lorton's eyes narrowed. "What about him?"

Will tried to figure out the best way to play this. It wasn't as if he could just come out and ask if Fenske was dirty.

"I'm looking into some things that were happening inside the unit a few years back, right around the time I left."

"You mean got kicked out?"

Will looked away but didn't say anything. Speakers mounted high up in the corners of the room played "Under the Bridge" by the Red Hot Chili Peppers.

The waitress came back with their drinks and set them down on the table. She was middle-aged and wore a T-shirt with an American flag silk-screened on the front. Lorton stared at her chest as she leaned over the table. It looked like the woman wasn't wearing a bra, her large breasts straining against the pattern of stars and stripes.

Lorton swiveled his head to watch her walk away. "God bless America," he said.

Will took a hit of the beer. "What can you tell me, about Fenske?"

"That he was a good man."

Will waited for more, but there wasn't any. "Did you ever notice anything . . . I don't know, funny about him?"

"Funny *how*?"

Will hesitated. There was no delicate way to put this. "Like he might've been mixed up in something illegal."

"No," Lorton said. "But that's a pretty ironic question, coming from you."

Will looked at him. "You don't like me. I get that. But I could really use your help here."

"With *what?*"

"Fenske and Ray Miller worked in the same unit, now they're both dead. I think it's more than just coincidence."

Lorton used a bevnap to pat dry his mustache. "You wanted to know about Fenske, you should've asked your friend Ray Miller."

"Why's that?"

"'Cause they were partners."

"What're you talking about? *You* were Fenske's partner."

"Not for long. Right after you got the boot, they bumped Fenske to Detective Two, partnered him with Ray."

Will nodded. "I didn't know that."

"You been gone a long time, there's all kinds of shit you don't know."

A man in a rumpled suit nodded at Lorton as he walked by their booth. He opened the door to the men's room, the chemical smell of urinal cakes wafting out.

Will looked at Lorton. "How long were they partners?"

"Not long. Fenske ended up getting killed pretty soon after they started working together. I remember it was a few days after Thanksgiving. At least with the promotion, his family ended up getting a bigger pension."

"I know Fenske was killed in the line of duty. But what happened?"

"They got an anonymous tip about a drug dealer. Went to check it out. Fenske ended up getting shot."

"Who's *they?*"

"Fenske and Ray Miller."

Will sat up on the padded bench. "Ray was with Fenske when he was killed?"

"What'd I just say?"

Will finished what was left of the beer. He could feel it working, nothing in his stomach except for the Dodger Dog he'd eaten at work. "The shooting, how'd it go down?"

"The way I heard it, Ray had gotten a tip on this dealer. The two of them went to look into it, no warrant. Dealer let them into his crib to talk.. But then he pulled a piece and shot Fenske in the face. Ray was lucky, got his gun out in time to put the dealer down."

"The dealer, what was his name?"

"Fuck if I remember. You're talking five years ago."

"Was he by any chance from Angelino Heights? Went by the nick-name Chongo?"

Lorton stared at him, a look of astonishment on his face. "How the fuck did you know *that*?"

FIFTY-THREE

Will pulled loose the duct tape that held the red ledger in place against the bottom of the desk drawer.

The window was thrown open, the early morning air already heating up. Buddy was curled up in his usual spot beneath the desk, his fur against Will's bare foot.

Will set the ledger down on top of the desk and flipped through the pages until he came to the final set of entries. They stopped halfway down the page. Ray and Fenske had each received payments of $150,000 on 10/13/03. AB had received the same amount a day later.

After that, the payments had just stopped.

Lorton had said that Fenske was killed just after Thanksgiving, almost a month after the wave of fentanyl ODs.

He ran through it in his mind. With thirty-one people dead from the stolen dope they'd been dealing, it made sense that they decided to shut the operation down. But Ray and AB could have also decided that they needed to cover their tracks, that they couldn't risk leaving anyone walking around who could tie them to the deaths.

If Ray and Fenske had been working with Victor Luna, a.k.a.

Chongo, all along, the dealer would have let them inside his apartment. Will closed his eyes and pictured the scene in his mind's eye, Ray pulling a throwdown to shoot a surprised Fenske, then drawing his duty weapon to blow away Chongo.

The Force Investigation Division would've looked into it, but Ray had enough experience to know how to make it play.

Will opened his eyes and saw Laurie standing in the open doorway. "I'm going."

She was dressed in her work clothes, a rolled-up yoga mat in a hemp bag slung across her shoulder. Her pregnant belly was enormous, her protruding navel pushing out the stretch fabric of her shirt. The obstetrician had given her the okay to keep teaching, but there were certain poses she had to avoid. She'd probably have to stop working any day now.

"What're you working on?" she asked.

Will closed the ledger. "Nothing much."

Since his arrest, an uncomfortable tension had settled in between them. There was a strained politeness, as if they were two office workers who'd just been assigned adjoining cubicles.

She studied him. "Well, you look pretty serious."

He shrugged. "Just waking up, I guess."

"Whatever," she said. "I'll be home around four."

He started to get up to kiss her good-bye, but she turned and walked away.

He waited until he heard the front door close, then flipped the ledger open again. He leafed through the pages, studying the amounts. AB had made more money than either Fenske or Ray, since his payments were always equal to the larger of what had been paid to the other two.

Will opened the desk drawer and took out a pocket calculator. He went through the ledger from beginning to end, punching in the amounts paid to AB. After he'd entered the last payment, he hit the EQUAL key:

1995

He mentally tacked on the missing three zeros. Almost two million dollars, more than he'd probably end up making in his entire life.

He sat up in the chair, remembering something. He got up, taking the ledger with him. Buddy followed him into the kitchen and out through the door that led to the garage.

He hit the wall switch, the fluorescent tubes mounted to the ceiling flickering to life. The garage was big enough to fit one car, but like everyone else in the neighborhood, they'd always used it for storage, leaving the cars parked outside. The walls were lined with cardboard cartons on metal shelving units. Hand tools hung from sheets of pegboard.

He went over to one of the shelving units. The ends of the cartons were printed with the name of a local moving company. He remembered that he'd taken home an LAPD phone directory when he'd been with the department. If he could find it, he could go through the names, might be able to find someone with the initials AB.

He'd always intended to label the boxes but had never gotten around to it. He took down a carton and set it on top of the workbench. He picked up a box cutter and ran the exposed blade along the strip of packing tape.

He unfolded the flaps, drawing in a breath when he saw that the box was filled with things that had once belonged to Sean.

The clothing was laundered and neatly folded, pastel-colored shirts and shorts, all of it impossibly small.

He felt his anger flare at Laurie, didn't know why the hell she insisted on hanging on to this stuff. Maybe she was planning on letting the baby wear it when he got older, but he'd talk to her about that, the idea of it making him feel queasy.

He closed the box, taped the flaps shut, then put it back on the shelf. He rested his palm against the rack, trying to steady himself. Buddy sat on the concrete floor, looking up at him.

Will had to go through two other boxes before he found the right one.

The carton was filled with things from his desk at Rampart. He remembered the day he'd been fired, going back to his desk and dumping its contents into the box.

He hadn't paid much attention to what he was doing at the time, just wanting to get the hell out of there, the eyes of everyone in the room boring into his back.

He pulled out a photograph in a black wood frame. It had been taken after a Police League softball game, the team from his unit standing together in front of bleachers that were painted green. He picked out younger versions of Lorton and Fenske. Ray Miller smiled out at him, his cap on backward, his sunburned and muscular arm wrapped around Will's shoulders.

He set the photo down on the workbench and continued digging through the contents of the carton. He felt a pang of guilt when he saw the covert surveillance equipment he'd never bothered to return to the department.

He picked up a small body-mounted wireless transmitter that was about the size of a pack of cigarettes, only thinner. The tiny microphone and cable were wrapped around the body of the transmitter. A handheld receiver and small tape recorder were down at the bottom of the box.

He'd found the equipment in the trunk of his personal car a few weeks after getting fired. He'd intended to bring it back but couldn't stomach the thought of walking back inside the station.

He pressed the PLAY button on the recorder, surprised that the batteries were still good, the reels of the microcassette turning.

Then he spotted what he was looking for.

A blue vinyl loose-leaf binder. He opened it up, the first page printed with a warning in bold letters:

OFFICIAL USE ONLY
Not to be removed from the premises of the
Los Angeles Police Department.

He sat down with the binder on the step that led into the house. The pages listed the names and phone extensions for both sworn and classified LAPD personnel.

He turned to the *B*'s, saw a couple of hundred names listed there. He started at the top, running his forefinger down the column.

When he reached the end, he let his breath out in frustration. Then he checked again, going slower this time, hoping that he'd missed something.

But no one was listed there with a first name that began with the letter *A*.

Buddy came over and began to lick Will's forearm. He reached down and stroked the fur on the dog's neck, trying to think.

Because of the pattern of payments in the ledger, it seemed logical that the mysterious AB was the leader of the operation. But if Ray had killed Fenske and Chongo, it was conceivable that he might have killed AB as well.

Of course, there was also another possibility.

AB might be the only one left who was still alive.

FIFTY-FOUR

Crandall loved the gun.

It was the best thing he'd ever bought. Shit, it was the best thing he'd ever *owned,* period. He couldn't stop playing with it.

He sat on a stool at the kitchen counter inside his apartment, dry firing the gun. He pointed it into the kitchen, lining up the sights on the picture of the guy on the cylindrical container of Quaker Oats. He squeezed the trigger, imagining the dude's forehead imploding, his strange black hat flying from the top of his head.

Crandall picked up a plastic tumbler and took the last sip of the protein shake he'd made in the blender. He swallowed, the sweetness of protein powder mix covering up the taste of the raw eggs.

He thumbed the button on the gun to eject the empty magazine, then set the mag down on the counter.

He opened the flap on the box of bullets. He picked up one of the bullets, surprised at how heavy it felt.

The tip of the bullet had a dimple in it. Crandall knew that this was part of the bullet's design, so that once it entered someone's body, the slug would mushroom.

He used his thumb to slide the bullet into the opening at the top of the magazine. Then he picked up another bullet, repeating the process seven times, until the magazine was full. He fitted the mag inside the butt of the gun and used the flat of his palm to drive it home. He pulled back on the slide to feed a round into the chamber.

He slid off the stool and walked over to the mirror that hung on the living room wall. He was stripped to the waist, nothing on but the cargo shorts and his Nikes without socks.

He could swear that he could feel the Equipoise coursing through his veins, doing its thing. He stared at the mirror, studying his body, trying to see if he could see himself becoming bigger, like one of those stop-motion scientific films that let you watch a flower growing.

He held the enormous gun down at his side and squeezed the tops of his shoulders inward to fire his pecs, thick veins rising up beneath his skin like water moccasins surfacing in a pond.

The sliding glass doors to the patio were closed, only the blackness of the night out there on the other side. He could hear his neighbor's TV, an announcer speaking rapid-fire Korean.

He shoved the gun into the cargo pocket on the side of his shorts. The Eagle was heavier now that it was loaded, pulling down the shorts to reveal a strip of his trimmed pubic hair.

He squinted his eyes and lifted his chin, speaking to the mirror. "You talking to me?"

He cocked his head to the side. "You talking to *me?*"

Crandall reached down for the gun and drew it from his pocket. The front sight snagged on the fabric, but he tugged it free. He extended his arm and pointed the gun at the face in the mirror, holding it in a one-handed grip.

The Eagle was heavy, but Crandall's hand was steady. He rotated it so that the gun's frame was parallel to the floor, gangsta style.

He reached his thumb up and cocked back the hammer all the way, the gun making a satisfying mechanical click.

He lowered the gun back down to his side and turned away from the mirror. Then he swiveled his head back, trying his best to act surprised.

"You talking to me?"

Crandall had caught the movie, *Taxi Driver,* a bunch of times on the little television in his cell. He knew there were more words he was supposed to be saying, but right now he couldn't remember any of them.

"You talking to *me?*"

He brought the gun up fast, like a Western gunslinger, squeezing the trigger just a little as he aimed at the face in the mirror.

BLAM

When the gun went off, it was the loudest thing he'd ever heard. His face disappeared as the mirror shattered into a million tiny pieces.

The spent cartridge ejected from the gun, just missing his chin before landing on the carpet by his right foot.

Holy shit. Crandall looked at the gun, not quite believing that it had really gone off. He hadn't squeezed the trigger that hard.

He waved his hand back and forth in front of his face, trying to clear away the Sheetrock dust. His ears were ringing, and the air smelled like fireworks. The mirror was gone now, just the top of the wooden frame left hanging there.

The bullet had made a hole in the wall, about the size of a quarter. The edges of the hole were clean, like it'd been made with a drill bit.

He leaned forward and put his eye up to the hole. He could see light coming from the other side. He squinted and saw the arm of a green sofa and a color television playing inside an oak entertainment center.

An Asian-looking dude was on the TV screen. He stood in a kitchen talking Korean while he used a cleaver to chop up some kind of raw meat.

Crandall held his breath, listening. He didn't hear anything out of the ordinary, no one screaming, or any footsteps running down the hallway. He stood there, waiting for a knock on the door. The minutes felt like hours, but it never came.

He slid open the patio doors and stepped out onto the balcony, holding the gun down at his side. He stepped up to the iron railing and looked down. There was no one out on the sidewalks, the street quiet. He closed his eyes and listened for sirens but didn't hear any. It was as if it never even happened.

Fucking L.A. You had to love this town.

A stucco pony wall separated Crandall's balcony from the one next door. He leaned over it, trying to get a look inside the neighboring apartment.

Pink curtains were drawn across the sliding glass doors, so that he couldn't see anything inside. The doors were opened a few inches, the sound of the Korean television station coming through the gap.

Crandall climbed over the low wall and onto the other balcony. He reached out and moved the curtain aside. He saw the TV set in the entertainment center and a green leather living room set that was wrapped in protective vinyl covers. The floor was carpeted with white wall-to-wall that looked brand-new.

He raised the gun a little and took a step inside the apartment. He sniffed at the air, the place smelling of vinegar.

He spotted something on the floor, sticking out from behind the sofa. A pair of white rubber sandals, like what the inmates in prison wore to the showers.

Crandall took a step closer. The sandals were pointing straight up at the ceiling. There were little feet inside them, covered by sheer black stockings.

He raised the gun and went around the couch. The stockings came up to the woman's knees, her bare thighs spiderwebbed with veins. She was wearing a pink terrycloth bathrobe with a matching belt that tied at the waist.

She was old and looked Korean. Her hair was gray, one side of her head dark with blood, a ragged hole above her ear. Blood and what Crandall thought was pieces of brains came out of the hole and onto the white carpet.

A little dog, some kind of terrier, ran back and forth on the carpet next to her body. The dog looked like a rat, a blue ribbon tied into a bow on top of its head.

The Korean lady's eyes were open, but she wasn't moving. Crandall used the toe of his Nike to kick her in the side.

She didn't react.

The little dog did, though, jumping around on the floor and barking at him.

"*Shut up.*" Crandall tried to keep his voice down. His headache was raging now, out of control. "Shut the hell *up.*"

The dog turned in frantic circles, the yapping an ice pick jabbing into Crandall's brain. He thought about just stomping the little fucker, crushing it like some kind of bug. He took a step toward the dog. It cowered and then started to take a leak right there on the carpet, its piss mixing with the lady's blood.

Unbelievable. Crandall shook his head, the sight of this freak show making him feel sick to his stomach.

He looked down at the little dog and made a low growling sound. The dog whimpered and then went and hid under the couch, leaving a trail of pee on the white carpet.

The old lady's robe was open a little down at the bottom, revealing the crotch of her flesh-colored nylon panties. Crandall forced himself to turn away, feeling like looking at her down there was somehow wrong.

He crouched down next to the woman's head. He could see himself reflected in the black pupil of her unblinking eye. He held his palm under her nose.

She wasn't breathing.

One of her hands was closed up, like she was holding on to something. Crandall used the barrel of the gun to pry open her fingers. Brightly colored pieces of candy spilled out onto the carpet.

He took a closer look, saw that they were M&M's.

Crandall grabbed a green one and popped it into his mouth. He chewed, looking up at the hole in the wall, then down at the dead lady.

He pretended he was the dude on *CSI,* trying to re-create inside his mind how it had gone down.

On this side of the wall, the hole was a little bigger and ragged. He figured that the Eagle must have gone off just as the lady was coming back from the kitchen with her handful of treats, so she ended up taking one square in the *cabeza.*

Crandall swallowed the piece of candy, shaking his head from side to side as he looked at her face.

Goddamn, he thought. Some people just *cannot* catch a break.

FIFTY-FIVE

The offices of the Campaign Finance Disclosure Section of the Los Angeles Registrar-Recorder/County Clerk were on Imperial Highway.

Will stepped inside the building's elevator and pressed the button for the second floor. Last night, he'd come up with an idea for how he might be able to identify the mysterious AB.

He remembered getting a letter from Ray Miller a few years back. It was obviously a form letter, Ray saying that he was supporting Dennis Byrnes's election campaign and asking Will to consider contributing as well.

Will figured that if Ray had been helping to raise money for Byrnes, he would've reached out to people he knew who had money—and based on the red ledger, AB certainly had money.

State law required political candidates to disclose the names of the individuals that contributed to their campaigns. If AB had made a contribution to Byrnes, his name would be listed on the campaign filings.

Will got off the elevator and walked down the hallway until he found the right door. A long wood-grain counter separated a small sitting area from the rest of the cavernous office. A heavyset African American woman wearing yellow plastic hoop earrings rose from her desk and stood on the opposite side of the counter.

"Can I help you, sir?"

"I'd like to see Supervisor Byrnes's campaign filings."

She didn't look happy about it. "We close in five minutes."

"I'll be quick."

"You're talking about a whole lot of paper. Is there anything specific you're looking for?"

"A list of his campaign contributors."

"Cash or nonmonetary?"

"Cash."

She nodded. "Schedule A."

"Great," Will said. "Can I see it?"

She looked at her watch and then turned away. She disappeared into a maze of tall metal shelves. Will looked around but didn't see anyone else working in the office.

The woman came back carrying a bound document as thick as a phone book.

She dropped it onto the counter. "You've got three minutes."

Will opened the cover. The pages were printed in landscape format and laid out like spreadsheets. Columns listed the contributor's name and address, occupation, contribution date, and the amount of the contribution.

The names were in alphabetical order. He scanned the M's until he found Ray Miller. Under the column for occupation it read RETIRED N/A. The amount received was $1,000, which was the maximum that could be donated by an individual.

Will flipped toward the front of the document until he came to the F's. Mike Fenske was not listed, which made sense given the fact that he was already dead at the time of Byrnes's campaign.

But his wife's name was there. Her occupation was listed as HOME-MAKER N/A, along with a contribution of $1,000.

Will felt his pulse quicken as he flipped to the *B*'s. He began to go through the names, running his forefinger down the column.

The clerk walked up on the other side of the counter. "We're closed."

He gave her a smile. "Please, just one more minute."

He looked back down at the document. There were dozens of individuals listed whose last name began with the letter *B*. But he could only find one whose first name began with an *A*.

It was a woman named Anne Bender. Her occupation was listed as STUDENT N/A, along with a UCLA campus address. Her contribution amount was $200.

He stared down at the listing. It didn't feel like what he was looking for; he didn't think Anne Bender was the AB listed in the red ledger.

The clerk cleared her throat. "That's it, sir. You can come back tomorrow."

Will pretended that he hadn't heard her, checking the names again, trying to make sure he hadn't missed something. But he didn't see anything.

He closed the document and slid it to the woman. "Thanks."

He turned and walked toward the door. A bulletin board hung on the wall. A laminated printout thumbtacked to the board caught his eye. The heading read GENERAL ELECTION TOTALS.

Will went down the list until he came to the supervisor race. There were two candidates, Byrnes's name with a check mark next to it, indicating that he had been the winner.

The first column on the chart was headed TOTAL CONTRIBUTIONS.

It showed that Byrnes had raised $137,892. It didn't seem like that much money, not for election to such a highly sought-after office.

Will took a step closer to the chart and saw that the runner-up had raised more than ten times as much, $1,462,765.

But Byrnes had still managed to win.

The overhead fluorescent lights switched off. The clerk swung up a section of the countertop and stepped into the sitting area, carrying a paper shopping bag. It was darker now inside the office, but enough natural light came in through the windows for him to see.

He looked back at the chart. There was another column headed PERSONAL FUNDS.

The other candidate had $0.00 listed in this column. But not Byrnes. He showed $1,860,479.

The clerk came up to him. "You're about to get locked in, sir."

Will pointed at the listing for Byrnes. "Does that look strange to you?"

She let out a breath through pursed lips, but then she craned her head forward and looked.

"Strange?" she repeated. "I wouldn't say that. It just looks like he basically financed his own campaign."

FIFTY-SIX

Crandall hated bars. He usually tried to steer clear of them, but he'd been going stir crazy locked up inside the motel room.

After he'd found the dead Korean, he'd gone back to his apartment and packed up his things. It pissed him off, since he'd come to think of the apartment as home. At least it hadn't taken him long to pack, since he didn't own much.

It wasn't going to take a Sherlock Holmes to figure out where the bullet that had killed the old lady had come from. Fortunately, he'd always paid his rent in cash and never given the landlord his real name. That would buy him a little time.

The bar was out on Abbott Kinney in Venice. A yuppie kind of place with a blender behind the bar that was seeing heavy action from the after-work crowd.

The bartender stepped up to the other side of the dark wood bar. He was a good-looking dude in a prep-school, My-name-is-Chad kind of way.

"What can I get you?"

"Club soda, with lemon."

"Anything else?"

Crandall stared at him. "Did I ask for anything else?"

Crandall couldn't handle alcohol anymore, was starting to wonder if something was wrong with his liver. Even one drink would set off the bad headaches. Not that it really mattered, since they'd become semi-permanent fixtures in his life now, even when he didn't drink.

The bartender grabbed a highball glass from the back bar. He looked like he lifted, but he was one of those lean types. Lots of definition but no mass. Crandall figured he could take one of the loser's skinny arms and snap it clean off.

Crandall held his left hand underneath the bar, working the stress ball. He was wearing his red Fila tracksuit, the jacket unzipped to his navel, a white guinea tee underneath. He hadn't taken a shower today, but he'd sprayed himself down with the bottle of Axe body spray before heading out.

The bartender set a cardboard coaster on the bar and then put the glass of club soda down on top of it. A piece of lime floated at the top.

Crandall squeezed the stress ball faster. He couldn't stand limes.

He pointed a finger at his glass. "That look like a lemon to you?"

The bartender looked at the drink. "No, why?"

"'Cause that's what I ordered."

The bartender picked up the glass and made a big deal of dumping it out into the bar sink. Then he refilled the glass from the gun and tossed in a wedge of lemon.

"That's four twenty-five."

"For a club soda?"

"With *lemon*."

Crandall felt a vein on his temple begin to throb. "I'll run a tab."

The place was packed with a middle-aged crowd, business types in sport jackets and collared shirts. Mostly guys, but also a few babes dressed in career clothes. None of them was anything to write home about, soft bodies and bad skin. No mystery why they had to work for a living.

He took a sip of the club soda, wondering if he'd made a mistake by keeping the Eagle. After he'd finished packing up the apartment, he'd driven out to Venice, walked out to the end of the pier to toss the gun into the Pacific. But he just couldn't bring himself to go through with it. He knew it was risky to hang on to the gun, but he just couldn't bear the thought of getting rid of it.

After, he'd gotten back into the Town Car and driven south on Lincoln until he'd spotted the motel—$119 a night for a room with two twins and the stink of mildew.

The bartender came over and put a check down in front of Crandall. "Can I get you anything else, Chief?"

Chief? Crandall willed himself to stay seated on the stool. He pointed at the empty glass. "Yeah, I'll take another one of these."

The bartender rolled his eyes. Crandall knew he was taking up valuable real estate at the bar, but the bartender could go blow himself. Last he checked, it was still a free country.

The bartender came back with his new drink. He pointed at Crandall's chest. "Dude, you're bleeding."

Crandall looked down and saw that the front of his white T-shirt was spotted with blood.

He grabbed a paper napkin off the bar and pressed it to his nose. Goddamn nosebleeds had started a few days back, seemed like they were somehow connected with the headaches. He tore a corner from the napkin, rolled it into a loose ball, and shoved it up inside his right nostril.

The bartender watched him, a look of disgust on his face.

Crandall lifted his chin. "What's the matter, you never seen blood before?"

The bartender walked away. A plasma television was mounted on the wall, the local news playing. The sound was switched off, the bar's sound system playing a Lionel Richie song he'd always hated, was pretty sure the name of it was "Hello."

Crandall froze when he saw the front of his apartment building come up on the TV screen. Flashing red lights washed across the entrance of the building, a barrier of yellow police tape set up on the sidewalk. Letters at the bottom of the screen read:

LAPD INVESTIGATES KOREATOWN SHOOTING

Crandall brought his hand up to shield the side of his face, afraid that his mug shot was about to come on the screen. But the program just cut away to a commercial.

Crandall knew he'd have to move fast now, step up his game plan. He'd given the address of the apartment in K-town to his parole officer, so it was only a matter of time before the police would connect the dots.

He needed to get his money, then get the hell out of town. He'd spent too much time fucking around with the cop as it was. Now it was time to shit or get off the pot.

He drained the last of his drink. The news came back on the plasma, video footage of a tall man in a suit standing in front of a construction site, reporters sticking microphones in his face.

Crandall looked up at the screen, staring at the guy in the suit. He had the feeling he knew the dude from somewhere.

Crandall waved the bartender over and pointed up at the television. "You know who that is?"

The bartender looked at him. "You're serious?"

"Yeah, who is it?"

"Dennis Byrnes."

"Who?"

The bartender shook his head. "County supervisor."

Crandall stared at the screen. The man in the suit turned to take a question. When Crandall saw his profile, he *knew*. Crandall had always been good with faces.

The last time he'd seen him, the man had been wearing a Dodgers cap and dark sunglasses, sneaking into the cop's backyard.

It had been dark that night, but the more he looked at the television, the more certain Crandall became.

FIFTY-SEVEN

The mansion was red brick, sections of the facade hidden by thick vines of English ivy. Will drove slowly past, the driveway filled with cars and trucks. A white party tent was set up on the lawn beside the house.

He'd called Byrnes's office first thing that morning. The reception-ist had told him that he would be out all day at a charity event. A quick Internet search had turned up the event in question, a benefit for a local organization that helped children with physical disabilities.

Will had changed into his suit and driven out to the address in Han-cock Park.

The mansion was surrounded by a black iron fence. A guard in a dark double-breasted suit stood at the front gate clutching a clipboard. A coiled wire snaked from his ear and down into the collar of his shirt. An elegantly dressed crowd was lined up on the front walk, waiting to get in.

Will thought about just trying to talk his way inside but didn't like his chances. He looked around for another way in and saw the catering truck parked in the brick driveway.

Will walked toward the truck. Waiters in tuxedos were busy

unloading platters of food from the back of the truck and carrying them inside through a service entrance at the rear of the house, where another security guard was stationed.

The roll-up door on the back of the truck was raised. When no one was watching, Will reached inside and grabbed a silver platter of cocktail shrimp off the tailgate. He hoisted the platter onto his shoulder and fell into step behind another waiter.

As Will approached the guard, he shifted the platter from one shoulder to the other, hoping the activity would distract the guard from noticing that he wasn't dressed like the other waiters.

It seemed to work, because the next thing he knew he was standing inside the large industrial kitchen of the house. He set the platter down on a granite countertop. A man dressed in chef's whites gave him a look that seemed filled with suspicion. Will nodded to him and walked out of the kitchen.

The dining room was empty, the long table covered with plastic racks of glassware and other party supplies. A pair of French doors at the end of the room looked out onto the lawn. On the other side of the glass, he could see the white party tent and people milling around, cocktails in hand.

Will went out through the doors and down a couple of steps onto a small flagstone patio. The sun was bright, and he began to sweat inside his suit.

A mariachi band dressed in matching matador jackets and sombreros played on a stage set up next to the tent. The lawn area was crowded with guests, waiters circulating among them with trays of appetizers.

An oval area of the manicured lawn had been sectioned off with rope. A Hispanic man dressed like a cowboy led a donkey in a counterclockwise direction around the inside perimeter of the oval, a little girl in a pink dress in the saddle mounted on the donkey's back. A line of other children waited their turn, some of them in wheelchairs, others propped up on forearm crutches.

Will made his way through the crowd, looking for Byrnes. He

recognized a male actor who played a cop on a cable television show and a blond teenaged movie actress, but didn't see Byrnes anywhere.

A bar table had been set up beneath the spreading foliage of a mimosa tree. Will walked over to it and asked the bartender for a mineral water.

From behind him, Will heard the sudden squeal of electronic feedback and turned toward the stage. A handsome woman in a sage-colored gown stood on the stage holding a microphone. She said a few words about Byrnes and then called him up to the stage.

The woman waited, but Byrnes didn't appear. The woman held a flattened hand above her eyes, like a visor, and scanned the crowd. She spoke into the microphone. "*Dennis? Dennis, are you here?*"

The French doors at the back of the house opened, and Dennis Byrnes stepped out into the sunlight, followed by the female aide from his office.

The crowd burst into applause as Byrnes strode across the lawn and climbed up onto the stage. He hugged the woman in the sage dress, then took the handheld microphone from her.

Byrnes was dressed in a dark suit with a solid red necktie. He said a few words, then picked up an oversized check mounted on a piece of foam core. He handed it to the woman, and the crowd applauded.

Will was still holding his glass of mineral water, so he didn't clap. He looked around at the crowd and saw a security guard standing off to his left. The guard had a blond crew cut and was staring at him.

Will took a sip of his drink and looked away. Another guard was standing off to the other side of him, maybe ten feet away. This one was also looking right at him.

Will took a step back into the crowd. The guard to his right raised his wrist to his mouth and spoke into a microphone. Then a hand closed around Will's left bicep.

He turned to see the blond guard standing beside him. He wore wraparound sunglasses. The tailored suit he was wearing didn't hide the fact that he was built like a fullback.

Will acted surprised. "What the hell is this?"

"What do you think?"

Will turned and started to walk away from him, but the other guard blocked his path. This one had dark hair but was just as big as his partner. The two of them grabbed him at the same time, one on each arm.

"I'm a friend of Dennis Byrnes," Will said.

The blond guard looked at him. "Sure you are. That's probably why you snuck in."

The crowd began to applaud. Will turned to see Byrnes descending the stairs at the front of the stage.

Will called out to him. "Dennis."

Byrnes looked over, and for a moment their eyes met. But then Byrnes tried to pretend he hadn't seen him and continued to walk in the direction of the house.

Will yelled louder. "Dennis, *wait*—"

People in the crowd turned to look. The security guard's grip tightened on his arm.

Byrnes stopped. He strode over, probably just hoping to avoid a scene.

He spoke through clenched teeth. "I have to admit I'm surprised to see you here."

"I need to talk to you."

"This is hardly the appropriate time."

"I think it is. This has gone on long enough."

"I don't know what you're talking about." Byrnes looked at the blond guard. "Call LAPD. This man is trespassing."

The guards tugged on his arms, trying to move him in the direction of the street. Will planted his heels and held his ground. A crowd had gathered around, watching.

Will looked at Byrnes. "I've got some things to say. If you want me to say them here, in front of everyone, fine. But trust me, I really think you'd prefer to hear it in private."

Byrnes addressed the crowd. "I'm sorry, folks. This man was a police detective who used to work under me. Unfortunately, he's had a spate of problems lately, of a personal nature."

He turned back to Will and lowered the volume of his voice. "I think you're out of your mind," he said. "But I'll give you two minutes, for old time's sake."

FIFTY-EIGHT

Byrnes told the two guards to wait outside and closed the door to the sitting room.

The walls of the room were painted the color of butter. A large glass vase shaped like a globe overflowed with cut flowers, and the air inside the room was perfumed with the scent of them.

Byrnes dropped into a tufted leather chair across from the couch that Will sat on. "Let's get on with it," he said. "I've got to get back out there with my guests."

Will swallowed. "You remember the thing I came to see you about at your office? The drugs being stolen when we were all at LAPD?"

Byrnes looked at him. "That's what this is about? When I didn't hear back from you, I assumed you decided to let that drop."

"I kept following up, on my own."

Byrnes put his feet up on the glass coffee table, making the top rattle. "And?"

"After all those people ended up overdosing, the operation was shut down. But they didn't want to chance leaving anyone behind who could tie them to the fentanyl. Ray Miller shot Mike Fenske and the dealer they'd been using to move the dope."

Byrnes raised one of his eyebrows. "That's quite the conspiracy theory."

"Ray made it look like a drug bust gone bad."

Byrnes crossed his legs on top of the table. "Listen to yourself, for chrissakes. The man was your partner. Now you're accusing him of being a murderer?"

Will was still holding the glass of mineral water. He took a long sip of it. "I think Ray and Fenske were working with someone higher up inside the department."

"What makes you think that?"

"The whole scheme was tied into Narcotics Division. They timed it so that they'd be putting the stolen product out right after the department ran street sweeps."

Byrnes looked at his wristwatch. "That sounds a little far-fetched."

"I looked at your campaign statements."

Byrnes shook his head. "You're interested in politics now?"

"You financed your own campaign."

Byrnes shrugged. "Something wrong with that?"

"Where does an ex-LAPD officer come up with almost two million dollars?"

Byrnes took his feet down from the coffee table. "So that's what this is about? That's why you felt the need to barge in here? Because you think this drug thing has something to do with *me*?"

Will looked at him. "How else did you come by the two million dollars?"

"My wife comes from money," Byrnes said. "Happy now?"

"Can you prove it?"

"I don't have to prove anything to you. If you're concerned, take it up with the county."

Will watched the other man's face. He didn't know what he'd been expecting, but Byrnes didn't seem to be concerned by what he'd just heard.

Byrnes stood up. He took off his suit jacket and draped it over the back of his chair. "I can see why you were thinking what you were. But trust me, you're barking up the wrong tree."

Will looked up at him. His light blue dress shirt had a contrasting white collar and cuffs. On the chest of the shirt, where a pocket would normally go, initials were stitched in navy blue thread:

Will pointed at the monogram. "What's the *A* stand for?"

"Aloysius," he said. "My first name. You can understand why I don't tend to use it."

"It starts with an *A*."

Byrnes smiled. "Very perceptive."

Will looked at him. "The other name in the ledger, the one that got the biggest payoffs? The initials were AB."

"Would you stop already? There must be fifty thousand people in this city with those initials."

"But how many of them used to be the commanding officer of Narcotics?"

Byrnes looked down at him. "You're a washed-up junkie, Will. Do you really think anyone's going to believe you?"

"I don't need them to believe me," Will said. "I've got the ledger."

"So what? That doesn't prove anything."

"Maybe not by itself. But what do you think's going to happen when someone checks the date of the payments made to AB against your bank accounts?"

Byrnes sat back down. "What about you, Will? If there's an investigation, aren't you concerned about what might come out in the wash?"

Will smiled. "For some reason, I don't think anyone's going to be paying much attention to me."

Byrnes gazed through the large casement windows at the far end of the room. They looked out onto the lawn, the Hispanic man still leading the donkey around the makeshift paddock. A boy wearing thick eyeglasses sat atop the animal's back, his small body jerking with each step of the donkey.

Byrnes leaned forward on the edge of his chair. "I don't need to sit here and justify myself to you. But at this juncture, I should probably point out that I'm in a position to help you."

"How's that?"

"My sources in the district attorney's office tell me you've been indicted on some rather serious charges."

Will looked at him.

Byrnes laced his fingers together. "If you get convicted, you're looking at prison. Which would be a real tragedy, because I also understand you have a child on the way. So let me ask you: Is it really worth throwing your life away, over something that happened over five years ago?"

"What are you saying?"

"That I have the power to help with your legal situation. But if you persist with this ludicrous mission of yours, my influence can also cut the other way."

"You're threatening me?"

"No, just clarifying. That I'm willing to help my friends—not my enemies."

Will stood up. "Thanks for the drink."

Byrnes looked up at him. "Where are you going?"

"To turn you in."

"You never were one to do the smart thing." Byrnes shook his head. "Take your best shot. I don't think you're going to find many sympathetic ears inside LAPD."

"I've got a contact at FBI. I'm pretty sure he'll have the right kind of ears."

Something shifted behind Byrnes's eyes. It wasn't much, but Will could tell that he'd finally succeeded in getting to him.

Will turned and walked across the carpet. When he reached the door he turned back toward Byrnes. "Enjoy the rest of your party."

FIFTY-NINE

Crandall cracked open the fortune cookie.

He pulled the little strip of paper out and popped the broken pieces of the shell into his mouth. He took a moment to enjoy the familiar vanilla taste, then read his fortune:

DON'T WORRY ABOUT THE STOCK MARKET. INVEST IN FAMILY.

What the fuck? He hated when this shit happened. Every once in a while he'd end up with a fortune that seemed like it was meant for somebody else, like when babies in a hospital got switched at birth.

He rolled the fortune into a ball and put it in the ashtray of the Town Car. Then he took the other cookie off the top of the dash.

He cracked it open. This time he read the fortune before he ate the cookie.

THE FIRST STEP TO BETTER TIMES IS TO IMAGINE THEM.

Now that was more like it. Crandall took out his wallet and tucked the fortune inside.

He was parked three houses down from the cop's, on the other side of the street. That way, when the cop went out, he'd drive off in the opposite direction, toward the freeway.

That was *if* the cop would ever leave. Crandall had been sitting there for close to two hours already, waiting for his chance to get the wife alone. He wanted to do it today, was getting worried about how much time he had left before the cops figured out that he was the one who'd been living in the apartment next door to the Korean lady.

Before he'd left the motel, he'd called his parole officer to tell him that he was really sick and wouldn't be able to make it in for his appointment today. Crandall had caught a break when the guy wasn't there. He'd left a message with the receptionist.

Crandall had never missed a parole appointment before. Always showed up on time to piss in the little plastic cup. The tests always came back squeaky clean, since they were only testing for narcotics, not for steroids.

He could feel the clock running out now, figured he probably only had a day or two left before he'd have to blow town. But once he got with the wife, he didn't think it would take very long to find out what he needed to know. No, not long at all.

He leaned over and picked up the shopping bag off of the passenger seat. It had the name of a self defense store in Canoga Park printed onto the white plastic. The bag held the supplies he'd picked up.

Crandall reached inside the bag and pulled out an aerosol canister that was the size of a can of spray paint. The canister had a drawing of a bear's head on it. The drawing made it look like the bear was jumping right off the can, its sharp teeth bared. Above the picture were the words BEAR REPELLENT.

Crandall looked at the directions on the label. A big warning was printed in red letters: KEEP OUT OF REACH OF CHILDREN.

Well, no shit.

The canister had a plastic trigger on top of it. Crandall put his finger through it and practiced pulling back the safety clip. He pointed the canister at the floor and pretended to press down on the trigger with his thumb.

When he felt like he had it figured out, he fitted the canister into its black nylon hip holster and put it down on the passenger seat.

He reached his hand back inside the shopping bag and pulled out a small cardboard box. The box was white except for some words stamped on the side: MADE IN CHINA.

Crandall opened the end flap and slid out the stun gun. It was the size of a pack of cigarettes and had two metal prongs sticking up from one end. Crandall held it out in front of him and flicked the switch on the side.

The thing started to make a snapping sound. Crandall jerked his head back to avoid getting electrocuted.

He'd thought about bringing the Eagle along but decided to leave it back in the motel room. He couldn't imagine needing it. Not for the woman.

He slid the stun gun into the side pocket of his cargo shorts and zipped the pocket closed.

Crandall lowered the driver's side window. He was so sick of being stuck inside this goddamned car, couldn't wait to say good-bye to the thing. When he got himself down to Honduras with the money, he'd just walk along the beach to get everywhere, maybe ride a bicycle. He was done with cars for a long while.

He looked out through the windshield. The cop's piece-of-shit Volvo was still sitting there in its spot in the driveway, a ball of sunlight reflecting off the window of the tailgate. He wondered when the cop would leave already.

He watched as a FedEx truck rumbled down the street and came to a stop at the corner.

Crandall reached down and flicked the switch on the base of the power seat. The motor whirred, and the seat slid backward on its tracks. He stretched out his legs as best he could, then reclined the seatback, trying to get comfortable.

He'd waited all these years to get his money back, he supposed he could afford to wait just a little bit longer.

SIXTY

A FedEx truck rumbled down the street, rattling the panes of glass in the window of Will's home office.

Will spun the knob on the side of the Rolodex until he found the business card for Steve Fong, Supervisory Special Agent, Federal Bureau of Investigation.

He hadn't talked to Fong since they'd worked a joint investigation when Will had been with LAPD, but he felt confident that Fong would remember him.

He picked up the phone and dialed the number on the card, listened to the electronic ringing, then heard Fong's recorded voice asking him to please leave a message. Will hit zero and was connected to a female operator.

"I'm trying to reach Steve Fong," Will said.

"Agent Fong is out of the office. Would you like me to connect you to his voice mail?"

"No," Will said. "I'll call back later. Any idea when he'll be back?"

"I can't give out that information, sir."

Will thanked her and then hung up. He'd call back later in the afternoon.

He picked up the red ledger and reused the pieces of duct tape to secure it to the bottom of the desk drawer. Then he slid the drawer back into place.

Laurie was in the baby's room.

She used a pair of scissors to cut a piece of wallpaper from a roll that lay on the wooden floor. Buddy was curled up in a corner of the room, watching her with one opened eye.

The wallpaper was vintage, something she'd found at the Rose Bowl flea market. It was patterned with illustrated circus elephants lined up against a yellow background.

"Hey," he said.

She looked up. "Hey."

Her blond hair was pulled back into a ponytail. She wore one of his old button-down shirts and a pair of white painter's pants. The shirt was big on her, but it was still pushed out where it draped over her pregnant belly.

She used a paintbrush to coat the back side of the piece of wallpaper with paste, then pressed the paper in place on the wall opposite the crib.

"That looks great," he said.

She stepped back to admire her handiwork. "I just wish I had more of it, so I could do the other wall."

He looked around the room. It seemed perfect the way it was, like something out of a design magazine. A room any kid would be lucky to have.

"You got a letter from Barry Feingold," she said. "I opened it."

"What'd it say?"

"Something about how he got a continuance. The hearing's pushed back until early November."

He walked over to her. "It's going to be okay, Laurie. Trust me."

She looked at him, then nodded her head once.

He hadn't told her anything about the situation with Byrnes. He didn't like keeping secrets from her, but he didn't want to get her hopes up until he made sure the FBI was interested in what he had.

He reached out and put his hand on the back of her neck. He could feel the tension that was there, and he used his fingers to massage the muscles hidden beneath her warm skin.

She didn't resist him, dropping her head forward so that he could work a little deeper. He used both hands now, moving the balls of his thumbs in small circles across the top of her shoulder blades.

She reached up and took hold of his right hand. "You better stop," she said. "Before we get carried away."

"I'm good with carried away." How long had it been since they'd last made love? He couldn't even remember. Not since he'd been arrested, anyway.

She smiled. "Not right now."

He parsed the words for meaning, like a semantics scholar. He was able to find a molecule of hope in them. After all, she could have said "no" or "never," but she hadn't.

Not right now. At least she'd left the door open a crack.

"I was heading to the store," he said. "You need anything?"

"Where're you going?"

"Just down to Gelson's, pick up some stuff for dinner. It's going to be a nice night, I thought I'd buy something to grill. We could eat out on the patio."

She nodded. "That sounds good."

"I can get you a bottle of that nonalcoholic wine."

She lifted one of her eyebrows. "First the massage, now you're trying to ply me with nonalcoholic beverages?"

She smiled at him, her skin glowing. He stared at her, trying to take a photograph in his mind, so he could always remember the way she looked at this moment.

"*What,*" she said.

He shook his head and leaned forward.

He pressed his lips to hers and kissed her good-bye.

SIXTY-ONE

Crandall watched the front door of the cop's house swing open as the cop stepped out into the sunlight.

About fucking time.

The cop fitted a pair of shades onto his face and got inside the Volvo. The engine sputtered to life, the station wagon backing out of the driveway. It headed off in the opposite direction, just like Crandall had planned it.

He watched the Volvo disappear from view, then clipped the nylon holster that held the canister of bear spray to the waistband of his cargo shorts. He patted the cargo pocket, double-checking that the stun gun was there.

As he did this, he noticed wet splatters of blood down the front of his brand new white T-shirt.

Goddammit.

He looked at his face in the rearview mirror. Blood dripped down from his right nostril. He opened the glove compartment and took out the box of Kleenex, but it was empty. He looked around the car's interior for a napkin, something to use on his nose, but couldn't find anything.

Another drop of warm blood landed on his chest.

He took out his wallet and unfolded the fortune. He rolled it up into a ball and looked in the rearview as he shoved the wad of paper up inside his nostril.

He looked out at the cop's house. He decided to give it a few minutes more, just to play it safe. Make sure that the cop hadn't forgotten anything, that he wasn't coming back.

Crandall reached into the front pocket of his shorts for his stress ball. He felt around, starting to feel a rising panic when he realized it wasn't there. He must've left it back in the motel room.

He checked the clock on the dash.

It was time.

He opened the car door and climbed out of the Town Car. He stood there for a moment, tucking the tail of his T-shirt down inside the waistband of his shorts.

His legs had gone stiff, causing him to lurch as he crossed the street toward the house.

SIXTY-TWO

Laurie was using the scissors to cut the final piece of wallpaper when the doorbell rang.

Ding-dong.

She was sitting in a half lotus on the hardwood floor. The sound caused Buddy to lift his head from where he lay in the corner.

She decided to just ignore the bell. She wasn't expecting anyone; it was probably just the UPS guy letting her know that he was leaving a package on the porch. She'd go and get it later, but right now she wanted to finish this job before the paste started to dry.

Ding-dong. Ding-dong.

It didn't sound like whoever was at the door was just going to go away.

She unfolded her long legs and climbed to her feet. It wasn't easy, not with her stomach sticking out in front of her like a medicine ball, messing with her balance. She slid the scissors into the brush holder on the side of her painter's paints.

She walked barefoot through the house. Buddy trotted along behind her.

Ding-dong.

She looked through the peephole, but there was no one out there. She opened the door, figuring that someone had left a package after all.

It was bright outside, and she squinted her eyes. She looked down at the porch floor but didn't see a package. She took a step out onto the porch.

There was a sudden movement from her left, an enormous figure moving into her field of view. She turned and saw that it was the man from the park.

Erik Crandall.

The front of his shirt was covered with blood.

Her heart stopped beating for a horrible moment before it started up again and began to jackhammer inside her chest.

She jumped back inside the house, slamming the door closed.

It stuck on something before it could latch, daylight coming in through the gap. The man's thick fingers were wrapped around the edge of the door. She pushed harder, throwing her weight into the effort, not caring if she hurt him. But then the door suddenly flew inward with a force so powerful it was as if it had been struck by a tornado.

The edge of the door caught her in the shoulder, and she staggered backward into the living room, fighting to stay on her feet.

The man stepped inside the house and kicked shut the door. He seemed even bigger now that he was indoors, the familiar objects of her life serving to put him in scale. His eyes were red and had a feral look.

Buddy began to growl, the sound low and guttural. He bared his fangs, his eyes locked on the man. Laurie had never seen him act like this before. He'd never been much of a watchdog, but it was like he was remembering what the man had done to him in the park.

The man stood frozen in place, watching the dog. His bare arms bulged with muscles, but he looked unhealthy.

Buddy lowered his rear and started barking, the sound of it too loud inside the room.

The man reached down to a black holster that hung from his waist.

He took out a canister that had a red plastic handle on top. He aimed the canister at Buddy's face and pulled a trigger at the top of the plastic handle.

She screamed as a stream of reddish brown mist shot from the can and enveloped Buddy in a cloud. The dog let out a yelp and struggled to turn around, his claws scrabbling against the hardwood floor. He took two meandering steps and then collapsed.

The man slid the canister back inside the holster and stepped toward where Buddy lay on the floor whimpering. He bent over and grabbed hold of Buddy's rear legs.

He shuffled backward, bent over at the waist, dragging the dog across the floor. He opened the door to the hall closet and began to shove Buddy inside.

Laurie's throat was on fire, her eyes tearing from the chemical spray. Everything in the room had gone blurry, nothing but shapes.

She considered whether she should try to make a run for the telephone to call 911. She thought about it, but the phone was cordless, and for the life of her couldn't remember where the handset was.

Then her fingertips brushed against the scissors resting inside the brush holder of her pants. She wrapped her sweaty fingers around the plastic handle and blinked her eyes in an attempt to clear her vision. The man had his back to her, bent over as he tried to shove Buddy's legs inside the closet so that he could get the door shut.

She raised the scissors and took a step toward the man. She hesitated before bringing them down because the man had somehow managed to turn around, was now staring straight up at her, watching. She gasped, then realized that the eyes were unblinking and two-dimensional, only some kind of bizarre tattoos.

She took another step forward and swung the scissors downward in an arc just as the man began to straighten up. The blades missed their mark and stuck high up on his shoulder blade.

She was surprised by how it felt. She'd expected the scissors to plunge inside him, but it was like trying to stab a block of wood. The blades sank in a couple of inches and then came to a stop against something solid.

The man let out an angry howl that made her freeze. He turned and looked at her, the expression on his face more about shock than pain.

"You fucking *bitch*."

He reached around behind him to pull out the scissors, but his upper body wasn't flexible enough. He tried to reach them with his other hand, up on tiptoes and turning in a little pirouette as he struggled.

She saw that this was her opportunity. She took a step forward and kicked him in the balls as hard as she could.

She wasn't wearing any shoes, and when she connected she ended up stubbing her big toe. The pain rocketed up from her foot and made her feel nauseated. She hopped on her good foot, watching as the man grabbed his crotch and doubled over with pain.

He looked up at her like a bull lanced by a picador, the scissors still sticking up from his back.

Laurie tried to think of what to do next. But as she looked around for something else she might use as a weapon, he charged her. He was crouched over as he came, his shoulder catching her just above the pubic bone, the pain from that taking her mind off her toe.

The man's massive arms wrapped around her waist, and she was driven backward into the living room. She felt her calves knock over the coffee table, then went airborne for a moment before landing on her back on the couch.

The big man came down on top of her, knocking the air from her lungs. Her mind went to the baby as she felt it give a familiar kick inside her.

The man grabbed hold of both her wrists and pinned them against the couch cushions above her head.

He spoke to her through clenched teeth. "Pull out the scissors."

She shook her head.

"Pull them out, or this is going to go a lot worse for you."

She tried to wriggle her wrists free, but he was too strong. "What are you going to do?"

"Just talk," he said. "As long as you cooperate. Now, pull them out."

She tried to focus on her breathing, as if she were meditating. She needed to stay present, not let herself get carried away by the fear. She found that it was almost impossible to do this, jumbled thought fragments racing through her mind.

Then she knew what it was she had to do, the idea coming to her all at once, like a gift.

"Okay," she said. "But you need to let go of my hand."

He loosened his grip on her right hand but kept his weight pressing down on her left.

She reached her hand around his massive back. Her fingers found the plastic handles of the scissors and wrapped around them.

His eyes widened with pain as she worked them free.

She brought her hand back around the man's torso, the scissor blades coated with blood. She tightened her grip on the handles and pointed the blades at him. Then she stabbed them toward the center of his chest.

The man's hand caught her wrist as it came forward, arresting her arm in midstab.

He smiled as he looked into her eyes. Then he twisted her wrist backward, his strength impossible for her to counter. A bolt of agony exploded inside her brain. The scissors clattered down onto the floor.

He pinned her wrist against the cushion, the pain even worse now. She began to wonder if it was broken, then pushed the thought from her mind. She'd worry about it later, if there was any later. Right now she had to be present, try to find a way out of this.

"What do you want from me?" she said.

His breathing was labored, the air making a whistling sound as it passed through his nostrils. "We were interrupted," he said. "I thought we could pick things up where we left off."

She struggled, trying to get away from him. But he was straddling her, his bulk pressing her down into the couch, pinning her there.

"What's the matter," he said. "Not used to having a man on top of you?"

She didn't say anything, just tried to stay with her breathing so that she wouldn't lose her mind. The smell the man gave off was overpowering, cheap cologne that didn't quite manage to mask his body odor.

He looked down at her. "In the park, you told me that your husband stole *some* of my dope but not all of it. Did you really expect me to believe that?"

"It's the truth."

He shifted his weight on top of her. "Bullshit."

She winced. "Please, you're hurting the baby."

His eyes looked as if they'd been dipped in nail polish. There was something stuck up inside one of his nostrils.

Laurie forced herself to hold his gaze. Trying to make a connection with him, to try to get him to understand. "You've made a mistake. He doesn't have what you're looking for. But if you leave now, I promise we won't call the police."

"The only way I'm leaving here is if you tell me what I want to know."

The man forced her hands together on top of her head, as if she were doing a jumping jack. He grabbed hold of both her wrists with one of his hands, pinning them to the couch.

He took his free hand and reached down toward the front of his shorts. She heard a zipper being unzipped, her body going stiff at the sound.

He brought his hand back up holding some kind of black plastic device that had two metal prongs sticking up from one end.

She lost control of her breathing, her panic running free. *"What is that?"*

He held it up in front of her face. "I'm sorry I have to do this to you. But I'm running out of time. And I'm all out of patience."

SIXTY-THREE

Will unloaded the groceries from the plastic basket, placing them on the moving surface of the conveyor belt.

The checkout clerk was a middle-aged blond woman wearing a Hawaiian shirt patterned with green coconut palms. She seemed to be moving in slow motion as she picked up each item and passed it over the window of the scanner.

"So how's your afternoon going?" she asked.

"Can't complain." Will didn't ask her how she was doing. He didn't want to be rude, but Laurie had warned him not to strike up a conversation with the checkers. She said that it distracted them, so that they made mistakes when they rang you up.

The store's sound system was tuned to an oldies station that was playing the Badfinger classic "Day After Day." The clerk hummed along to the chorus.

She picked up the package of fish that was wrapped in white butcher paper and ran it back and forth over the scanner, trying to get the price to read.

Will remembered something. "I couldn't find the nonalcoholic wine."

"It's in aisle seven, with the regular wines."

"I know, but the space on the shelf is empty."

She shrugged. "Sorry, we must be out."

She totaled up the order, and Will ran his MasterCard through the slot in the machine. He helped her bag the groceries to try to speed things along.

As he walked out of the store, he flipped open his cell phone and hit the speed dial for home. He listened to it ring.

He was surprised when Laurie didn't pick up the phone and the ringing switched over to the answering machine.

Laurie heard the phone start to ring, the man freezing on top of her.

He was still holding the stun gun in his hand, and he swiveled his bald head in the direction of the ringing.

The answering machine was in the kitchen, on top of the counter.

Laurie heard Will's voice coming through the speaker, like he was there inside the house with her.

"It's me," his voice said. "Can you pick up?"

For some reason, the sound of Will's voice made her lose it. She began to cry, tears rolling down her face.

"I'm all finished at the store," Will's voice said.

She felt the man's body tense on top of her.

Laurie tried to think. Gelson's was five minutes away. She would tell this to the man, and if he had any sense of self-preservation, he'd leave. This would all be over.

Will's voice kept going. "If you're listening, I'm calling because they're out of that nonalcoholic wine you like, and I just wanted to see if you could go without."

She closed her eyes and tried to send him a telepathic message.

Yes, I can go without it. I'll gladly go without it for the rest of my goddamn life. Now, please just hang up the phone and get your ass back home.

His voice paused, as if he were giving her a chance to come to the phone. It was like torture, the silence stretching out for an eternity.

"All right," Will said. "I guess you must be in the shower. I'm gonna drive over to Full o' Life . . ."

No—don't do that. Full o' Life was all the way over in Burbank.

"Call my cell if you need anything else from there. I'll see you in about forty-five." There was a brief pause, and then he added, "Love you."

There was a click as he broke the connection and the answering machine fell silent.

SIXTY-FOUR

The man held up the stun gun. "So where were we?"

Laurie shook her head and tried to squirm out from underneath him. She was still crying. "Please, you don't have to do this."

"You're not giving me a choice."

"We don't have any money. Everything we had, it all went to hire the lawyer."

The man shook his head. "You people are pathological, you know that? Every time I talk to you, it's a different fucking lie."

She shut her eyes for a moment, hoping that when she opened them again he'd be gone. She grasped at the idea that she was asleep, that this was all just a nightmare.

Her eyes flew open again when she felt the man's hand on her chest. She lifted her head and watched as he fumbled with the top button of her shirt.

She bucked her upper body to make it harder for him to work the buttons, but then he simply yanked on the shirt's placket, the buttons popping off into the air. He spread the shirt open and then brought the device toward her exposed chest.

He pressed the metal prongs into the flesh of her left breast, above the cup of her maternity bra. "I have a feeling this might change your attitude."

She twisted and tried to pull her wrists free from his grip, but it was futile. Why the hell hadn't she taken karate or something useful, instead of the yoga?

His thumb moved on the side of the device, and she heard a mechanical click as he flipped the switch.

She closed her eyes and took a deep breath through her nose, bracing for the pain. She thought of something her meditation teacher had once said at a dharma talk. How we only become truly aware when we stop trying to avoid the things that make us suffer.

The moment went on forever. She waited, continuing to focus on her breath, but the pain still didn't come.

She felt the metal prongs being taken away from her breast. She opened her eyes. The man held up the device in front of his face, looking at it, flipping the switch over and over.

Nothing happened.

His face grew flushed with blood as he shook the device. He flipped the switch, his eyes fixed on the twin prongs.

When nothing happened, he turned and threw the device away into the corner of the room. "Cheap Chinese piece of crap."

His nostrils flared as he breathed. "Don't think you're off the hook," he said. "I'll just have to find some other way to make you talk."

He looked down at her, studying her as if she were a laboratory animal, his gaze moving slowly down her body: over her throat, lingering on her breasts, then along the mound of her exposed and pregnant belly.

He ran the palm of his hand over the curve of her naked stomach. "Boy or girl?"

She began to tremble, nothing that she could control.

He stroked the skin of her belly, the skin of his fingers calloused. She thought she could feel the baby moving inside her, as if it were trying to get away.

"What are you doing?"

"Are you pro-life?" he asked. "Let's find out where you stand on the issue."

He stopped stroking her and formed his hand into a fist. He cocked back his arm at the elbow, his muscles rising and going stiff, his fist poised six inches above her stomach.

"Please, don't hurt my baby." She squirmed and began to moan, begging him over and over to *please don't hurt the baby,* her words coming in an unbroken stream.

Hot liquid ran between her legs as her bladder let go.

Erik Crandall didn't seem to notice. He sat astride her, implacable. "Last time I'm going to ask," he said. "Where's my money?"

Everything was blurry now, tears streaming from her face. "I swear on the baby's life. We don't have it."

The man paused, as if considering her words.

Then he drew back his fist and punched her in the stomach.

SIXTY-FIVE

The traffic was heavy on Burbank Boulevard, so Will took Vineland up to Victory and took that the rest of the way home.

He turned into the driveway behind Laurie's Volkswagen and switched off the ignition. He went around to the tailgate and took out the two paper sacks of groceries.

On the front porch, he shifted both bags into the crook of his left arm so that he could work the latch on the front door. He used his hip to push the door, the hinges creaking as it swung inward.

There were no lights on inside the house. He was still wearing his sunglasses, so at first he couldn't see anything. He caught a whiff of something strong, almost like Mace.

He spun to his left when he heard the strange sound coming from inside the hall closet. It sounded like scratching. He stood there, staring at the closet door and listening.

He set down one of the bags and opened the closet door. Buddy staggered out of the closet, like a drunk exiting a bar.

Will tore the sunglasses from his face. Buddy looked up at him.

His eyes were swollen, the fur surrounding them coated with a shiny discharge.

Will looked into the living room, his breath catching in his throat. *"Laurie?"*

The house was a disaster area. The coffee table was knocked over onto its side, books pulled from the bookshelves, drawers hanging out from the end tables.

Will took a step into the living room and saw Laurie. She lay on her back on top of the couch. Her wrists and ankles were bound with silver pieces of duct tape.

He dropped the bag he was still holding, the one from the health food store. It landed on the floor, glass shattering. The fake wine ran from the bag and spread out into a puddle.

"Laurie?"

She didn't answer or move.

He rushed over to the couch. He was praying to himself, silently, not really conscious that he was even doing it. Her shirt was ripped open, her bra and pregnant belly exposed. Her eyes were shut.

He reached down and touched her cheek with the back of his hand.

He said her name over and over, but she didn't respond.

SIXTY-SIX

Valley Presbyterian Hospital is on Vanowen, just off Sepulveda.

Laurie was in a semiprivate room in the antepartum ward, the room's other bed unoccupied. The head of her hospital bed was raised at a forty-five-degree angle, the plastic drip tube from an IV bag running down to where it was taped to the back of her hand. A tangle of wires snaked out from beneath the hem of her faded green examination gown and were hooked up to a fetal heart monitor.

LAPD had already come and gone. They'd taken Laurie's statement and shown her a photographic lineup card. Even in her drugged state, she'd been able to positively ID Erik Crandall's mug shot.

Will had been glad to see the detectives leave. He'd worry about Crandall later. Right now, the only thing he cared about was Laurie and the survival of his unborn son. He sat in the room's vinyl-upholstered guest chair, trying to focus on what the doctor was saying.

He was a hospital resident, young and African American. He wore his hair in short dreadlocks that reminded Will of the musician Lenny Kravitz.

"I'll start with the good news," the doctor said. "There's no sign that the uterus has been ruptured."

Will sat up in the chair, waiting for the other shoe to drop. Was his son going to be born deformed, or with some kind of brain damage?

The doctor continued. "Whenever we get this kind of blunt trauma to the uterus, there's always the risk of placental abruption."

"Could you put that into plain English please, Doctor?" Will said.

The doctor nodded and held up one of his hands. He formed it into a tight ball and then wrapped his other hand around it. "An abruption is when a portion of the placenta becomes detached from the uterine wall." He pulled his curled hand away from the fist. "Not good—to put it in plain English."

"Is that happening?" Will asked.

"No, I don't see any evidence of that."

Will couldn't stand it anymore. "So what's the *bad* news?"

"Your wife is starting to have contractions. At only thirty-two weeks, we'd obviously prefer not to see her going into labor. I'm giving her terbutaline to slow the contractions."

Will swallowed. "What about the baby? Is he okay?"

"It seems like the fetus is stable. The heart rate is normal, no decelerations."

Will couldn't believe it. "But she said that this guy, he punched her right in the belly, right where the baby—"

The doctor held up a hand, cutting him off. "Amniotic fluid is the world's best shock absorber. I'm not seeing any signs of fetal distress."

"So he's not hurt?"

The doctor spread open his hands and smiled. "What can I say? The kid knows how to take a punch."

Laurie cleared her throat. Will turned to look at her, realizing they'd been talking about her as if she weren't even there.

She sipped water through a straw from a plastic hospital tumbler. "So what happens next?" she asked.

"As a precaution, I want to keep you here for two to three days. If there's no change in the cervix length, and the contractions resolve, you'll need to spend the rest of your pregnancy on bed rest."

"Here?" Laurie asked.

"No, I'll send you home. But I won't want you moving around."

Will stood up and began to shake the doctor's hand, as if he'd just performed some kind of miracle.

After the doctor had left and they were alone inside the room, Will slid the chair over to the side of the hospital bed. He took hold of Laurie's hand, being careful to avoid the IV. He saw that her wrist was ringed with blueish bruises, like a bracelet.

She was staring at the television mounted to the wall, even though it was switched off. The pillowcase was stenciled with the initials of the hospital, Laurie's blond hair spread out on top of it. The room held the familiar hospital smell of disinfectants trying to mask the odors of bodily excretions and pain and fear.

His heart was pounding inside his chest. He didn't know how to put into words all the things that he wanted to say to her.

He finally managed to get some words out. "I'm sorry."

She kept staring at the television set that wasn't on.

He said it again.

She turned her head and looked at him. "In the back of the ambulance, on the way here? I was so angry at you. Because I kept telling myself that all this was because of you."

He looked at her, not knowing what he could say.

"But it's not true," she said. "I was just taking the easy way out, trying to put it all on you."

He swallowed. "I deserve it. I should've paid more attention to looking out for you."

"I'm not exactly the easiest person to look out for. You tried, but I didn't want to live my life in fear. I never thought he would actually do something this bad."

Will looked over at the fetal monitor, a scroll of paper unfurling from a slot on the front, tracing the activity of his unborn son's heart.

"I was so scared, Will. I tried not to be, but I couldn't deal with my fear."

He squeezed her hand tighter. "Under the circumstances, I'd say that's pretty normal."

"When I heard your voice coming through the answering machine, when you called from the store? I was sure I'd never see you again."

A single teardrop ran out from the corner of her eye and landed on the pillowcase, a dark blot on the green fabric.

He got up from the chair and leaned over the bed and laid his head down on her chest. He felt her arms wrapping around his neck.

Outside the open door to the room, an orderly pushed a metal cart down the vinyl-tiled corridor. One of the cart's wheels was broken so that it fluttered back and forth, making a chattering noise.

"So what are you going to do now?" Laurie asked.

"Stay here, with you."

"What do you mean?"

He stood up. "I'll sleep on the other bed, until they let you out."

"That's crazy. You heard the doctor, they're only keeping me here as a precaution."

"I don't care. I'm not letting you out of my sight again."

"I'm in a hospital. I'm safe now."

"You've obviously never seen *The Godfather.*"

She smiled. "I'm stuck here, Will. You don't have to be."

She reached out and ran her fingertips along the side of his face. "Go home."

SIXTY-SEVEN

The house was dark.

Will pulled into the driveway, expecting LAPD to be here. To see evidence techs doing their thing, or at least some uniforms standing guard over the scene. But the place was deserted.

His thoughts began to well up in the silence, turning on him. He tried to push them away by focusing on the things that he knew he had to do. First thing in the morning, he'd drive down to the Federal Building on Wilshire and hand over the red ledger to Steve Fong. After that was taken care of, he'd allow himself to start thinking about Crandall.

He went up the front walk and saw that there was a sticker attached to the front door. An LAPD emblem was printed at the top, along with bold letters declaring that his home was now an official crime scene.

He reached inside the pocket of his pants for the house key, then saw that the door was ajar. He let out his breath in frustration as he pushed it open.

He flipped the switch, and the recessed ceiling lights came on, illuminating a scene that made him groan.

He took in the overturned furniture, the books dumped out onto the floor, the drawers sticking out; all pretty much as he remembered it from when he'd come home and found Laurie. Added to this now was the detritus from the police. The scene techs must have already been there; he could see the residue of fingerprint powder clinging to the room's hard surfaces. A paper cup of takeout coffee topped with a plastic lid sat on top of the wooden fireplace mantel.

Will looked around for Buddy before remembering that he was at the veterinarian's. They were keeping him there for a couple of days, but it looked like there would be no permanent damage to his eyes.

Will turned on lights as he walked through the house. The chaos was not limited to the living room. It was as if someone had gone through the house searching for something. Not in an organized way, but by opening every cabinet, pulling out every drawer, dumping everything out onto the floor. It would take him days to get it all cleaned up.

He went down the hallway that led to the bedrooms. The lights were off inside the baby's room, but he could see the elephant wallpaper, a rectangle of bare wall standing out down near the baseboard.

Will flipped on the light in the office. This room had been gone through as well. The framed photographs that had hung on the walls had been thrown onto the floor, the glass inside the frames shattered. The top drawer of the metal filing cabinet was pulled out, hanging down at an awkward angle. Paperbacks from the shelves above the desk were piled on the floor.

The desk drawers were closed. Will sat down in the swivel chair and held his breath as he slid out the middle drawer.

He worked the drawer up and down to free it from its tracks. Then he pulled it out and flipped it over.

He let out his breath, staring down at the plywood drawer bottom. There was white residue in the shape of the strips of duct tape that had held the red ledger in its hiding place.

But the strips of tape were missing now, and so was the ledger.

SIXTY-EIGHT

Will's eyes snapped open at the sound of the doorbell.

Ding-dong.

He rolled over in the bed. He hadn't been able to sleep last night, his thoughts coming in a nonstop onslaught. He'd finally managed to doze off sometime after the sun had come up.

He looked at the glowing red numerals of the alarm clock and saw that it was already after eight.

Ding-dong.

Will flung off the tangled covers and got out of the bed. He threaded his way through the obstacle course of toppled furniture in the living room.

Ding-dong. Ding-dong.

Will opened the door. Bright sunlight came in through the doorway, setting off a stabbing in his forehead.

"Sorry, I didn't mean to wake you," the man said.

Will held up his hand to block the sun and saw that it was Ed Denslowe, the LAPD homicide detective who had investigated Ray Miller's death. He was holding a tall paper cup covered with a plastic lid.

"What's up?" Will asked.

Denslowe smiled. "Thought I'd come by to check on you."

"What is it you want?"

Denslowe took a sip through a hole in the lid of his cup. "I just wanted to tell you how sorry I am. About what happened to your wife."

Will didn't say anything. His mouth had a bad taste, probably from all the cognac that he'd drunk before going to bed.

"What?" Denslowe said. "You think this is my fault?"

Will held the man's eyes. "What do you think?"

"I did everything I could in terms of checking Crandall out for the Ray Miller thing. But I admit, we should've been paying more attention to him."

"*Attention?* You should've put Crandall away for murder."

"Ray Miller committed suicide."

Will shook his head in disbelief. "It takes a small man to be unable to admit his mistakes."

"You're jumping to conclusions here. Crandall's a bad egg. Obviously. But just because of what he did to your wife, it still doesn't mean he killed Ray Miller."

Will let out his breath. "You're unbelievable."

Denslowe took another sip from his cup. "Are you going to let me in or not?"

"I think we're done here." Will began to shut the door.

Denslowe held up his hand. "Hold up. I need to talk to you."

"About *what?*"

"What happened to your wife. I caught the case."

Will was confused. "Why? You're Homicide."

"Because of my experience with Crandall. Also because the DA is hoping to charge him with attempted murder, for what he did to the fetus."

Will shook his head. "That should really generate some gangbuster headlines."

"You should be happy. It means more resources on your wife's case."

The smell of Denslowe's coffee made Will feel desperate for a cup of his own. He opened the door to let him in.

The detective followed Will into the kitchen, looking around at the disarray. "Crandall did all this?"

Will nodded. "And your guys."

Will managed to find a package of ground coffee among the items that had been dumped out onto the kitchen counter. He measured it out into the basket of the coffeemaker.

"You want some?"

Denslowe held up his cup and shook his head. "I'm good." He leaned his tall frame against the stainless steel front of the refrigerator. "You know, if I was in your shoes—"

Will spun around. "Which you should be glad you're not."

"Granted. But if I *was*, right about now I'd be thinking about taking matters into my own hands. After all, it's my wife we're talking about here."

Will chewed his bottom lip. "You mean *my* wife."

"You know what I'm trying to say. I'd be thinking about tracking this guy down, an eye for an eye and all that. Well, let me give you some advice: Don't do it. Don't even think about it."

"Did you come here to talk to me or browbeat me?"

Denslowe smiled. "I guess maybe a little of both. I'm asking you to stay out of this. You'll only end up making things worse."

"I don't see how that's really possible."

The coffeemaker began to make a hissing sound, brown liquid dripping down into the glass carafe.

"Listen to me," Denslowe said. "The department, we're all over this thing now. When the lab work comes back, the blood on the scissors will match Crandall. Your wife gave us a positive ID. It's a slam dunk."

"Assuming you can find him."

"I've got half the department doing door-to-doors. We've got an APB out to county and federal. It's only a matter of time."

"What if he tries to get in the wind?"

"We've sent flyers to TSA, Customs, bus and train stations. There's nowhere for him to go."

Will looked over at the coffeemaker. The carafe was only half full, but he pulled it from the machine and poured some coffee into one of the few mugs that hadn't been shattered.

Then he began to walk toward the front door. "Thanks for stopping by," he said.

"Hold up. I want to hear you say it."

"Say *what?*"

"That you won't go after Crandall."

Will looked at him. "I don't have to tell you shit."

"Remember what happened the last time you tried to take matters into your own hands. It didn't turn out too well, am I right?"

Will took a sip of the coffee. It needed milk, but he was all out.

Denslowe was staring at him. "At least try and look out for yourself here."

"In what way?"

"Think about it. After what Crandall just pulled, odds are the DA's going to drop the charges against you. But you go after him again, all bets are off."

SIXTY-NINE

After Denslowe had left, Will drove over to the hospital and visited Laurie.

He watched the morning talk shows with her until she fell asleep. Then he continued to sit there looking at her, reassured by the rhythmic sounds of her breath moving in and out.

As it grew close to lunchtime, he decided he should go back home and begin the daunting task of trying to clean up.

Back at the house, he took a broom and a long-handled dustpan from the hall closet and made his way through the rooms, sweeping up shards of broken glass into the dustpan, the sound of it like the rattling of chains.

It was too quiet inside the empty house, every creak of the floorboards sounding like they were amplified. Thoughts swarmed into his mind, but he tried to focus on the task at hand, squinting down at the wood floor to make sure that he swept up every last piece of glass.

He went into the kitchen to empty the dustpan into the garbage. The light on the answering machine was flashing. He hit the button and played a message from the veterinarian's office. They said that they were giving Buddy steroids to treat the swelling in his eyes and that Will could pick the dog up tomorrow morning.

In the disarray of the living room, he stood on the area rug and tried to decide where to begin. The air held a strange odor, like air freshener or cheap cologne. He bent down and flipped the coffee table up onto its legs and then put the magazines, photography books, and remote controls back on top of it.

One of the sofa cushions had fallen down onto the floor. He started to put it back into place but then stopped, noticing something.

A faint yellow stain spread out across the white canvas fabric, the edges convoluted like the shoreline of a lake. Will stared at the stain, trying to figure out what had caused it. He bent over and sniffed. Then he froze as it hit him all at once, certain now of what had created it.

Outside the living room window, a car coughed, the engine coming to life.

Will held the cushion with both hands, his stomach fluttering. An image flashed into his mind, Laurie and Crandall there on the couch. He stared down at the stain, imagining just how much fear and pain it would have taken to make her do this.

Will blinked and let go of the cushion as if it were too hot to hold. It fell down onto the rug. He swallowed as the wave of nausea roiled his abdomen. He stood there, not daring to move, waiting for it to pass. When he realized that it wasn't going to, he bolted for the bathroom. He managed to throw open the lid of the toilet seat just in time.

He stayed there on his hands and knees on the ceramic tiles of the bathroom floor, his insides emptying until there was nothing left except for strands of viscous bile and wracking dry heaves.

He climbed up and went to the pedestal sink, using the liquid soap to scrub his hands. Then he cupped them together and rinsed out his mouth and splashed cold water onto his face.

He looked at his reflection in the mirrored front of the medicine cabinet. He almost didn't recognize the face that stared back at him. His eyes were sunken back in his skull, blue-black ringing the sockets.

His hair was disheveled, more strands of gray there than he'd ever noticed before, as if they'd been busy breeding while he'd been otherwise distracted.

He stared into his own eyes. There was no way to stop the thinking now, his thoughts coming at him in a jumbled stream, breaching the spillway of the dam. He stood there, gripping the porcelain corners of the sink.

Finally, he straightened up and took a hand towel from the rack. He wiped his face, certain now of what he was going to do.

Will set his nylon backpack on top of the dining room table and unzipped it. He went through the house, trying to gather the things that he might need.

His mind kept wandering off, and he would find himself standing in place in front of a closet door or an open cabinet, having forgotten what it was he had come looking for.

He began tossing anything he could think of into the pack. A flashlight and extra batteries, bottles of water, a roll of duct tape. A pair of binoculars, energy bars, notebooks, his cell phone and the charger. A digital camera, a toothbrush and toothpaste, his sunglasses. He jammed all of it into the backpack until it was full. Then he zipped it closed.

All he needed now was a weapon.

LAPD had seized his gun, keeping it for evidence in the case still pending against him.

Sitting on top of the kitchen counter was a maple block filled with knives. The knives were German, a wedding gift from Laurie's parents. Will pulled out a chef's knife and ran the ball of his thumb along the edge of the blade, testing its sharpness. He wrapped his hand around the black handle and held the knife pointing out in front of him, feeling its satisfying heft.

Then he recognized just how ludicrous the idea was, pictured himself driving along with the big knife lying on the seat beside him, or trying to carry it through the streets of the city.

He slipped it back into the block.

He went out into the garage and flipped on the overhead fluorescent lights. He looked around at the metal racks and the tools that hung on hooks from the walls, his eyes running over the rusted blades of a pair of garden shears.

He took down a claw hammer, then put it back on the pegboard.

A plastic bucket sat in the corner, by the overhead garage door. The bucket was filled with old sports equipment. The handle of a softball bat stuck out from it.

He pulled out the bat and used his palm to wipe away cobwebs. The bat was aluminum, its white barrel decorated with orange and black flames.

Will gripped the bat with both hands and brought the barrel up to his right shoulder. He took a swing in the tight confines of the garage, the bat making a whooshing sound as the head whipped through the air.

He would have to make it work.

He took the bat back inside the house, shutting off lights and locking windows and doors. He checked the answering machine and then slung the backpack onto his shoulder.

He carried the bat in one hand as he locked the front door behind him.

It was time to hunt.

SEVENTY

An unseasonable low pressure system had dropped in from the north-west. A light mist began to fall against the windshield as Will drove along Ventura Boulevard, then became raindrops as he turned onto Laurel Canyon.

Will switched on the wipers, thinking the same irrational thought he always did every time it rained. About Sean, worrying about him getting wet and cold down in the ground.

He found a parking space on Santa Monica. Even though it was early in the afternoon, the neon nautilus shell above the front door of the gym was switched on, glowing with a dull red light.

A young Indian woman was behind the front desk, the same one who was here the night he came after Crandall. Will took this to be a positive, figuring that she would at least know who Crandall was.

There were maybe half a dozen men inside the weight room, work-ing the machines. Will didn't recognize any of them from the last time he was here.

He stepped up to the desk.

"Can I help you—" The woman's eyes widened with recognition. "You need to leave. Right now."

He spoke in a soothing voice. "I'm not going to hurt you. I just want to ask you a couple of questions."

She rolled her chair back, moving away from him. "If you don't leave, I'm calling the police."

"Hold on, I just want to talk to you."

She picked up the phone. "I don't care. I'm calling right now."

Will reached out and put his hand on top of hers. He was gentle, but she pulled away, as if he'd given her an electrical shock.

He looked into her eyes, desperate to make a connection. "That man beat up my wife, she's in the hospital right now. She's seven months pregnant."

A man stood off to the side of the desk, staring at Will. "This guy bothering you, Varsha?"

He took a step toward the desk. He was tall and wore a sweatshirt with the sleeves cut off, the exposed skin of his thick arms glistening with sweat.

The woman looked at the man, then back up at Will, as if trying to decide what to do. The sound of iron plates clanking together came in from the other room.

She smiled at the man. "No, it's fine."

The man stood there a moment longer, giving Will a hard look. Then he turned and headed back toward the weight room.

The woman set the phone back in its cradle. "He really did that? To your wife?"

"Yes."

She nodded. "That guy really creeped me out. I kept catching him staring at me all the time. He'd have this sleazy look on his face."

"Have the police been here looking for him?"

She shook her head. "No, why?"

Will let out his breath. It was an obvious place. If they hadn't even been here, then what the hell were they doing?

"When does he normally come in?"

She pursed her lips. "Now that you ask, I don't think he ever came back here. After what you did to him."

Will looked at the computer on her desk. "You keep members' information in there?"

"Like what?"

"Their addresses?"

"Yes, but I'm not allowed to give that out."

He looked at her. "Please."

She glanced around, as if to make sure no one was watching. She slid the keyboard closer to her but didn't begin to type.

"What's wrong?"

"I don't remember his name."

"Erik Crandall. Erik with a *K*."

She nodded once. "Right. I always thought that was kind of weird." She typed in the name. "We only have his home address."

"That'll work." He smiled as he pulled a reporter's notebook from the back pocket of his jeans. He grabbed a ballpoint from a cup that sat on the counter.

She leaned a little closer to the screen and read from it. "5941 Vesper Avenue, Van Nuys."

She looked up at Will, waiting. "Aren't you going to write it down?"

He didn't answer, just stood there gripping the plastic barrel of the pen, not seeing any point in writing down his own address.

SEVENTY-ONE

The name of the travel agency was Happy Holidays. It was located in a small storefront stuck in the middle of a minimall in Culver City.

It had been tough for Crandall to even find a travel agency; there were less of them around now than before he'd been sent away.

"How can I help you today?" The lady was white but old, with a big nose and half-glasses that hung on a gold chain around her chicken neck.

"I need a plane ticket," Crandall said.

"Great," she said. "Where to?"

"Honduras."

"Honduras? What makes you want to travel down there?"

He hadn't figured on having to answer this question, didn't have an answer prepared. He glanced around the open office. Framed travel posters hung from walls covered with fake wood paneling.

"Just want to get away," he said.

She nodded. "Let me ask you something. Have you ever heard of Sandals?"

Crandall didn't understand what she was asking. "You mean like the shoes?"

She shook her head. "*Sandals*. It's an all-inclusive resort, down in Jamaica."

Crandall didn't get it. "Did I say I wanted to go to Jamaica?"

"No, but if you're looking for some fun in the sun, it's a terrific value."

Crandall looked at her. "Like I said: I want to go to Honduras."

She spun her office chair, so that she faced a computer that sat on one side of her desk. "Why don't we start with your name?"

"Roman," Crandall said. "Roman Follis."

Crandall was wearing the San Francisco Giants cap he'd bought at Dodger Stadium. Below that he now had a full head of long blond hair that reached almost down to his broad shoulders. The hair was a wig, something he'd picked up at a store on Fairfax.

He was also wearing a pair of noncorrective contact lenses that made his normally brown eyes appear light blue. The lenses made his eyes hurt, as if he'd been swimming too long in a public pool.

Crandall had picked up the wig and contacts for the purpose of disguising his appearance, but he also thought they made him look pretty cool, a little like the guy in the commercials for I Can't Believe It's Not Butter.

"Okay, Roman," she said. "What departure date did you have in mind?"

"How about tomorrow?"

She punched some keys on the computer. "There's a direct flight, but it's a redeye, at midnight. Otherwise, you'll need to change planes in Houston."

"I'll take the redeye."

"And the return?"

"Don't worry about it."

She looked at him over the top of the half-glasses. "One way? You really don't save as much as you think. You're better off buying a round-trip now."

Crandall pulled the stress ball from the pocket of his cargo shorts and began to squeeze it.

This lady was really beginning to piss him off. "Just the one-way."

Her long red fingernails made clicking sounds as they tapped the computer keys. "One way in economy is six hundred and fifteen dollars. But I can upgrade you to business for only a hundred and fifty more."

"Economy is good," Crandall said.

She looked at him and smiled. "A big guy like you, you'll be a lot more comfortable in business."

"Economy."

"All right." She cleared her throat. "Do you need a hotel, Roman?"

"No."

"Where will you be staying?"

Crandall stared at her big nose. He wondered what it would be like to snap it off, teach her not to be sticking it in other people's business. He worked the stress ball, telling himself he needed to be cool, not do anything that would make her remember him after the fact.

He forced himself to smile. "I'm late for work. I'd really like to just buy the ticket. Please."

"Forgive me, Roman. I'm just trying to make sure you have a great trip."

"That's nice of you. But can we move this along?"

She cleared her throat again. "How will you be paying?"

"Cash."

"May I see your driver's license, please?"

Crandall looked at her. "I just said I was paying cash."

"I understand. But the rules say I need to see some form of photo identification."

Crandall reached up and scratched his head, the wig itching the shit out of him. He hoped he'd get used to it. He reached into the side pocket of the cargo shorts. He took out a driver's license and passport and held both of them out.

She took the license. "I don't need your passport."

He laid the passport on his lap and flipped open the cover. He looked at the photograph of himself wearing the blond wig and contacts.

The passport looked official, because it was. He'd gotten it from an Armenian he'd met in Quentin, $1,500 for a driver's license, passport, and Visa check card. He hated the name, Roman Follis, but he wasn't given a choice.

The lady handed him back the driver's license, and he counted bills out onto the desk. He was running low on cash, but there was nothing he could do about it.

He was sure now that the cop's wife didn't know where the money was at. When he'd hit her in the stomach, right where the baby was, and she still hadn't given it up? That's when he knew.

He was beginning to think that the cop didn't have the money, either. Maybe he'd gotten it wrong. He wasn't sure who ended up with his dope, or where the money had gone to. Maybe the cop's partner, but he was dead.

In any event, he couldn't afford to burn any more time worrying about it right now. It was time to move on.

"Roman? . . . *Roman?*"

Crandall looked up at her, trying to figure out who the fuck she was talking to. He looked around, but there was no one else inside the office.

Then he realized she was talking to *him*. "Sorry, I was just thinking about something."

He'd have to pay better attention to the name from now on. If he wasn't careful, he could really screw himself up.

"Well, here you go." She handed him his change and a little folder with the name of the travel agency printed on the front. "You have a safe trip."

SEVENTY-TWO

Will used his pen to cross the name of another gym off the list.

He'd torn three pages from the yellow pages, listings for gyms and health clubs. This one was called Equinox, out on Hyperion Avenue in Silver Lake.

He'd been working his way steadily eastward, going from gym to gym, asking people if they'd seen Crandall. So far he'd come up empty. Will figured someone would remember him, thinking that a huge man with eyes tattooed on the back of his bald head would tend to stick out in a person's mind.

He started up the car and continued to head east on Hyperion. The rain had stopped, but the streets were still wet, the potholes filled with shallow puddles that were iridescent with the sheen of motor oil.

He caught a red light at Riverside, staring out through the windshield at the sign for 5 South. He began to think about how easy it would be to just drive onto the ramp and head downtown. To go back to the open-air drug dispensaries on Alvarado.

He wondered if any of his old connects were still around to cop from. He doubted it, given the career longevity of the average urban drug dealer. But he had no doubt that there would be young blood that had stepped up to take their place, ready and willing to come to the aid of a man in need.

There were times when the urge to get high was more than an idle thought, moments when the old and familiar craving became over-powering, making him feel like he needed to lash himself to the near-est mast.

The sensations of what it was like to boot the stuff were permanently etched into his brain, the memory of watching his blood mix with the milky white residue inside the syringe as he drew upward on the plunger, stretching out the moment before he thumbed it back down.

A car horn was honking somewhere behind him. He glanced up and saw that the light had turned green. He looked at the beckoning entrance of the freeway ramp, his knuckles white on the steering wheel. Then he floored the accelerator, cutting off an SUV as he hung a sharp left onto Riverside.

He worked his way to Hollywood Boulevard and drove west, figur-ing that he could count on plenty of visual distractions.

He passed a Thai massage parlor and a storefront fortune-teller, a Scientology Test Center and a bus stop bench with the graffiti-covered face of a real estate agent smiling out from an ad printed on the seat-back.

Backlit signs advertised tacos and tortas, Popeye's Fried Chicken, and foot-long hot dogs, but he was only vaguely aware of the gnawing that came from his stomach, empty after vomiting breakfast.

The sun had already set and the sky turned black. He glanced over at the torn pages of the phone book, thinking that he should get back to work. But he knew that he was only kidding himself. In a city where everyone was obsessed with body image, there were too many gyms.

He crossed Formosa, the neighborhood now becoming more resi-dential, first with low-slung apartment buildings that had canvas aw-nings covering their entrances, then with flat-roofed houses hiding behind clipped hedges and painted stucco walls.

He dropped down onto Sunset and took Coldwater up to Mulholland, climbing up into the Cahuenga Pass.

He looked down at the lights. Red lights that blinked from the top of high-rises in Century City and the warm lights that glowed from behind the picture windows of houses, houses spreading out in every direction, hundreds of thousands of them.

He thought about all the people inside the houses, wondering what they were doing at this moment, imagining scenes of idealized domesticity, families seated at candlelit dining tables, gathered around board games, tucking children safely into beds.

He grabbed the 101 at Cahuenga, the oncoming headlights making his head throb. His eyes felt like they had receded and were now located at the back of his skull.

His exit was coming up, so he merged into the right lane. He wanted to see Laurie more than anything, just to sit there beside her hospital bed.

But how could he? He wasn't about to lie to her; when she found out what he was up to, she'd freak out. He knew that he couldn't see her until this was done. Even then, she might not understand.

He kept driving, afraid of what he might do if he stopped.

The luminous green sign for the Encino exit zoomed past overhead. In his mind's eye he saw Suzie Miller sitting alone inside the empty house, her reflection trapped in the blank screen of the television set, an insect preserved in amber.

He got off the freeway and drove through Reseda and Northridge, eventually making his way over to the 5 and heading north. He threaded the Volvo through convoys of semitrucks until he had to stop for gas outside of Castaic.

He pumped gas beneath a soaring metal canopy, the underside lined with glowing fluorescent tubes, an oasis of light surrounded by the empty darkness. The credit card reader on the pump was broken, so he went inside the mini mart to pay.

He attempted to strike up a conversation with the attendant behind the counter, but the man's vocabulary seemed limited to the minimum number of English words he needed to perform his duties at the cash register.

He continued to head north, driving the freeway. He kept to the middle lane, going with the flow of traffic. At one point, he caught himself falling asleep and lowered the window. The night air smelled like rain.

Well after midnight, the thoughts came. He argued with them, trying to hold them back, but they started coming at him too fast, in waves that made him grit his teeth.

He reached into the door pocket and grabbed the first CD he touched, feeding it into the mouth of the player without bothering to see what it was. He cranked up the volume, desperate to drown out his thoughts.

From the first strummed guitar chord he knew what he was listening to.

Dylan, *Blood on the Tracks.*

When "You're a Big Girl Now" came on he tried to focus his mind on the lyrics, but for some reason they only made him think of Laurie.

The headlights of the oncoming cars began to blur, and he switched on the windshield wipers. When they had no effect he realized that it wasn't raining.

He managed to steer the car onto the shoulder of the freeway and switched off the engine. The car shook, buffeted by the big rigs that thundered past.

He sat alone inside the car, the only light coming from the green glow of the dashboard.

He laid his forehead down on the rim of the steering wheel and let the tears come.

SEVENTY-THREE

The sunlight woke him.

Will sat up, not sure where he was at first. Then everything came flooding back, and he realized that he'd just spent the night in the car. Just like the old days.

He managed to get his sunglasses onto his face and looked out through the windshield. He was parked on the side of the freeway, somewhere he didn't recognize. He saw trees and dun-colored rocks, but no landmarks that were familiar to him.

The dashboard clock read 7:19. He was both surprised and relieved that CHP hadn't discovered him sleeping there.

He started the engine and drove north until he came to the first exit. He got off and turned himself around, heading back toward the city.

The South Central parole office of the California Department of Corrections and Rehabilitation was located on South Alameda, not far from the Rampart police station.

Will parked in the fenced lot and went inside the building.

A receptionist sat behind a thick Plexiglas window, the rest of the offices on the other side of a steel security door with a web of chicken wire set in the glass of its window.

Will stood there, trying to figure out how to play it. He hadn't really thought through his plan, knew only that he needed to somehow get Crandall's address from his parole officer. He knew that if he just told the receptionist who he was and what he wanted, Nguyen would blow him off.

He stepped up to the window. "Detective Denslowe for Tony Nguyen."

He felt self-conscious about his appearance after sleeping in the car. He'd used a gas station restroom to freshen up, but it was a lost cause. Hopefully, she'd think he was working undercover.

The receptionist was an African American woman with colorful plastic beads adorning the ends of her braided hair. "I'll let him know you're here."

He paced the lobby, afraid he might not be able to get back up again if he sat down.

A few minutes later, the security door buzzed, and the receptionist held it open for him. "Follow me."

She led him through a maze of cubicles that had low walls covered with a gray hopsack fabric.

She stopped in front of one. "Here you are," she said as she walked away.

Tony Nguyen was a short and fit Asian man with a crew cut. He got up from his desk and extended a hand. "I apologize for not returning your call, Detective. I've been out on vacation."

"Nice." Will shook his limp hand. "Where to?"

"Cancún," Nguyen said. "Time-share."

"Then I guess you haven't heard the news." Will looked at him. "I mean, since you were on vacation."

"What news is that?"

"Erik Crandall assaulted a pregnant woman."

Nguyen cocked his head. "Erik who?"

Will tried to keep from screaming. "Erik Crandall."

"I'm sorry," Nguyen said, "but what does this have to do with me?"

Will tried to breathe, looking around Nguyen's cubicle. File folders were strewn over every inch of his desktop.

"Crandall's one of yours," Will said. "I called you a while back to tell you that he'd threatened me. But you didn't do anything, and now my wife's in the hospital."

"Your wife? I don't understand." Nguyen stared at Will as if seeing him now for the first time.

He pointed a finger at Will. "You're not Denslowe."

"No, I'm not."

Nguyen took a step toward the cubicle's exit. "I can respect that you're looking for someone to blame here, but this isn't my fault."

"No? So what exactly did you do to prevent it?"

"You need to calm down."

Will took a step toward him. "I am calm."

"Look, you need to understand, I'm carrying a full caseload. I'm completely swamped."

"Then how come you just went on vacation?"

"We can't carry it forward. If I don't take it, I lose it."

"I hope you enjoyed it. Because my son might not live."

"I'm sorry to hear that, but you shouldn't even be back here. You need to leave."

"I'll leave as soon as you give me Crandall's home address."

"You know I'm not allowed to do that. Technically, I shouldn't even be talking to you."

Will tried to remember a training course he'd been required to take when he was with LAPD. The course had been called Verbal Judo, and its purpose was to teach cops how to handle confrontations without resorting to the use of force.

The instructor had used a lot of acronyms as memory aids, but Will found that he couldn't remember any of them. The only thing he could now recall was that it was important to let the other person save face.

To give him some way to comply with what you were asking him to do without making him look bad.

Will nodded his head. "I realize you've got an impossible job to do here, and that you're trying to do your best."

It almost killed Will to say it, but there it was.

"Okay," Nguyen said. "But you still have to leave."

"Will you give me Crandall's address?"

Nguyen shook his head. "If I did that, I'd lose my job."

Will now remembered something else from the training. That it was important to make the other person see that it was in his best interest to go along with what you were asking him to do.

"I want to see you keep your job, too," Will said. "That's why you need to give me that address."

"What're you talking about?"

"If you give me the address, I won't talk to the newspapers."

"I'm afraid I don't understand."

"Think about how much the press is going to love this story: Bureaucratic ineptitude results in a parolee assaulting a pregnant woman. They'll eat that shit up."

Nguyen's mouth tightened. "You do whatever you feel you need to."

"You're not thinking this through, Tony. This story hits the papers, you know there's going to have to be some kind of an investigation. That's just the way it works. Someone's head is going to need to go on the platter, am I right?"

Nguyen didn't argue, but Will could tell that he was thinking about it.

Will looked away, giving Nguyen some space. A bagel smeared with cream cheese sat on an open piece of deli paper on the desk. His empty stomach rumbled.

Nguyen cleared his throat. "Hypothetically, let's say I did try to help you out here, how do I know it's not going to come back to me?"

Will spread open his hands. "It won't. But even if it did, it would be your word against mine. Who do you think they're going to believe?"

Nguyen took a step over to his desk and looked down at his hoard of file folders. "What's this guy's name again?"

Will gritted his teeth. "Erik Crandall. E-R-I-K—"

Nguyen gave him a sharp look. "I'm not an idiot."

It took every ounce of Will's self-control to keep his mouth shut.

Nguyen started to shuffle through the folders. He grabbed one from a stack and flipped it open. Then he set it down in the middle of his desktop.

"I've got to take a leak," Nguyen said. He tapped his index finger against the cover of the folder, looking straight at Will. "Please don't touch anything on my desk while I'm gone."

Will nodded. "Thanks."

After Nguyen was out of sight, Will opened the folder and flipped through the pages inside until he came to a blue form.

He ran his eyes down the page until he came to the lines that listed Crandall's residence address. He grabbed a Post-it from Nguyen's desk and wrote down the address.

As he was closing the file he noticed a pink message slip that was stapled to the inside of the file jacket. At the top were the words WHILE YOU WERE OUT.

The slip was dated two days ago. It indicated that Crandall had called to say that he was going to miss his appointment. There was a phone number on the slip. Will wrote it down on the Post-it.

Then he closed the folder and walked away.

SEVENTY-FOUR

Crandall stood naked in front of the full-length mirror on the bathroom door, checking himself out.

He'd just come back from the indoor tanning place, thinking it was a good idea for him not to look so white when he showed up in Honduras.

He'd sprung for the "Full-Body Spray Tan," like going to Earl Scheib the way they'd painted his body with the spray nozzles.

He smiled at his reflection, his teeth now looking unnaturally white. He turned in place, looking to make sure they hadn't missed any spots.

Maybe it was the bathroom's fluorescent lights, but he thought the color of the tan looked off, more yellow than brown, like he'd been dipped in Gulden's mustard.

He went over to the dresser and put on a sleeveless white undershirt and his red Fila tracksuit.

He winced when he pulled on the shirt, his upper back killing him from where the bitch had stabbed him with the scissors. The way it was throbbing, he was starting to worry it might be infected. He wondered if it'd been a mistake to get the tanning spray into the wound.

He thought about whether he should try to see a doctor before he blew town. He wasn't sure what the medical care situation was like down where he was going. Maybe later, if he had any time left. Right now, there was something more important he needed to take care of.

He looked down at the twin bed, the things he'd stolen from the cop's house laid out on top of the bedspread. His plan was to take it all downtown and pawn it, get himself some road money.

A far cry from what he figured he'd be walking away with, but he was out of options.

He picked up a small nylon duffel bag that had a Tommy Bahama logo silk-screened onto one side. He unzipped it and started tossing in the stolen goods.

He grabbed a handful of the wife's jewelry, none of it looking all that expensive.

Just a gold necklace with a heart-shaped locket that had a photograph of a gray-haired old lady inside. A bunch of Indian-looking bracelets with pieces of turquoise on them. He'd also taken some forks and knives and spoons that he was hoping might be made out of real silver.

With any luck, this stuff would net him enough cash to make it down to Honduras, get himself settled. Then he'd have to look for some kind of job. He didn't think it was going to be too much of a problem, figured they could probably use somebody like him down there, knew how to speak English. Maybe he could even open a gym, teach the Hondurans—or whatever the fuck they called themselves—about bodybuilding.

He drained what was left in his can of grape soda, looking down at the final item that lay on the bedspread.

He picked up the little red notebook and leafed through the pages.

It'd been hidden inside the cop's house, duct-taped to the bottom of a desk drawer. He'd taken it, figuring it had to be important.

Crandall had looked at it over and over, trying to figure out what it was about, but it was filled with random letters and numbers, none of it meaning anything.

He stared at the pages, trying one more time to figure out if there was anything that he could do with the notebook, but couldn't come up with anything.

Just another dead end.

Fuck it. He turned and threw the notebook into the trash can.

SEVENTY-FIVE

Will stood listening outside the steel door.

It was hard for him to tell for sure, but he thought that he could hear Crandall moving around on the other side. He tightened his grip on the padded handle of the softball bat, his palm sweating.

He found it difficult to think because his heart was hammering so fast. He wondered if he should call the police, then rejected the idea.

The door casing was also made of steel. He doubted he'd be able to kick in the door with one blow, and couldn't afford to lose the element of surprise. He thought that he might be able to use his driver's license to spring the lock but was afraid it would make too much noise.

He reached out and put his hand on the door latch. He was just testing it and was surprised to find that it moved, not even locked.

He took a deep breath to gather himself and then twisted the latch as he threw his shoulder into the door. He raised the bat up to his shoulder as he went through the doorway.

Bright sunlight came through a set of sliding glass doors, blinding him as he tried to scan the room.

He gripped the bat handle with both hands and cocked it back, ready to swing.

The apartment was a single rectangular room, a small kitchen on the other side of the laminate counter. There were some pieces of furniture, but otherwise the room was completely empty.

The door to the bathroom was ajar. Will went inside and flipped on the light switch.

The fluorescent fixture over the mirror flickered to life. Pink tiles lined the walls. He used the barrel of the bat to slide open the shower curtain. The metal rings made a metallic scraping noise as they slid along the chromed rod, but no one was hiding inside the tub.

The white porcelain of the sink gleamed, as if it had just been scrubbed.

He felt light-headed as the adrenaline drained out of him.

He went back into the kitchen and began to throw open cabinets and pull out drawers. He found nothing inside, everything empty.

Something on the living room wall caught his eye. A spot where the paint didn't quite match, darker than the lighter shade of white that surrounded it. He ran his fingertips over the wall and could tell that the Sheetrock had been patched, the section of wall freshly painted.

The apartment felt stuffy, as if it had been sealed up for a while. The air smelled of cleaning chemicals. He went through the closets but found nothing to indicate that the apartment was occupied.

He went over to the patio door and slid it open. A preprinted plastic sign was taped to the outside of the glass, orange letters on black, the kind of thing you could buy in a hardware store:

FOR RENT

Will stepped out onto the small balcony. The sunlight was too bright, and he could hear the traffic moving along the street down below. He felt his shirt pocket for his sunglasses but realized he'd left them in the car.

Had he somehow gotten the address wrong? He pulled the yellow Post-it note from his pocket and looked at it. There was no doubt about it; he was certain that he was in the right place.

His chest tightened with anger. Could Parole really be that inept? Not even capable of keeping track of a parolee's address?

He started to put the Post-it away but then noticed the phone number he'd written down from the message slip.

The phone number Crandall had left had a 310 area code, meaning it was on the west side. Not out here in K-town.

Will took out his cell phone and flipped it open. He punched in the number from the Post-it, the blank windows of the neighboring buildings staring out at him.

He listened to the electronic ringing.

A male voice answered. "Good morning, Sundowner Lodge."

SEVENTY-SIX

The Sundowner Lodge was a two-story 1960s motel designed in a Polynesian theme. The facade was covered with fake rocks, the building's two wings bracketing a swimming pool that was shaped like a kidney.

The motel sat at the southwest corner of a busy intersection, close to LAX.

The man behind the desk was young and had thick eyebrows that almost joined together above his bent nose. "Checking in?"

"I'm looking for one of your guests."

"Name?"

"Crandall. Erik Crandall."

The clerk tapped keys on a dated desktop computer. A cardboard sign thumbtacked to the wall invited Will to ASK US ABOUT OUR HOURLY RATES.

"Sorry, he's not registered here."

"Are you sure?"

"Positive. We're pretty empty right now."

"Maybe he checked out? He said he was staying here."

"When was this?"

Will tried to recall the date on the message slip. "Couple of days ago."

The clerk clicked more keys on the computer, then shook his head. "No one with that last name."

Will struggled to think straight through the haze of exhaustion. "It's possible he registered under a different name. He's a big guy, bald. Has a pair of eyes tattooed on the back of his head."

The clerk's eyes widened. "Oh, *that* guy. Yeah, he's staying here."

"Can you please give me his room number?"

"I'm not allowed. But I can ring the room for you."

Will didn't want to tip Crandall off that he was here but wasn't sure how else to get up to his room.

Will smiled. "That's okay, I'm a friend of his. Is the room next door available, something with an adjoining door?"

The clerk began to say something, then changed his mind and went back to the computer. A television set in the office was on, the actors speaking what sounded like Arabic.

The clerk stopped tapping the keys. "I think I've got something."

"Great."

The clerk looked at him. "You guys looking to party?"

"What do you mean?"

"You interested in some girls, anything like that? I can hook you up."

"I'll let you know."

"No problem."

"What about the room?" Will pointed at the computer. "Does it have an adjoining door?"

The clerk nodded. "Looks like you're in luck."

The room was up on the second floor. All of the motel's rooms were accessed by an exterior corridor that had a metal safety railing along its outer edge.

Will used the plastic key card to open his room. He stepped inside and switched on the light, carrying the softball bat in one hand. A full-length mirror hung on the door that led to the adjoining room. He opened the door, exposing a second door that was closed from Crandall's side.

Will put his ear up against the painted wooden surface of the door and listened. A plane roared as it passed overhead, shaking the thin walls of the motel. No sound came from the other side of the door.

Will pushed against the door, but it was locked. There was no lock hardware on this side of the door.

Will took a step back. He paused there for a minute until he heard another plane passing overhead. He counted silently to three, then raised his right foot and drove the sole of his hiking boot hard into the edge of the door.

Wood splintered as the door flew inward, glass shattering as it banged against the wall of Crandall's room.

Will raised the bat in both hands as he went through the doorway. Crandall's room was dark, the only illumination what came in through the open adjoining door.

The two twin beds were both made, covered with floral-patterned bedspreads. He checked the bathroom, but it was empty.

Will switched on the table lamp that stood on the dresser. Shards from the shattered mirror lay in a heap on the green pile carpeting.

The room was a mirror image of the one next door: worn furniture, peeling wallpaper, and water stains on the cottage cheese ceiling. The air held the scent of the same cologne he'd smelled in his living room.

Folded clothes were laid out on top of one of the twin beds. They looked like they would belong to Crandall: nylon tracksuits, Under Armour shirts, pairs of white anklet socks rolled into tight balls.

He began to search the room, starting with the low dresser. The top drawer was empty except for a white envelope that had the name of the motel printed in the upper left corner. Will picked it up.

The flap of the envelope was not sealed.

Will peered inside it, saw confetti-like strips of white paper. They were printed with red ink.

He pulled out one of the strips and read it:

KEEP YOUR PLANS SECRET FOR NOW.

He put the fortune back inside the envelope and used his index finger to poke through the rest of the strips of paper, nothing but a collection of fortunes.

The rest of the dresser was empty. So was the open closet.

He slid open the drawer of the night table.

Lying beside the Gideon Bible was a gun.

He picked it up. The gun was heavy and oversized, like something out of a comic book. He turned it over and saw that the safety was off. He switched it on and pulled back the slide to check if the gun was loaded.

There was a round in the chamber, the clip full.

Will slid the gun down inside the waistband of his jeans at the small of his back. It felt too heavy, like carrying around a brick.

A black metal garbage can sat beneath the desk. Will started to reach his hand inside before thinking better of it.

He upended the can and emptied the contents out on top of the desk. He jumped back when a syringe fell out, not wanting to get stuck.

The syringe was huge, not like anything Will had seen before.

He took a pen from his shirt pocket and used it to sort through the other objects from the trash can.

A cardboard Chinese takeout container with a pagoda printed on its side leaked dark sauce. He pushed aside an empty can of grape soda and spotted a glass vial. He turned it over, the label warning that it was for veterinary use only.

He used the tip of the pen to move aside some wadded-up balls of Kleenex, his breath catching in his throat when he saw what else was there on the wood-grain surface of the desk.

He picked up the red ledger. He opened the cover and flipped through the pages, relieved to see that they were all still there. He slid the ledger inside the back pocket of his jeans.

Then he froze in place when he heard a key card being fitted into the lock of the motel room's door.

SEVENTY-SEVEN

Crandall slid the plastic card into the slot above the door handle.

He yanked the card back out, but the little light flashed red. He checked the number on the door to make sure that he had the right room, then tried again, pulling the card out slower this time.

The light flashed green.

He pressed down on the metal lever to open the door, then stepped inside the motel room. He left the door open as he bent over to untie his sneakers.

He'd stepped in a mound of dog shit when he was on his way back to the car, didn't want to track it onto the carpet.

He pulled off his left shoe and turned it over to examine the extent of the damage. The pair of Nikes was almost brand-new, and now look at them. He caught a whiff of the mess, no idea how he was going to clean it out of all the little indentations of the rubber sole. He'd probably have to scrub it out with his toothbrush.

What the fuck was it with people? Couldn't even be bothered to clean up after their pets, as if the sidewalk was their dog's personal toilet, no concern whatsoever for someone who might actually want to use it for the purpose it was actually intended.

Crandall got the other sneaker off, then started to close the door.

The table lamp on the dresser was on. He could've sworn that he'd switched it off before he left. He stared at it, figuring the maid must have turned it on.

He shut the door, almost jumping when he saw the cop standing there. He must've been hiding behind the open door the whole time.

Crandall was caught off guard. "What the fuck?"

"Hello, Erik," the cop said.

He looked different now than Crandall remembered him. His hair was messy, sticking up in tufts. He was pale, and his eyes had a look that reminded Crandall of the way guys looked after they'd pulled a long stretch in the hole.

Then Crandall saw what the cop had in his hand.

A gun.

He looked closer and realized it wasn't just any gun—it was *his* gun. Crandall's head started to throb at the sight of the *lying-thieving-conniving-asshole* cop's dirty hands touching the Eagle. Without even thinking about it, Crandall reached out to take it back.

The cop must have been looking out for it, because he stepped back and brought his gun hand up in a smooth motion.

The gun was now pointing right at the center of Crandall's chest. He could see that the hammer of the gun was already cocked back.

"Don't move," the cop said.

"That's my fucking gun."

"What's wrong, Erik? You don't like it when people take your things?"

Crandall's head felt like it was about to explode. He was seeing everything now through a film of red.

The cop motioned at him with the gun. "Now put your hands up against the wall."

SEVENTY-EIGHT

At first, Will almost didn't recognize Crandall.

He was wearing a ridiculous-looking wig under a San Francisco Giants baseball cap. His skin had an ugly jaundiced coloration, and something about his eyes seemed different.

Crandall turned and placed his hands up against the peeling wallpaper.

"Spread your legs apart," Will said.

Crandall didn't move.

Will kicked his feet apart.

"Take it easy," Crandall said.

"Then start listening to what I say, Erik."

Will used his left hand to pat down Crandall's powerful arms and torso, then ran his hand over Crandall's legs, his thighs like tree trunks.

Will straightened up, confident that Crandall was unarmed. "Place your hands on top of your head and turn around."

He wished that he still had his handcuffs, but they'd been confiscated by LAPD along with the gun.

Crandall turned. "Now what?"

Will looked him in the face as he spoke. "This ends now. You crossed the line, you shouldn't have touched my wife."

"You didn't give me any choice."

Will shook his head. "Every criminal I ever arrested, you know what they all had in common?"

"No, but I've got the feeling you're going to tell me."

"They all had a reason for the things they did. Some justification."

"What's your point?"

"I don't want to hear your bullshit."

A plane flew overhead, making the window rattle.

Will used the gun to motion in the direction of the beds. "Move over there."

Crandall cocked his head, searching Will's face. "What're you going to do? Shoot me with my own gun?"

"Now you know why they say it's dangerous to keep a gun around the house."

"You're not worried about going to prison? Because believe me, you wouldn't make it a day inside."

"I'm not going to get caught. I'm going to make it look like you committed suicide. Just like the way you did Ray Miller."

Crandall looked at him. "Who?"

Will felt like shooting him right where he stood. "Move, asshole."

"Wait, I'm being serious. Who're you talking about?"

"My ex-partner."

Crandall's mouth dropped open. "I already told you, I didn't kill him. I swear."

"Have it your way. Now move."

Crandall held up his palms in a placating gesture. "You expect me to beg?"

"No, Erik. I expect you to die." Will gestured again with the gun. "Get down on the bed."

Crandall looked at him. "What for?"

"So you don't make noise when you hit the ground."

"I've got to hand it to you. You really know how to think things through."

Will shook his head. "If that were true, I wouldn't be here. Now shut up and sit down on the bed."

Crandall sat. "You don't want me to write a note or anything?"

"I think the situation speaks for itself: Lonesome fugitive with nowhere left to run takes the easy way out. Besides, it's not like LAPD's going to be busting their ass trying to investigate the situation. They'll just zip up the bag and call it a day."

Will took a step toward Crandall, putting the muzzle of the gun up to his right temple. Close but not quite touching. He tried to think it through, trying to picture how Crandall would hold the gun in his own hand, wanting to get the angle right.

He kept an eye on the other man's hands. He didn't like standing this close to Crandall, knowing how easy it would be for him to grab the gun.

He looked at the pillow lying on the bed, thinking that maybe he should wrap it around the barrel of the gun to muffle the sound. He rejected the idea, since there was no way it would fit with the suicide scenario.

He took some of the slack out of the trigger. He watched Crandall's eyes, wanting the satisfaction of seeing his fear, some measure of payback for the hell he'd put Laurie through.

But there was nothing there. Crandall just sat on the bed and looked up at Will, his palms resting on top of his thighs. Almost serene.

"I warned you," Will said, talking to himself now as much as to Crandall. "I told you to stay away from my family."

Crandall didn't say anything. He just sat there, gazing up at Will.

Will wished that Crandall would open his mouth. If only he'd start talking again, spinning his lies, it would make it easier to do what he needed to do.

Will's hands poured sweat, the checkered grips of the big gun becoming slick. This was the situation he'd been fantasizing about, this very moment, but now that it was real everything felt wrong.

He'd forgotten just how tough it is to pull the trigger, to shoot another human being at close range. He'd done it three times before, but for some reason he found that only made it more difficult now, the looming knowledge of what it was like to carry around the fallout.

Crandall didn't move. He sat on the edge of the twin bed and stared up at Will. He looked somehow smaller now, childlike. His lips turned upward in a beatific smile.

Will made himself picture Laurie in his mind, trying to psych himself into action, the way she looked when he found her lying there on the couch.

He told himself to just squeeze the trigger, but he was having a hard time doing it with Crandall looking at him.

The room started to shake as a jet rumbled up in the sky, and then Crandall's left hand was somehow up in the air, too close to the gun. Will pulled his gun hand back, but Crandall's fingers wrapped around the barrel, crushing Will's forefinger inside the trigger guard.

Will tried to fire the gun, but his finger wouldn't move, nothing but pain.

Crandall grinned a jagged jack-o'-lantern smile.

He twisted the gun, forcing the top of Will's hand back toward his wrist. Will gritted his teeth as he tried to resist, but he was overwhelmed by Crandall's strength.

Crandall gave another twist on the gun, and Will felt bone grind against bone.

He tried to block out the pain, to focus on just holding on to the gun, but his palms were too slick with sweat, and then his hand was suddenly empty.

Crandall rose up from the twin bed, moving surprisingly fast for such a big man.

He pointed the gun at Will's chest, his grin wider now. "You stick a gun in my face, you best be prepared to use it, jackass."

Will watched as the hand that was holding the gun began to move, the dark metal finish becoming a blur.

The side of Will's head exploded with pain. The world spun away and then went dark.

SEVENTY-NINE

Will regained consciousness on the dirty carpeting of Crandall's motel room.

He blinked his eyes and saw that he was in the back corner of the room, just outside the bathroom. The left side of his head throbbed, the worst headache he'd ever experienced.

He tried to reach up to cradle his aching skull, but his wrists were bound behind his back. He looked down at his legs and saw a wide strip torn from the bedsheet knotted around his ankles.

He heard a toilet being flushed. Crandall walked out of the bathroom and passed in front of Will without looking down at him. Will held his breath, trying to keep quiet.

Crandall went over to one of the twin beds and began to pack the folded clothes inside a nylon duffel bag. Will watched him, trying to get his aching brain to figure out what he might do next.

A wave of nausea hit, and he leaned over to vomit. He retched, but nothing came up.

Crandall stopped what he was doing and looked at Will, no trace of emotion on his face.

"You're weak, dude. I knew you wouldn't be able to use that gun."

Will swallowed. "Want to give me another try?"

Crandall snorted. "You should've killed me while you had the chance."

He put the last items of clothing inside the duffel and walked over to Will. He stood there, towering over him, a giant in a long blond wig. He reached his right hand inside the bag.

Will was sure he was about to pull out the gun. He tried to work his wrists loose from the bonds, but they were tied too tight, no give in the fabric.

Crandall's hand emerged from the duffel. It wasn't holding the gun.

He held out the red ledger. "I found this in your pocket."

Will stared up at the ledger but didn't say anything.

"Want to tell me what it's about?"

"What do you mean?"

"It must be pretty important. You hide it inside your desk, then try and steal it back from me."

"It's nothing."

Crandall stared down. "Nothing."

"It's personal, is all. Believe me, it's not important."

Crandall's foot shot forward and kicked Will in the forehead. Crandall didn't have shoes on, but Will still felt like he was about to pass out from the pain.

Crandall crouched down, staring into Will's eyes. "You sure it's nothing important?"

"Yeah."

"Then I guess you won't mind if I hang on to it."

Crandall stood and put the ledger back inside the duffel bag. He turned away and walked toward the door of the motel room. He looked around the room, as if checking to make sure that he wasn't leaving anything behind.

He bent over and pulled on a pair of sneakers, then tied the laces.

He went to the door and put his hand on the lever and looked at Will. "It's been real."

"What happens to me?"

"Nothing. I'd like to shoot you, but the last thing I need right now is a murder beef hanging over my head."

Will felt the tension drain from his muscles. He'd been sure that Crandall was planning to kill him.

Crandall opened the door, late afternoon sunlight spilling in through the opening.

Will shivered even though it was too warm inside the room. He tried to think of something he could do or say. Once Crandall walked out that door, Will would have nothing. He'd have no shot at Byrnes, and Crandall would waltz off into the sunset.

"Hang on."

Crandall turned and looked at him. "*Jesus.* I thought this was what you wanted, right? Me out of your life?"

Will couldn't think of anything to say. It was too hard to think with all the pain. He concentrated, the roughest outline of a plan taking shape inside his mind.

"I know a way to get you back your money."

Crandall cocked his head. "I thought you didn't have it."

"I don't, but I know who does. And I know how to get him to give it to you."

Crandall shut the door. "I'm listening."

"His name is Dennis Byrnes."

"The politician?"

"That's right."

Crandall walked through the room and stared down at Will. "I watched the dude you're talking about break into your house."

"Bullshit. You're the one who broke into my house."

Crandall shook his head. "I'm telling you, it was this Byrnes guy. I only broke in your house the one time, to scare you with the blood."

Will stared up at him. "What do you mean, you saw him break into my house?"

"What I said. I was watching your place. One night, he showed up and snuck in through the back."

"When was this?"

Crandall rubbed his hand against his chin. "I don't know, about a month ago."

Fuck, how could he have been so stupid? Laurie had noticed the break-in right after he'd told Byrnes about the ledger. He'd been so obsessed with Crandall that he'd completely missed it.

"So tell me something," Crandall said. "Why is it he broke into your house?"

Will used his chin to point toward the duffel bag Crandall was holding. "Because of that ledger."

"Why is it everyone wants it so fucking bad?"

"There was a conspiracy inside LAPD. Some cops were selling the dope from drug busts—"

"I fucking knew it," Crandall said.

"That ledger implicates Byrnes. Trust me, he'll pay you your money to get it back."

"Five hundred grand?"

Will nodded. "He should be able to swing that."

Crandall stood there, breathing through his mouth as he thought it through. "Say I did want to do this, how would we work it?"

"I'd call Byrnes, set a meeting. Tell him you'll trade him the ledger for cash."

"I wish you could've told me this a little earlier. I've got a plane to catch."

"What time?"

"Midnight."

"That should work. Let me give him a call."

Crandall nodded his head. "You better not be bullshitting me."

"I'm not. Hand me your cell."

Crandall pulled a cell phone from the pocket of his warm-up jacket but didn't give it to him. "What's in this for you?"

"Everything that's happened? It's all because of Byrnes. I want to nail him, and you're going to help me."

Crandall held up his hand. "Who said anything about helping you?"

"You want revenge on the guy who stole your drugs? Well, he's the one. Do you want to let him just walk away, after what he did to you?"

"The only thing I want is my money."

Will nodded. "We can kill two birds with one stone."

EIGHTY

Crandall steered the Town Car through the dark streets.

Will sat alone in the backseat, like a businessman being chauffeured to a meeting. The headlights of passing cars were knives inside his skull.

He shifted forward on the leather seat and tried to loosen the knot in the strip of fabric that bound his wrists. Crandall had already freed his ankles before they'd left the motel room.

Will winced when he broke off a fingernail, but couldn't manage to make any progress with the knot.

Crandall glanced up at the rearview mirror. Will stopped what he was doing and sat back in the seat.

"You sure we really need to get this thing?" Crandall asked.

They were on their way to Will's house to pick up the wire and recorder that Will had found in the box in the garage.

"Like I told you, I want to record Byrnes when he pays you off for the ledger."

"Then I'll be on the tape, too. It'll incriminate me."

"You're already incriminated, remember? Besides, I thought you were leaving the country."

"I never told you that."

"You didn't have to. You said you had a plane to catch. I figured you weren't headed for New Jersey."

"I still don't like it."

"We had a deal, Erik. We do it this way, or I'm not going to tell you where the meet is."

Crandall grinned. "I listened to you talking to him on the phone. I heard you say something about a sanitarium, by the academy."

"So you know where that is?"

Crandall didn't answer.

"I didn't think so," Will said.

"Whatever. But if it comes down to it, I'm all about the money. I don't give a shit about your recording."

Crandall got off the freeway at Burbank Boulevard. He stopped for a red light in front of a Salvadoran restaurant that he and Laurie liked going to. On the other side of the restaurant's plate glass window, a couple ate dinner at a table lit by a votive candle set inside a small glass.

The air inside the car reeked of Crandall's cologne. The smell mixed with the artificial strawberry scent from a cardboard pine tree that dangled from the rearview.

"Do you think you could crack my window a little?" Will asked.

Crandall shook his head. "I got the air on."

The big car rolled along through the Valley, the interior of the Town Car as quiet as a tomb.

Crandall cleared his throat. "Just so you know? This hasn't exactly turned out the way I wanted it, either."

"Thanks for sharing."

Crandall kept checking him out in the rearview, as if trying to figure out whether to say something else. "What I did to your wife? It wasn't personal."

Will's hands clenched into fists behind his back. "That means a lot to me, Erik. That really changes everything."

"I mean it. I never meant to hurt her. All I wanted was to find my money."

Will gritted his teeth, but it only made the pain in his head worse.

Crandall looked at him in the rearview. "So is she going to be okay?"

"Do me a favor, Erik," Will said. "Just shut up and drive."

Will unlocked the front door of the house and walked through the living room, Crandall following a step behind.

Will used his chin to gesture at the disorder of the room. "Look familiar?"

He led them out into the garage and told Crandall to turn on the overhead fluorescents.

Crandall looked around at the boxes set in racks and the tools hanging from their hooks on the walls. "You keep things real neat in here. Organized."

Will's wrists were still bound. He gestured at the boxes on the top shelf of the metal rack. "It's up there."

Crandall reached up but grabbed the wrong box. He began to take down the one that was filled with Sean's old clothing.

Will stepped forward, not wanting Crandall touching it. "Not *that* one."

Crandall turned and looked at him. "*Jesus.* Calm down."

"The one to the right."

Crandall pulled the box down and set it on top of the workbench. He started to take off the lid but then stopped. "This better not be some kind of trick."

Will stared at him. "Like *what*?"

Crandall hesitated for a moment, then took off the lid. The framed softball photograph lay at the top, Ray's face smiling up at Will.

"It's in there," Will said.

Crandall began to root through the objects from Will's glory days as a police officer. He pulled out the handheld receiver and the small tape recorder.

"This it?" Crandall asked.

"That's the receiver. We still need the wire."

Crandall stuck his hands back inside the box, shoving things around until he came out with the wireless transmitter. The tiny microphone and its cable were still wrapped around the body of the transmitter.

Crandall held it up, studying it. "This the same one you used to bust me?"

"Could be," Will said.

EIGHTY-ONE

Crandall turned the Town Car into the deserted parking lot of Barlow Sanitarium and switched off the engine.

A single streetlight stood in the center of the parking lot. The moon was almost full. The trees on the hillside across the street were etched with silver light, the boarded-up cottages dark forms climbing up the scrubby slope.

They sat inside the darkness of the car's interior, the engine making a ticking sound as it began to cool. The digital clock on the dashboard read 9:10. Byrnes was due to arrive at ten.

Crandall climbed out of the driver's seat and walked around the front of the car to let Will out. The wire and tape recorder lay beside him on the backseat.

Crandall opened the door. "Let's go."

Will managed to get out, his hands still bound behind his back. When he stood up he became light-headed, on the verge of passing out. He wasn't sure if it was from exhaustion, hunger, or being struck in the head. Most likely, a combination of all three.

The sound of crickets was loud, almost drowning out the roar of the nearby freeway.

Will looked at Crandall. "You have any flashlights?"

"In the trunk."

They went around to the back of the car, and Crandall used a button on the key to pop the trunk lid. He took out a metal-bodied flashlight and switched it on. The beam was weak and yellow against the pavement.

"Do you have any batteries?"

"What do I look like, a 7-Eleven?"

Will spotted a tire iron inside the trunk. "You should grab that."

"What for?"

"We need something to get the plywood off the cottage door."

Crandall picked up the tire iron and closed the trunk.

"Will you please untie my hands now?" Will asked.

"No way."

"Come on, Erik. You can't do this all by yourself."

"Who says?"

"We're running out of time, there's too much to do."

"Like what?"

"I need to get the wire on, set up the recorder. You don't know how to do that."

"Like I said, I don't give a shit about your recording." He grinned. "And now I know where the meeting is."

Crandall reached out and gave Will a shove in the direction of the cottages across the street. "Let's roll."

Will stumbled but managed to stay on his feet. "Look, I'm the one who knows Byrnes. If you want this to go right, you're going to need my help. So untie my hands."

Crandall looked at him, as if trying to decide what to do.

"What is it you're so worried about?" Will asked.

"That you're gonna run off."

Will shook his head. "These are my *wrists*, Erik. They're not going to help me run any faster. Besides, you've got the gun."

Crandall patted the front pocket of the warm-up jacket. "Have it your way. But you try anything, I'll use it."

Will used a roll of surgical tape to attach the small microphone to his sternum. Under normal circumstances, he would have shaved the area, but since he didn't have a razor he just stuck the tape to his chest hair.

His fingers weren't working right, still numb from his wrists being bound for so long. He ran the wire down his side and taped the transmitter in place at the small of his back. He put his shirt back on and then twisted from side to side to make sure the equipment stayed in place.

Crandall leaned against the fender of the car, watching him with a bored look on his face.

Will switched on the tape recorder and watched as the reels of the microcassette began to turn.

He turned toward Crandall. "Say something."

"Like what?"

"Anything."

Crandall stood up and cleared his throat, an actor preparing to take the stage. "If you want the rainbow, you must to put up with the rain."

Will pressed the STOP button.

He hit REWIND and played back the recording, listening to Crandall's voice as it recited the trite aphorism. "Very profound."

Crandall nodded. "It's D. Parton."

Will set the receiver and the tape recorder down on the passenger seat of the Town Car and closed the door.

"We're good," he said.

They went across the road and climbed up the scrub-covered hillside. The anemic beam from the flashlight swept along the earth in synchronization with Crandall's gait.

The cottages were simple structures, rectangles with gabled roofs and tan stucco walls. The walls were overgrown with vines, webbed with dark cracks. The windows and doors were covered with weathered sheets of plywood.

They went ten yards up the hill, stopping in front of one of the cottages. The cottage sat parallel to the parking lot, the front door situated on the short wall.

Will used the tip of the tire iron to try to pry loose the sheet of plywood that covered the door. Crandall stood there and held the big gun on him.

It was hard work, the plywood attached to the door frame with dozens of long screws. He began to sweat but had only managed to loosen one side of the plywood by an inch.

Crandall shoved him in the shoulder. "Move over."

Crandall reached out with his empty left hand and dug his fingers behind the loosened edge of the plywood. He blew air out through his nostrils as he pulled.

The wood made a shrieking sound as the sheet of plywood came free and then clattered to the ground.

Crandall brushed his hand off against the leg of his warm-up suit. "Isn't it nice to have a man around the house?"

He pointed the gun at Will and motioned for him to go inside.

There was no light inside the cottage. Will was momentarily blind while he waited for Crandall to come inside with the flashlight. The cool air held the smell of mold and rodent droppings.

Crandall played the yellow beam of the flashlight over the cottage's interior. It was a single large room, a small kitchen down at the far end, set off by a framed archway. The rafters were exposed overhead, dirty white paint hanging down in strips.

The cottage was empty except for a rectangular dining table, the top hidden below a carpet of gray dust. There were no chairs.

Will stepped farther into the room, something brushing against his face. He reached up and swept away a spiderweb loaded with snared insects.

He walked to the far end of the dining table. He motioned to Crandall. "We should stand here."

"Why?"

Will wondered how Crandall had been able to make it this far without him. "So we're facing the door."

Crandall nodded. "Makes sense."

He came around the table, his shadow monstrous on the wall.

Will pointed at the tabletop. "Put the flashlight down there."

"What for?"

"To keep your hand free for when Byrnes shows."

Crandall stood the flashlight on its end, shining upward. Motes of dust swirled in the beam of light.

Will went over to the window. The sheet of plywood attached to the outside had warped, so that there was a gap he could look through. He could see the parking lot across the road, empty except for Crandall's car.

He reached down and felt the microphone through the material of his shirt, making sure that it hadn't shifted when he was working on the sheet of plywood.

He took another look around the room. There was no place to sit, so he leaned against the wall.

There was nothing left to do now but wait.

EIGHTY-TWO

Car tires crunched over pavement.

Will peered out through the gap in the window and saw headlights sweeping across the parking lot. A Ford Taurus pulled into the space next to the Town Car.

The car's headlights went dark. The driver's door opened, and Dennis Byrnes climbed out holding an aluminum briefcase. He swiveled his head, his eyes sweeping the area.

He looked up at the cottage for a long moment, then started to walk toward it.

Will turned to Crandall. "Get ready."

Crandall straightened up, holding the gun low, in front of his crotch.

Byrnes came through the front door of the cottage carrying the briefcase. His well-tailored suit and red silk tie seemed out of place inside the room.

He stopped at the opposite end of the long dining table and looked around. "Nice place you've got here."

"Dennis, this is Erik Crandall."

Byrnes nodded at Crandall. "Love the hair."

"It's a wig," Crandall said.

Byrnes raised an eyebrow. "Who would've guessed?"

Crandall took a step forward. "Fuck you, asshole."

Will held out an arm to stop him. "Let's just get this done."

"Fine by me," Crandall said. He looked at Byrnes. "Did you come alone?"

Byrnes studied Crandall. "Let me ask you something, genius. If the whole reason I'm here is to keep this secret, why the fuck would I bring someone?"

"Whatever." Crandall squeezed something in his left hand, over and over. "Did you bring my money, asshole?"

"Two things," Byrnes said. "One, I'd appreciate it if you'd stop calling me 'asshole.' And two, let's see this ledger."

Crandall put whatever he'd been squeezing away in the pocket of his warm-up jacket. Then he reached inside his pants pocket and took out the red ledger. He held it up for Byrnes.

Byrnes reached out his hand. "I want to look inside."

"What for?" Crandall asked.

"I wouldn't want to judge a book by its cover."

"Let's see the money first," Crandall said.

"I'm afraid I've got some bad news on that front."

Crandall raised the big gun. "I fucking *knew* it."

The light being cast upward by the flashlight left Byrnes's eyes in shadow. "I could only manage to come up with three hundred thousand, this being short notice and all."

Will felt his palms begin to sweat. He looked at Crandall, not sure how he would react.

Crandall lowered the gun. "Let's see it."

Byrnes set the aluminum briefcase down on the dining table. A cloud of dust rose from the tabletop, particles swimming around in the beam from the flashlight.

The latches on the case snapped open. Byrnes raised the lid and turned the case around so that Crandall could see inside. Stacks of hundred-dollar bills bundled with rubber bands were piled inside.

"Satisfied?" Byrnes said.

Crandall nodded.

Byrnes turned the case back around, the raised lid blocking the money from view. "Now, let's have a look at that ledger."

Crandall hesitated.

"It's okay," Will said. "Let him see it."

Crandall stepped forward and put the red ledger down in the center of the table.

Byrnes picked it up and started leafing through the pages. "How do I know you didn't make any copies? I wouldn't want this to become a habit."

When Crandall didn't say anything, Will spoke to Byrnes. "You're just going to have to trust us."

Byrnes studied Will's face. It was quiet inside the cottage; Will could hear Crandall's breath moving in and out through his mouth.

Byrnes nodded once. "I guess I'll have to."

He reached his hand down into the open case. When it came back out it was holding a nickel-plated automatic.

Will started to say something, but the words were drowned out by the blast from the gun.

Will's face was sprayed with warm blood as the top of Crandall's head flew off and collided with the plaster wall. The ejected cartridge from the pistol pinged off the tabletop and then fell to the floor.

Crandall's knees buckled as he began to collapse. Will stepped forward and grabbed him in his arms. He could see down inside Crandall's open skull.

He struggled to hold Crandall up, the other man too heavy. He tried to lower him down gently, but Crandall hit the wood floor with a thud. Part of his brain came out of the opening at the top of his skull and out onto the dirty floorboards.

Will looked at Byrnes. "What did you do that for?"

Byrnes stood at the head of the table. He didn't answer. He was still holding the gun, pointing it at Will.

Will reached down and felt the side of Crandall's neck for a pulse but couldn't find one.

He straightened up. "He's dead."

"That was kind of the idea."

"What the fuck, Dennis?"

"What did you think, I was going to pay for the ledger and then let him go around telling everybody?"

"He was leaving the country."

Byrnes shrugged. "How was I supposed to know that?"

"Jesus. What're we supposed to do now?"

"*We're* not going to do anything, Will. But I think you can guess what's going to happen to you."

EIGHTY-THREE

The air inside the cottage reeked of gunsmoke.

Byrnes used his chin to gesture down toward Crandall's dead body. "Use your foot to slide me his gun."

Will's ears were ringing. He used the toe of his shoe, but the dead man's finger was caught inside the trigger guard and the gun wouldn't come loose from his hand.

"Try a little harder, you won't hurt him."

Will gave Crandall's hand a soft kick, and the big gun clattered loose onto the wooden floor. Will thought about trying to make a grab for it, but Byrnes had the muzzle of the pistol aimed right at his chest.

Will shoved Crandall's gun with his foot. The gun slid across the floor and came to a stop next to Byrnes.

Byrnes reached his empty hand into the pocket of his suit coat and took out a rubber surgical glove. He switched the automatic to his right hand and pulled on the glove. Then he crouched down and picked up Crandall's gun with the hand that was wearing the glove.

Will watched him. "You're just going to shoot me?"

Byrnes nodded, looking down at Crandall's body. "But since it's his gun, he'll end up getting all the glory."

"In that case, who is it that killed him?"

"I did, after he shot you in cold blood."

"Should I thank you now?"

Byrnes put the silver automatic back inside the briefcase. "You want to find somebody to blame for this cluster fuck? Take a look in the mirror."

"What's that supposed to mean?"

"You should have left things alone. None of this would've happened if you hadn't stirred things up."

Will stared at him. "You're unbelievable."

Byrnes shook his head. "No, you are. Let me ask you a question: Why do you think you ended up getting tossed from the department?"

"You know why."

"Because you're an addict? Is that what you actually believe? Because that would've gotten you a stay at a treatment center, not thrown out on your ass."

"What're you saying?"

"That you were fired because none of us could trust you."

"Bullshit."

"It's true. Ray was afraid you were catching on to what we were doing at LAPD. But we couldn't just cut you in, because we knew you wouldn't play the game. So when you slipped up, I jumped on the opportunity to get rid of you."

Will used his shirtsleeve to wipe Crandall's blood from his face. "You killed Ray."

Byrnes didn't say anything. He motioned with the gun. "Move over there."

Will touched his chest, checking that the microphone was still in place. "He was trying to tell me the whole time, but I missed it."

"What are you talking about?"

"Ray's suicide note. It said, 'It hurts so much that it *burns*.' How the fuck did I miss that?"

Byrnes grinned. "A pun is the lowest form of humor."

"Why did you have to kill him?"

"He couldn't be trusted." Byrnes looked down at Crandall's body. "When that nutcase tried to shake him down, Ray fell apart. I think he was starting to go soft in his old age. He told me he thought we should pay Crandall off. He actually said that."

"So you shot him."

Byrnes shook his head. "I gave him the choice: If he wanted me to do it, or whether he wanted to do it himself."

"Some choice."

"I'm sorry I can't offer you the same." Byrnes waved Crandall's gun. "Now move over here."

It was too quiet inside the room. Will heard the sound of a car on the road outside.

"You don't have to do this, Dennis."

Byrnes looked him in the eye. "Don't worry, I'll put one right in your heart. You'll be gone before you even know it."

Will grabbed hold of the table edge for support. "Can we at least talk about this?"

Byrnes's teeth were too white when he smiled. "Why do I get the feeling you're stalling?" He motioned with the gun. "Now move."

Byrnes directed Will over to the spot where he had been standing when he shot Crandall. Then he moved around to the opposite side of the table, next to Crandall's body.

Will watched him. "Don't make this any worse for yourself, Dennis. Put down the gun."

"Why would I do that?"

"What're you going to do, shoot me while this is being recorded? I'm wearing a fucking wire."

"Nice try."

"I swear, Dennis. Just let me show it to you."

Byrnes didn't look like he was buying it. "I almost forgot how good at this kind of thing you used to be."

His finger moved, taking some slack from the trigger. "All right, I'll play along."

Byrnes aimed the gun at Will while he unbuttoned his shirt. It was hard to do because his fingers were trembling.

He pulled open his shirt, exposing the microphone taped to his chest.

Byrnes's eyes narrowed. "You motherfucker."

Will held out his open hand. "Be smart and give me the gun."

Byrnes stood there, not moving, lit from below by the flashlight beam. "I've got a better idea. Since I'm the one holding the gun, how about you give me the recorder that goes with that wire?"

A gust of wind rustled the trees outside the cottage.

Will looked out through the gap in the window. "Go fuck yourself."

Byrnes shook his head. "It's good to know some things never change. You always were insubordinate." He looked around the interior of the cottage. "I don't see it anywhere in here. So if I were a betting man, I'd have to say that it's in that car, out in the parking lot."

Will concentrated on keeping his face blank as Byrnes stared at him.

Byrnes nodded. "I thought so."

He cocked back the hammer of Crandall's gun.

Will tried to keep his voice even. "You sure you want to do this, Dennis?"

"Why wouldn't I?"

"Because the receiver isn't in the car you're talking about. It's in the other car."

"What other car?"

"The one with the FBI agent sitting inside it."

Byrnes smiled. "You never give up, do you?"

Will gestured toward the window. "Take a look for yourself. In the parking lot."

"Do you really think I'm that stupid?"

"What have you got to lose? Like you said, you're the one holding the gun."

Byrnes kept the gun pointed at Will as he went over to the window. He swiveled his head and looked out through the gap.

Will's heart thundered inside his chest.

Byrnes spun away from the window. "You piece of *shit*."

He looked into Will's eyes as he brought up the gun. His index finger began to move against the trigger. Will opened his mouth, but then Byrnes turned his wrist and pointed the gun toward his own head.

He pulled the trigger. The blast from the big gun going off inside the small room was deafening. Will shut his eyes for a second, not wanting to watch.

When he opened them again, Byrnes was already lying on the floor.

Will came around the table and looked down at him. He gagged and then turned away. There would be no point in checking for a pulse.

He went over to the window and looked out through the gap.

The dark blue Crown Victoria was parked in its usual spot in the lot across the road. The driver's door swung open and Gary Ackerman climbed out, the orange tip of a joint glowing from his mouth.

EIGHTY-FOUR

Gary Ackerman stood inside the cottage, looking around at the bloodshed. "*Jesus,* that's Dennis Byrnes."

Gary was wearing his white Western suit, the sequined marijuana leaves and opium poppies catching the weak light from the flashlight on the table.

He looked at Will. "We better call the cops."

It was hard to hear because of the ringing in his ears. "That's a Los Angeles County supervisor lying there on the floor, Gary. Believe me, we don't want to get caught up in this."

"Then let's get the fuck out of here."

"Not yet. I need your help first."

"With *what?*"

"I need to fix things, so that I wasn't here."

Gary's eyes were wide. "I can't go to jail, man. I've got a kid."

"If the cops show up, I'll take the weight."

Gary shook his head. "I can't deal with this."

Will looked at him. "Please, Gary. There's not enough time for me to do this myself. And I need a ride."

"How did you get here?"

Will pointed at Crandall's dead body. "He drove me."

Gary ran a hand through his long hair. "Let's just hurry the fuck up. What is it you need me to do?"

"Do you have a clean rag?"

"I've probably got something out in the car."

"Can you please get it?"

Gary nodded and then walked back outside.

Will looked down at the bodies of Crandall and Byrnes laying on the floor. He stood there, beyond exhaustion now, trying to think how to begin.

He went over to Byrnes and crouched down. He peeled the rubber surgical glove from Byrnes's left hand. The hand was holding Crandall's gun, and as he took off the glove the gun fell onto the floor.

Will pulled the glove onto his own hand. He reached inside the open briefcase and took out Byrnes's silver automatic. He put it into Byrnes's left hand.

He took the red ledger from the inside pocket of Byrnes's suit coat and put that down on the ground next to his head.

Will listened for sounds outside the cottage, half expecting to hear a car driving away when Gary decided to abandon him.

Will picked up Crandall's gun with his gloved hand and carried it over to where Crandall lay on the floor. He knelt and placed the gun in Crandall's hand. It was difficult because Crandall's fingers had already begun to stiffen.

He heard footsteps and looked up to see Gary coming back inside the cottage, holding a faded red automotive rag.

He looked down at Will. "What are you doing?"

"Making it look like they shot each other."

Gary backed up a step. "You mean they didn't?"

"It's a long story. I'll explain in the car."

Gary looked at him. "Hold on, did you—"

"I didn't shoot anybody, Gary. Now hand me the rag."

Gary brought it over to him. Will went around the room wiping off any surface he remembered touching.

"Holy *shit*," Gary said. "There's a boatload of money in here."

Will turned to see Gary reaching a hand toward the open briefcase. "Don't touch anything."

Gary looked at him. "Don't tell me we're just going to leave it here? This is like a million dollars."

"Trust me, Gary. We need to leave it."

Will took a last look around the room, checking the angles of limbs and the spray pattern on the plaster walls. He hoped the scene would play as if Byrnes had shot Crandall and then Crandall had managed to shoot Byrnes as he was turning away.

The batteries inside the flashlight were almost dead now, the corners of the room lost in shadow.

He looked down at Crandall's body, facedown on the floor. Crandall's wig had been knocked off his head. The eye tattoos stared up unblinking from the back of his ruined skull.

He reached inside Crandall's warm-up jacket and fished out the keys to the Town Car, so that he could get the recorder on the way out.

"Let's go," Will said.

Will turned and went to the front door. He wiped down the knob and then closed the door behind them.

"Where am I taking you?" Gary asked.

"Valley Presbyterian."

Gary looked at him. "Are you all right?"

Will nodded. "I just want to see my wife."

Four Weeks Later

EIGHTY-FIVE

The Dodgers made the playoffs that year. Their final game of the season was played at home under the lights, the pennants set high up on the stadium walls fluttering in a fresh breeze that blew in from the Pacific.

The Dodgers trailed from the first inning on, their last batter popping out to record the final out of the long season.

Will stood on the concrete walkway behind home plate and watched the fans file from the ballpark. The grounds crew drove an electric cart out onto the field and used shovels to begin digging up the infield grass.

Will spotted Gary Ackerman coming toward him along the walkway, holding on to the hand of a small girl. The girl's long blond hair fell down from underneath a blue Dodgers cap.

Will hadn't seen Gary since the night at the sanitarium. The shooting had been all over the news for weeks. Ed Denslowe had stopped by the house to ask Will if he'd had anything to do with it but hadn't pushed hard. The questions had seemed perfunctory, as if the detective were only going through the motions.

"Thanks for hooking us up with the tickets," Gary said.

"Least I could do."

Gary looked down at the girl. "Will, this is my daughter, Emma."

Will crouched down. "Nice to meet you, Emma."

She pointed at Will's badge. "Are you a policeman?"

Will looked at her. She had Gary's eyes.

"No," he said. "Not anymore."

They said good-bye, and Will watched Gary and the girl climb up the stairs and disappear into the crowd of people leaving the stadium.

Will took a walk around the ballpark, not ready to go home.

Inside the Dodgers clubhouse, Latin music blasted from a boom box. The players were already showered and dressed in street clothes. They gave each other hugs and high fives, preparing to scatter like migratory birds, each of them about to fly off in a different direction for the off-season.

He felt a hand on his shoulder and turned to see Joe Gibbs. Gibbs wore a gold-colored suit with a green pocket square that stuck up from his chest.

"So what're your plans for the off-season?" Gibbs asked.

"I'm not really sure. My wife and I are expecting."

"Well, that should keep you busy. When's it due?"

Will looked down at the carpet and then back at Gibbs. "Nine months would be in November. But it's going to come early. My wife's on bed rest."

"Sorry to hear that. How's she holding up?"

"Better than I am."

Players moved past them, carrying bags, the clubhouse emptying out.

Gibbs looked at him. "I'll tell you something. You kind of surprised me. When I hired you I didn't think you'd make it past the All-Star break."

"For a while there, neither did I."

"You interested in coming back with us next season?"

"I don't know."

Gibbs squinted at him. "What's the matter? You don't like it here?"

"I do," Will said. "It's just that I think I might be making some changes."

"Like what?"

"My wife and I, we're talking about leaving town."

"Why's that?"

"I'm not sure I really want to raise a kid here."

"I did," Gibbs said. "Five of them, and they all turned out pretty good. More or less."

Will smiled. "We're still trying to figure things out. Let's see where I'm at next season."

Gibbs held out his hand. "You keep me posted."

EIGHTY-SIX

Laurie lay on her back on the living room couch. The couch was new, upholstered in a khaki-colored twill. Her bare feet rested in Will's lap.

The lights were switched off, but it was bright inside the room from the sunlight that came in through the open windows.

The television was on, the sound turned down low, neither of them really paying attention. He reached out and placed his hand at the crest of the rising slope of her belly.

She hadn't been out of the house in over a month, dividing her time between the couch and their bed. She'd started referring to herself as "The Veal Calf."

He felt her body suddenly go stiff, her back arching up from the cushions of the couch.

He looked at her. "You all right?"

"Contraction." She let out her breath. "That one was a real mother."

He'd already called Laurie's obstetrician. She'd instructed them to stay home until the contractions were five minutes apart. Then they were to go straight to the maternity unit of the hospital.

Laurie's breathing was loud as she sucked air in and out through her clenched teeth.

"Can I get you anything?" he asked.

"Got any more of that stolen dope lying around?"

"Not funny."

Buddy came in from the kitchen and went over to Laurie. He pushed his nose into her upper arm, and she reached out to pet him.

The dog had recovered physically from his run-in with Erik Crandall, but Will thought he could detect other changes in the animal. There was a new wariness when strangers approached him in public, a constant and stoic sadness in the dog's eyes.

Laurie pointed at the television. "Turn this up."

Will picked up the remote control. On the screen, a female newscaster stood on the steps in front of the Hall of Administration and spoke into a microphone. At the top of the steps, a man dressed in a dark gray suit rested his hand atop a leather-bound bible as he was sworn in as the new Los Angeles County supervisor.

Will raised the volume, the reporter's voice narrating the footage. ". . . taking over for Dennis Byrnes, who was killed on September nineteenth while trying to apprehend a parolee wanted in connection with the brutal assault on a Van Nuys woman. Byrnes, a former LAPD officer, rose to become one of L.A.'s most powerful officials, only to die the heroic death of a police off—"

Will pressed the MUTE button. "Those PR people must really be working overtime."

" 'When the legend becomes fact, print the legend.' "

He smiled at her. *The Man Who Shot Liberty Valance.*

She nodded. "That's what happens when you're stuck at home for a month watching TV."

"Always the silver lining."

He looked back up at the muted television, the gathered crowd soundlessly clapping their hands together.

For weeks, Will had been expecting Denslowe or some other detective to knock on the door, but the knock had never come. He'd hung on to the recording he'd made at the sanitarium, just in case. In all of the news coverage about the shooting at the sanitarium, there had never been any mention of either the red ledger or the $300,000.

Barry Feingold had called Will earlier in the week to tell him that the district attorney's office had dropped the charges against him in the wake of Erik Crandall's death. The attorney had told Will that the gun Crandall had shot Byrnes with had also been used in the killing of an elderly woman in Koreatown.

He switched the television off and looked at Laurie. "I came up with the name. For the baby."

"Nothing like waiting until the last minute."

"Do you want to hear it or not?"

"I suppose I probably should."

He paused a moment for effect and then said, "Thomas."

"Thomas?"

"After the kid who worked for me, up in Haydenville."

She looked at him and then nodded. "Well, I'll give you this, it's a lot better than Sailor."

They sat there for a while, not speaking. Then she grimaced and her head arched backward, exposing her throat.

Through the fabric of her shirt he could feel the power of the contraction. "Are you okay?"

She blinked her eyes, tears there. "I think it's time."

"Are you sure?"

She nodded her head once.

He helped her get up from the couch. He put his arm around her and walked her across the room and over to the front door. A leather overnight bag packed with her things sat on the floor. He picked it up.

He opened the door, and they went out together into the warmth of the afternoon.

ACKNOWLEDGMENTS

John M. Anderson, Coblentz, Patch, Duffy & Bass LLP

Billie M.

Officer Bruce Borihanh, Los Angeles Police Department

Bullseye Shooting Range and Firearms, San Rafael, California

John Calagna Bail Bonds, Van Nuys, California

Coastside Healing Arts, Half Moon Bay, California

Parole Agent Tom De La Rosa, California Department of Corrections and Rehabilitation

Detective Sergeant Ray Deleon (Retired)

Andre Dubus III

The Hon. Kenneth R. Freeman, Los Angeles Superior Court

Tracey Gant, Susan Goldsborough, Michelle Griffin, and Louise Gross

Acknowledgments

Robert W. Gluck, Mandelbaum, Salsburg, Gold, Lazris & Discenza, PC

Liza Heath

Mary "Mel" Heath (June 5, 1930–March 31, 2010)

Michael Homler, Andrew Martin, Kelley Ragland, Bob Berkel, Hector DeJean, Monica Katz, David Rotstein, and everyone else who pitched in at Minotaur Books

Judith Israel

Don Jung, Jung Novikoff Bellanca & Company

Frank Kosempa and Scarlet Colsen

Rick Kurnit and Maura Wogan, Frankfurt Kurnit Klein & Selz, PC

Hut Landon

Russell Laros, M.D.

Kurt Lighthouse

Los Angeles Public Library

Barry Mandelbaum

Elaine Markson, Gary Johnson, and Julia Kenny at Markson Thoma Literary Agency

Barbara Peters

Adam Perez, California Department of Corrections and Rehabilitation

Elaine, Bill, and Kathryn Petrocelli, Sheryl Cotleur, and Karen West at Book Passage, Corte Madera, California

Gigi Reinheimer

Lisa Scarsella

Amy Schiffman, Intellectual Property Group

Dan Wieden, Wieden + Kennedy

Mark Winitz, BlackBeltGuide.com

Special thanks and much love to my wife and daughter for putting up with all the things they had to put up with during the writing of this novel.